S0-BOJ-879

# Wildflowers in Winter:
## Aging with Alzheimer's

## Naomi Wark

Copyright © 2017 by Naomi Wark
All rights reserved.
Cover art by Sara Bargar

ISBN-13: 978-1539332480
Library of Congress Control Number: 2017902069
Dragonfly Press
Camano Island WA

Wildflowers in Winter is a work of fiction. The events are imaginary; the characters are fictitious and are not intended to represent actual living persons.

# Dedication

To the elderly, especially those suffering with dementia. And to their loved ones and caregivers who give their time and love so freely.

I'm now an old woman ... and nature is cruel;
'Tis jest to make old age look like a fool,
The body, it crumbles, grace and vigor depart,
There is now a stone where I once had a heart.
But inside this old carcass a young girl still dwells,
And now and again my battered heart swells,
I remember the joys, I remember the pain,
And I'm loving and living life over again.
I think of the years ... all too few, gone too fast,
And accept the stark fact that nothing can last.

Anonymous. Excerpt from "An Old Lady's Poem"
retrieved from http://www.poemhunter.com

# Acknowledgements

This book has been an effort and a dream for over a decade. During that time, many people have shared in my journey with encouragement, writing expertise, and valued insights. My appreciation to Pamela Goodfellow, and my classmates at the University of Washington where I learned the craft of writing and learned to find the correct voice for each of my characters. And, more than ten years later, thank you to each and every member of the Skagit Valley Writer's League whose encouragement and inspiration pushed me the final steps to bring this story to publication. The biggest thanks to my critique group who read my manuscript, helping me fine tune my words, grammar, punctuation and flow.

A final note of thanks to my husband and daughters who encouraged and believed in me throughout the long process.

# Prologue

Wildflowers in Winter is a work of fiction. Edna Pearson represents many aging individuals who live to a ripe old age, but are cursed by failing bodies and minds. Edna, like others, has outlived her spouse and her children. Suffering from progressive Alzheimer's, she fears spending the last years of her life alone and isolated. Although Edna's story is fiction, the Alzheimer's flashbacks portrayed in this novel are inspired by excerpts from diaries left behind upon the death of one much-loved but forlorn, old woman.

"If we ask Our Father he will grant our prayers if he determines the right to grant. The grants will be the ones God sees fit to grant."
EMP diary (August 1921)

# Chapter 1

The shrill of the phone jolted Edna awake. Fighting drowsiness, she blinked a few times, fixing her focus on the red lighted display of the clock. Five-thirty. Her heartbeat quickened. Early morning calls can only mean bad news. Restrained by the blue nightgown wrapped around her legs and hips, she trembled, groping for the old dial phone on the nightstand. For a brief moment, Edna closed her eyes and breathed deeply before lifting the receiver to her ear.

Choked back sobs from across the line made it difficult for Edna to make out Alicia's voice. "Grandma, Daddy's dead."

Edna paused as she struggled to absorb the news. Without her hearing aids, the words came muffled and faint, barely audible above her pounding heartbeat.

"Alicia, speak up, you're not making sense."

"Daddy's dead." This time, Alicia's words stung clear and sharp.

Edna's mind whirled, fighting to comprehend. She must have misunderstood. Her son couldn't be dead. She'd just seen him yesterday and he was fine. "Larry? Larry's dead? I don't understand."

"Yes, Grandma, he's gone."

A sharp pain gripped her chest. Wet with fear and perspiration, she flung back the bed covers that ensnared her, and pulled herself to a seated position. She flipped on the small white reading lamp on the nightstand.

"What happened?"

1

"He suffered a stroke last night and never regained consciousness."

A dam of emotion released in a torrent of sobs. Edna had worried about his health and nagged him to quit smoking, but he wasn't supposed to die. Not like this, so suddenly, or so young. He was only sixty-four. "What am I going to do without him?"

"I don't know, Grandma. We don't know how we're going to get by, either. Dad took care of everything. Mom will be lost without him. I'll call you later to let you know when we've made the arrangements."

Edna straightened on the bed, shivering from the cold. "When can I see him?"

"I'll let you know when he's been taken to the funeral home. It may take a while to harvest his organs."

"What are you talking about? What do you mean, harvest his organs?" Resentment rose like the taste of bitter coffee in her throat.

"Dad was an organ donor. His kidneys, eyes, and tissue are still viable for donation."

Edna shook her head. "There must be some mistake. He would have told me." Dazed, Edna returned the phone to its cradle. It didn't make any sense for Larry to want to be dissected upon his death. Surely Kora-Lee and her daughters had put him up to it. "It's not right." She pounded her fist into the pillow.

Too early to call anyone, Edna motioned for her only consolation. Missy, her black terrier, pounced on the bed and nestled into the crook of her arm. Salty droplets fell on the dog's long, matted fur. She cried out her frustrations, burying her head into Missy's fur. "Why, God? Why didn't you take me instead?" It wasn't fair. Parents aren't supposed to outlive their children. For a few moments, she let her shock dissipate through her tears. A swell of loneliness gripped her like a rogue wave, at the thought of losing her last child.

Though it had been over forty years since her daughter, Bernice, died, a rush of memories raced through her mind like a flash flood. Then she had Jacob and Larry for emotional support. Now, with her husband and son both gone, the hollowness in her heart echoed her grief. Drawing on all her physical and emotional strength, Edna climbed out of bed and plodded downstairs to the

2

living room. Hoping the sunlight would overcome the darkness filling her, she pulled the drapes open.

Instead of the hoped-for light, the opened curtains revealed a still darkened, gray sky skirted with low ragged edges, suiting the somber mood of the morning. Edna shuffled to the sofa and gathered her favorite cover around her. She buried her nose in the quilt which had warmed her babies and herself throughout the years. With closed eyes, she inhaled the mix of sweet and bittersweet memories. Each memory unique, just like the multi-colored, tulip shapes she had carefully crafted and sewn into the quilt. Fingering one corner of the worn cotton spread, a smile turned up at the corners of her mouth at the sight of the small rips where Larry had used the quilt for teething. Remembering the past helped keep the early morning chill at bay. Numb, she sobbed in the silent empty house until, drained of tears and emotion, she drifted off to sleep.

The brazen rays streaming through the exposed living room window reawakened Edna. For a single heartbeat, she welcomed the new day, but a dull pain pulsed in her clouded head. She closed her eyes to quell the pain. Blurred memories of anger and tears swirled in her mind. Maybe it had been a bad dream. She blinked to focus on the room around her. She didn't understand why she wasn't in her bedroom. Wads of tissue littered the gold shag carpet. Reality resurfaced ... reawakening her grief. She trudged to the kitchen, poured water into a cup, and turned on the microwave's timer. Opening her small steel canister adorned with white daisies, she pulled out a tea bag, inhaling the spicy blend which she favored and Larry always bought for her. Its smell alone always helped wake her up. Normally favoring a breakfast of bacon, mush, and maybe a piece of toast with homemade jam, her stomach rebelled at the thought of food. Instead, she stirred a single teaspoon of sugar into her tea and sipped. Her hands warmed clutching the cup and breathing in the blend of sweet apples and spicy cinnamon soothed her heart.

Missy barked at the ringing phone and she scurried to answer it. Without her sobbing, Edna heard Alicia's voice clear and harsh. "Grandma, the arrangements are set. There will be a viewing on Thursday evening. The cremation will take place early Friday before the funeral service later in the afternoon."

"Larry didn't want to be cremated. We talked about funeral plots next to Bernice and Jacob. How can I visit him and leave flowers?" Edna held the phone receiver at arm's length, too stunned to face any more news. She sat unable to move for a few beats before confronting Alicia again.

"Mom prefers to have him cremated. It's less expensive than a standard burial."

Edna snapped, "How can you talk about money? Doesn't anyone care what Larry wanted, or what I want? I have money if you need money."

"Daddy would have wanted to go along with Mom's wishes. There's a place at the cemetery for cremated remains. You'll still be able to visit and place flowers."

Edna fumed, but fought back her anger. After all her son had done for that woman, marrying her when she was with child and accepting her four-year-old daughter as his own. How could Kora-Lee have such disregard for what Larry wanted?

"I'll let you know the time of the service. We're still waiting for the final details from the funeral home."

Without saying goodbye, Edna disconnected the call. She sank down into the overstuffed brown recliner she no longer had the strength to tilt back. Though she expected Alicia to side with her mother, as always, she resented her for defending Kora-Lee's decision. It was hard enough accepting Larry was gone, now hearing he would be cremated was more than she could take. She never felt so alone in her life.

With Larry gone, Edna had no one who loved her and would care for her in her remaining years. She didn't think of Kora-Lee and her girls as family. They weren't blood. Kora-Lee's daughters called her Grandma, but Edna knew it was only to pacify their father. Besides, they didn't treat her like family. They often spoke in hushed whispers about her when she visited. Edna wondered what would happen now to the already strained relationship with her daughter-in-law and granddaughters. Would she continue to see Kora-Lee or her daughters? She fumbled in her handbag for her handkerchief and dried her eyes and swiped her nose. Her gloom overshadowed the brightness of the sun announcing a new day, a day Edna wasn't sure she could face. Her body and mind were numb and her will to go on was as dead as the body of her last child now lying in a morgue.

She reached for the phone and dialed her dearest friend, Barbara, her only friendly contact for caring, comfort and consolation.

# Chapter 2

David frowned at the intrusion of the persistent phone as the family sat down for Wednesday dinner. He set rules for phone use and refused to let a phone call disrupt the family meal. He glared across the table with raised eyebrows at fifteen-year-old Rachel and twelve-year-old Emily, guessing either was the recipient of the call.

David's wife, Jean, got up and glanced at the phone number displayed. "It's from a 509-area code. Do you know anyone in eastern Washington?"

David shrugged. "Far as I know, my birth father still lives there."

"You might want to get it." Jean picked up the receiver and hit speaker button on the phone, against her husband's frowning protest. "Hello."

"Hi, I'm trying to get ahold of David Bryant. My name is Alicia."

From the dining table, David shook his head, unable to recall the name. The unfamiliar voice continued, relaying a clue. "I'm Larry's daughter."

Stunned, David's mind wandered back to the father he had seen only twice since he and his twin brother were five and his parents divorced. He wrinkled his face as he recalled the lanky soldier who smoked constantly and was barely home for his sons. He nodded at the vague memory of his stepsister, Alicia, whom he'd met only once, when he was eleven, and the last time he saw his father.

"Hold on a moment please, while I see if he is available." Jean put the call on hold and held the phone out to her spouse. "You should take it."

"Why? We haven't spoken in thirty years."

"It must be important for her to call you."

His stomach tightened, in spite of his lack of concern over the stranger who was his birth father.

David rose reluctantly feeling all eyes were on him.

"Alicia? This is David."

"I'm so glad I located you. It took some work finding you in Washington. I thought you might still be in California."

David held his tongue from stating the obvious. Her sniffles through her breaking voice across the line stifled his wisecracks. A lot of time had passed since they were children.

"I've been trying all day to track you down. I thought you and Nathan should know your father passed away."

"Larry's dead?" David swallowed. He didn't know what to say to her. He barely knew her. Hell, he barely knew his father. "I'm sorry. I hope he didn't suffer much."

"No. He suffered a stroke Monday night, and he passed away early this morning, in a coma. He never knew what happened."

"How are you and your family doing?" The words spilled out like a well-rehearsed routine, out of formality and manners. What else was there to say? He wasn't sure why he should be concerned. David paced back and forth in the kitchen, uncomfortably aware his family was watching and listening between forks of potato salad and bites of baby back ribs. He walked into the living room and plopped down on the sofa with the phone.

Alicia struggled between sniffles. "We're all in shock. Mom isn't sure how she'll handle things. Lorraine's in Minnesota now, so she's not around to help out as much."

David shifted on the sofa trying to push aside the thoughts of his dinner getting cold, hanging on to each word. He remembered Larry's oldest daughter, Lorraine, about five years older than he. He'd only met her once, when she was already in high school.

"On top of that, Grandma's driving us crazy with her constant sobbing and complaining over the arrangements."

David straightened, his interest heightened at the reference to his paternal grandmother. "Grandma Edna's still around? How's she doing? I haven't heard from her since high school. She got mad when Nathan and I moved to California. She accused Mom of doing it out of spite."

"That sounds like her. She's having a tough time right now. Dad's always been there to help her. I don't know how she'll get by."

"Well, she still has you and Lorraine, and your mom."

"Yeah, we're around to help out. It's just that she's getting senile and she's a little difficult to deal with. We haven't exactly been close lately."

Alicia's comment seemed cold, under the circumstances. "Well, I guess being difficult is to be expected at her age. How old is she now?"

"Ninety-two."

David grinned. If there was one positive thing he could say about his family, it was a tendency toward longevity. Both of his maternal grandparents, mid-way into their eighties, were still alive, also.

"The funeral will be Friday, with a viewing Thursday evening. We're still working out the exact times. I'll call you with the final times and addresses tomorrow. I assume you and your brother will want to come."

David mulled over all he had heard in the past few minutes. His mind reeled with fragmented thoughts. It didn't make sense to shake up his whole life to rush off to the funeral of a man with whom he had no relationship, even though it was his father. He didn't need another interruption in his already hectic schedule of overtime, putting in a yard, and coaching Emily's soccer team. David stifled a groan and glanced toward the dining room, his family still watching him. He didn't know how he should respond to the recent news. "Nathan's in the army. He's stationed at Fort Bragg, North Carolina, but last time I spoke with him he was leaving for the mid-east, something fairly top-secret. I doubt he'll be able to get away." For a moment, David wished he had such a simple, built in excuse.

"No wonder I couldn't track him down. Is he married?"

"Nah, he's single. Career military." Wanting to stay focused on the reason for the phone call, David changed the subject. "So, the service is Friday?" He paused and decided to build in an excuse for not attending. "I'm scheduled for a flight on Friday. Let me call you after I've seen what I can do about work."

"That's fine. I'll give you my number so you can call if you have any other questions. Otherwise, I'll phone when I know anything for certain. Will you let Nathan know?"

"Sure." David returned to the kitchen and grabbed a pen. He jotted down the phone number. "Got it."

"You know, it's too bad." Alicia paused before she continued. "He used to talk about you and Nathan a lot. I think he would have liked to see you both again before he died. We were planning a sixty-fifth birthday party for Dad and talked about having you and your brother come." Her voice trailed off. "I guess you never know when it's your time. We should all have tried harder to get together."

David noticed the sun setting through his large living room windows. He shook his head. He didn't buy the line that Larry had ever talked about him or Nathan. Besides, why should he be concerned with any guilt Larry might have had, which he doubted anyway. God knows David wasn't about to feel guilty for not keeping in touch with a man who hadn't been a father figure in his life for nearly forty years. With a sigh, he let go of his bitterness. There was no point in taking it out on Alicia. She had nothing to do with Larry's decision to ignore his sons, though he suspected Alicia's mother, Kora-Lee, had plenty to do with it.

"Whatever. Keep me posted. My dinner's getting cold." He flinched at the coldness of his last remark before taking a deep breath. "Thanks for calling." Setting the phone down, he blew out a long breath and plopped down on his chair at the table next to Jean. Everyone looked at him. "Well, I guess my birth father passed away this morning."

"Are you sad?" Rachel exchanged glances with her sister. "You never talk about your dad. What was he like?"

David stared at his plate of cold ribs and congealed gravy. He hesitated knowing he should have shared more of the story about his father and his stepsisters with his children long before it came to this. "No. I've never had much of a relationship with Larry, so I don't feel any loss. He was gone a lot. I was young and he was in the army the whole time Mom and he were married. I haven't considered him my dad for a long time." David thought about his relationship with his step dad, who raised him. "You know I'm not particularly close to Ray, either. He could be a mean S.O.B., but I consider him my dad, not Larry."

David tried to remember what he could about his father. There wasn't a lot. He remembered the constant fighting and long absences. How could he respect a man who left his wife with two small sons and married another woman and her ready-made family? No. There was no way David was going to drop everything to go to the funeral of some stranger, father or not. He had no desire to take part in a memorial service for a man for whom he had no respect. How could he make small talk with two sisters he didn't know, or his father's wife who he later learned was the primary reason for his parents' divorce?

"How come you never see your dad or your sisters?" Rachel twirled her curly hair around her finger avoiding her mother's disapproving look.

"When Mom and Larry split, she brought us back to the states from Korea where Larry was stationed. Mom married Ray, and we moved closer to her folks in California. Larry married a Chinese woman, Kora-Lee, who already had a daughter, Lorraine, and was pregnant with my other stepsister, Alicia. After that, Larry pretty much ignored Nathan and me. He was never a part of our lives. He had a new family, and from what I gathered early on, Kora-Lee would just as soon Nathan and I never existed. It's been easier to let it be at that. The way I always looked at it, if he didn't care to see me, why put myself out to see him?"

"You have two stepsisters, cool. It would be neat to have more aunts." Emily looked at her mother with a nod, motioning to be excused.

"Can I just finish my dinner, please, since everyone else seems to be done?" David shook his head as he stormed to the microwave to zap his plate with a few rays.

Carrying her plate to the sink, Jean stopped to rub David's shoulders. "How's your grandmother doing? I heard you say she's still around. This must be very hard on her. Larry was her only child, wasn't he?"

Emily wiped down the counter then hung the dish towel on the hook and joined the conversation. "She's got to be getting old, huh, Dad?"

David took a deep breath. It wasn't fair to his family to take his jumbled emotions out on them. He smiled in answer to Emily's broad silver grin, dressed in recently acquired braces. "Grandma's ninety-two. I guess she's doing fine. Alicia says she's crying a lot. I guess that's to be expected, under the circumstances. Her only other child, Bernice, died before I was born. My granddad died close to twenty years ago."

Rachel, who took after her mother with her persistence, excused herself from the table and went to the sink. "I'd like to meet her. I think it would be cool to have another grandmother. Don't you, Emily?"

Half-heartedly, David responded. "Maybe some time." He opened the microwave, carried his plate back to the table, and sat down. "I never told you girls, but I lived with my grandmother and granddad for several months when Nathan and I were five, shortly after Mom divorced Larry. I guess having twin troublemakers was more than Mom could handle alone." David smiled. "Nathan and I had a great time with them. She was big on vegetables and made us clean our plates before we were excused from the table. But after dinner she always had homemade desserts. She loved baking." David took a few bites of dinner before sensing Jean was watching him. He glanced up at her smile. He knew the look and realized his mistake. He had unconsciously given her a reason to encourage him to go to the funeral.

She kissed him. "If you don't care about saying goodbye to your dad, at least think about going to the funeral for your grandmother's sake. The girls are right. It would be good for them to know their great-grandma. After all, who knows how she's really doing and how much longer you'll have the opportunity to get reacquainted with her."

David cringed. He hated falling into the guilt trap, unconvinced he owed anyone anything. His appetite diminished after the phone call, David excused himself and dumped his plate in the sink. He snatched the phone before one of his daughters could dash off with it for their nightly phone marathon. "I'm going to call Nathan." Once again, he retreated to the sofa and dialed his twin brother to share the news. Nathan answered after the third ring.

"Hey, brother, what's up? It's got to be important for you to be calling."

"Funny. You know I'm not much for talking on the phone. Besides, when was the last time you called me? Anyway, I got a call from Larry's youngest daughter, Alicia. Larry apparently died from a stroke this morning."

"A stroke, huh? I had him pegged as a sure-fire cancer or emphysema victim. He smoked like an eighteen-wheeler burning oil the last time I saw him."

David shifted in his chair. "I remember. You saw him not that long ago, didn't you? When was that? Early eighties?"

"Yeah. Right after I graduated from West Point. I guess it's still been twenty years though. I had this crazy idea I should visit him again since I was heading out to active duty and likely to see some heavy action. You never know, especially with all the shit that's going on over there in the desert. It was a stupid idea though, seeing him again."

David couldn't remember the specifics about the visit. "Why? What happened?"

"Nothing, really, I just got the feeling he didn't care if he saw me or not. I'm not sure if he just didn't give a damn or was uncomfortable seeing me again after so long. His wife, I can't remember her name, anyway she made it very clear she wasn't pleased to see me." Nathan took a breath before continuing. "So, are you going to the service?"

"I don't know. You know Jean. She thinks it's the right thing to do, especially for Grandma's sake."

"Is the old gal still around? How's she doing?"

"Yeah, I guess so. She's ninety-two. Alicia says she's senile, who really knows. Do you remember when we lived with the grand folks the summer after Mom and Larry divorced?"

"How old were we? Five? That was probably the best summer we ever had. Remember how Granddad always took us down to the creek and we'd go fishing? Funny thing is we never caught on that we were never going to catch anything in that tiny old creek."

The memory of the long ago summer lightened the discomfort roiling in the pit of David's stomach.

"Didn't Granddad pass away sometime back?"

David's, smile faded. He recalled hearing of his grandfather Jacob's last trip to Madigan Army Hospital in Tacoma. "It's been a while. Shortly after you left. Right after I moved back to Washington, following those few rough years in Los Angeles after college."

"Well, I won't be able to make the funeral. These classified missions don't make for an easy out. I figure I'll be here in the God-forsaken desert at least for another year. I'll make it back to Washington someday. Tell Grandma 'hi' from me and let me know what happens."

Sending his best wishes, David clicked the phone off and returned to the kitchen, replacing the phone with a sense of reluctance and defeat. He turned to Jean. "Okay, we'll go to the funeral. I'll call Alicia tomorrow. It's probably the right thing to do under the circumstances, and it will be nice to see Grandma again."

# Chapter 3

Edna's day lagged. Grief sheathed her like low-lying clouds on a rainy day. Her neighbors Fred and Marge came over to extend their condolences. Barbara dropped by with some freshly baked rolls and a macaroni casserole, offering her comfort and a sounding board upon which Edna could project her emotions. Edna had outlived most of the teachers with whom she had taught for over forty years, many of her garden club associates, and both her children. But Edna had acquaintances from a neighborhood church, and kind neighbors who looked in on her. Edna had met Barbara at the church she attended after two young men rang her doorbell one day. An unselfish woman who took joy in caring for others, Barbara could be counted upon for support, or as a last-minute chauffeur. She asked for no recognition or compensation for her deeds, believing her reward lay in the afterlife. As the day wore on, visitors converged upon Edna's home. Barbara greeted and welcomed them, offering coffee and tea accompanied by her home-baked cookies.

At last, as the dinner hour approached, with the house empty, Barbara set the table and brought out her heated casserole and rolls. "What time is Alicia coming to take you to the funeral home tomorrow?"

"Around five-thirty." Edna breathed in the sweetness of yeast and immediately her mouth watered. Realizing she had avoided food the whole day, she devoured her first roll in no time.

Barbara took a seat next to Edna. "Will you need any help getting ready?"

Edna patted Barbara's hand. "No. I'll be fine." Edna gobbled down the tuna and cheese macaroni. Looking up at her friend, she smiled. "I didn't realize how hungry I was."

With forks set down and plates pushed aside, Barbara cleared the table and washed the dishes. "Are you sure you're okay? Let me know if you need anything. I'll see you Friday at the funeral." Barbara hugged her friend and departed.

Alone in the house, Edna reflected upon how quickly Larry's life of sixty-four years had passed. She warmed, remembering the love that surged from her as she gazed into her newborn son's deep intense blue eyes. Edna shut off the lights. Her loneliness mirrored the quietness of the house. Peace and sleep would not come easy. Long ago memories flashed like old silent movies through her mind, tiring her. Still, sleep evaded her.

After a fitful night, Edna woke Thursday to a sharp pain squeezing her chest, her breaths came short and shallow. She mused over the irony of having a heart attack on the day of Larry's viewing. Panicked, she struggled to sit, but lightheadedness forced her back to her pillow. She rubbed her fingers to stop the tingling and to distract any thoughts that perhaps she, too, was dying. Edna tried to imagine Kora-Lee and her girls planning her memorial. She wondered if Lorraine would trouble herself with her already too-busy schedule to assist with the arrangements and pay her respects. She doubted they would expend much energy on a suitable service in the event of her demise. The thought both amused and saddened her. After a few minutes, the pain subsided and her breathing returned to normal. It was only stress.

Feeling stronger, she marched to the bathroom to prepare for the day. Nonetheless, she reminded herself to talk further with Barbara about her affairs. She certainly couldn't count on Kora-Lee or her granddaughters to carry out her last wishes, especially now, knowing they were disregarding what she and Larry had discussed for his arrangements.

Alicia arrived on time to pick her up for the viewing, as promised. She rang the bell several times before Edna could get to the door. "Are you ready to go?"

Edna frowned at the hint of impatience and grabbed her purse from the dining room table. She followed Alicia to the car, opening her own door and climbing onto the well-worn, black vinyl seat which had absorbed the intense heat of the day. Edna shifted uncomfortably, both from the sticky vinyl and the oppressive tension between them. "Where's Lorraine?"

"She was at the viewing earlier. She had some last minute arrangements to make with the funeral director, though maybe David will be there."

"David? You spoke with David?" Edna straightened, turning her gaze to Alicia.

"Yeah, it sounds like he and his wife are planning on coming to the funeral. I'm not sure if they will make it in time for the viewing though."

Edna's anger relaxed, and with it the tightness in her body. She couldn't remember the last time she had seen either of her twin grandsons. "What about Nathan? Is he coming, too?"

Alicia shook her head and shared what little she knew of Nathan's situation. Edna wiped the corner of her eye with her finger. "It would be nice to see him, too, sometime."

"Well, I wouldn't count on it. It's not like they've gone out of their way to keep in touch all these years." Alicia looked across with her dark eyes awaiting a response.

Edna's pulse raced. She knew Kora-Lee had never allowed Larry to keep in touch with his sons. She didn't blame the boys. They were so young, not even school-age when their parents divorced. Edna swallowed her words. She would not get into it. Not today. Today her mind was on her loss. But today God had answered a long sought-after prayer. After so many years, she was going to see David again.

# Chapter 4

Luggage and funeral attire in the car, David and Jean were ready to hit the road. Overcoming the urge to call off the trip, David hugged his daughters and his sister-in-law goodbye.

"I wish we could go." Emily wrinkled her brows in a pout. "I really wanted to meet Great-Grandma."

"I know." David offered a weak smile. "Another time. She's going to be overwhelmed enough getting over Larry and with seeing me again. I need time to find out how she really is doing. Besides, you don't want to miss your soccer camp this weekend."

Hugs and reminders out of the way, and dreading the excursion, David turned the key in the ignition. They were on their way, for better or worse, for the drive across the state to eastern Washington.

"Are you doing all right?" Jean rested her hand on her spouse's leg. "You're very quiet."

David shrugged. No point thinking too much about a relationship which had never existed with his father. Now, it never would. "I'm only doing this out of obligation. Don't go trying to make this some big happy family reunion, okay?"

Though Jean agreed, David knew her mind was spinning a fairy tale ending on the whole awkward situation.

"Did you grab the address to the funeral home?" Jean glanced toward the back seat of the car scanning for the usual forgotten items, which always was the case with family trips.

"I already have it in the GPS." Tired from waking at six o'clock to work a half-day before the five-hour drive across the state, David focused on the tedious drive ahead.

They arrived during the last hour of the viewing. A solitary older model, blue Ford Taurus with splotches of primer on the rear driver's side stood parked in front of the funeral home chapel, along with a few hearses lining the side of the building. Inside the lobby, David was taken aback at the sight of a woman taller than he'd expected, dark eyes, and shoulder length auburn hair, not black as he remembered, but then it could just be from a bottle.

"Alicia?"

The woman rushed toward David, arms open in embrace. Caught off guard, David half-heartedly put his arms around his stepsister, patting her back.

Jean approached offering a hug of condolence. "I'm Jean, David's wife. It's too bad we have to meet under these circumstances."

Eyes smeared with black mascara, Alicia swiped the tears tracking down her cheeks with a well-used tissue. She told them about the last time she had seen her father. "I never got the chance to say goodbye. It happened so fast and he never regained consciousness." Alicia sniffled as she reached for a fresh tissue from one of several boxes scattered around the lobby on side-tables. "Come on, I'll take you to the viewing room." Alicia led them down the gleaming, gray and crimson, marble, tiled hall.

David clutched Jean's hand, an unconscious show of affection, or maybe an indication of much needed emotional support. He only knew it was good to have her here with him. Glancing inside the small, dark wood, paneled room, David saw a single casket atop a wheeled cart, visible near the front of the room. David studied the stooped posture and slight frame of the solitary visitor. "Is that Grandma Edna?"

Alicia exhaled as if exhausted. "Yeah, we got here around six. She refuses to leave until closing."

The roughness of Alicia's words bothered David. Not overly emotional, he easily imagined the difficulty of saying goodbye to a deceased child. His shoulder and neck muscles clenched. He ignored it and breathed easier, thankful Alicia's mother, Kora-Lee wasn't present in the small private grieving room. "Your mother and sister aren't here?"

"No. Mom, and Lorraine came by earlier. I said I'd stay with Grandma until they close."

Impulsively, David patted Alicia on the shoulder, his best attempt at consolation. He grabbed Jean's hand and they approached Edna with short slow steps. He hadn't been to many funerals, with all his relatives living to a ripe old age. He had never viewed an open casket and was unsure how he would feel. Stopping a few steps short from where Edna stood, David watched her for a few moments. She stood hunched over the simple, blue satin-covered casket. She plucked a yellow rose from one of the few arrangements sent in memoriam. Placing the rose in Larry's hand, she bent over and with uncontrolled sobs, kissed him.

Alicia approached David and mumbled, "That's disgusting, kissing a dead person like that. She's still upset about Larry being cremated, but she knows Mom can't afford a fancy all-out funeral."

The comment seemed inappropriate. David turned to Alicia. "I didn't know he was being cremated. How does that work, since the funeral's tomorrow?"

Alicia explained after closing, the body went to the crematorium, and by the early afternoon ceremony, Larry's remains would be in the receptacle she and her mother and sister preselected. Alicia paused often to dab her eyes. David couldn't help feeling perhaps her sorrow was over dramatized, though he had nothing on which to measure her grief.

Alicia fumbled in her purse. Pulling out her keys, she looked imploringly at David. "I've had a long day and I need to get home to my daughter. Would you mind taking your grandmother home when you're through here? Also, I need to be here early tomorrow before the guests arrive. Do you think you could pick her up and bring her to the funeral?"

"Sure, it's not a problem." David shrugged. "As long as you think Grandma's okay with it."

"I'm a little tired. It's probably best if I take a break for a while." Alicia paused before managing a feeble indication of concern. "Of course, I'll still be here for Grandma, but I think it's best if I support my mother right now. You understand?" Giving David a pat on the back, she gave a slight nod. "Thanks for coming."

Convinced his eyes would give away his feeling of disbelief, David avoided eye contact. He guessed the seemingly obvious resentment between Grandma and Kora-Lee was Alicia's real motivation for inviting him to the funeral. His role was now clearly understood. Intermediary.

After Alicia walked away, David looked at his wife and motioned with his head toward his grandmother. "I'm going to check on Grandma." He approached the casket, wiping his clammy hands on his jeans. Reaching Edna's side, he hugged her. "Hi, Grandma, I'm here."

Edna turned and looked up. Her moist eyes widened. A Cheshire cat grin spread across her face. Her wiry trembling arms reached out in a posture of praise. "David? Is that you?"

Shocked by the deep set wrinkles of time and the folds of her turkey neck, David hesitated before welcoming her embrace. "Yes, it's me. I'm sorry Nathan can't be here. He said to say hello to you." David skimmed Grandma Edna's appearance. Unlike his maternal grandmother, Edna's appearance was far from groomed. Maybe the food-stained dress and untidy hair pinned back haphazardly were only signs of her advancing age. Maybe the added stress of burying her last child was more grief than she could take. Maybe she gave up any concern about her appearance. David tried to push the shallowness of his thoughts from his mind.

Edna continued to cling to David. "I couldn't believe it when Alicia told me she called you. After all these years, thank God you are here."

"It's great to see you too, Grandma. It's been a long time."

"I don't know what I'm going to do without Larry. No one else cares about me. What's going to happen to me?" His grandmother's grief spilled out.

David pulled back, troubled by the remark. "You'll be okay Grandma, I'm sure you have lots of people who care about you. You have Kora-Lee, and your granddaughters, and I'm sure you have a lot of friends." Already questioning Alicia and her family's commitment to his grandmother, he justified the white lie about their concern as the right thing to do under the circumstances.

Grandma's eyes narrowed. She glanced around, as if checking for spies. "No. Those people don't care about me. They've just been pretending to care all these years because of Larry. Besides they're not family."

Stunned, David studied the frail woman. His eyes widened at her resentment. He was certain she hadn't heard Alicia's earlier comment. He cocked his head and looked directly at her. "Of course they're family. Why would you say that?"

Edna shot a glance back. "No. They're not blood. You and Nathan are my only family now."

Jean approached, shaking her head with index finger to lip. She narrowed her gaze toward her husband. He knew the leave-well-enough-alone look. He gulped down his unspoken comments. She took Edna's hand. "Hi. I'm Jean, David's wife. We care about you and we'll be here for you."

The drawn lines of Edna's face relaxed. She smiled at the granddaughter-in-law she was meeting for the first time.

Seeing Grandma had calmed, David stepped forward reluctantly and glimpsed down at the casket. His stomach gurgled, probably simply the lack of any substantial food during the long and hectic day. He stared at the gaunt man in a medium, gray, pinstripe suit. His thin face showed deep set lines around the lips, obvious smoker's pucker. His wrinkled and mottled skin looked older than his sixty-four years. David drew back slightly, not sure what he was expecting, but the deceased who lay in front of him was unfamiliar and aged beyond his imagining. Somehow, he expected to feel his skin crawl and to inhale the scent of ammonia or some whiff of death hanging in the air. Instead, Larry looked at peace, as if simply asleep. David detected a faint lavender scent floating on the air, likely from the array of arrangements of white and purple flowers gracing the white pedestals around the room. Aware of Edna watching him, David swallowed, rolled his tongue, and wet his lips to stir some saliva to his parched mouth. "Larry looks nice, doesn't he, Grandma?"

"Yes, I bought that suit for him. You should have seen what Kora-Lee wanted to bury him in."

David smiled and patted her arm. "You did a good job."

Jean put her arm around David. "Are you okay?"

"Sure." David lowered his voice. "It's like I'm looking at a stranger. I'm more concerned about Grandma." Glancing at this once important person of his past, now near stranger, at his arm, a hint of weirdness made his head spin. He looked unconsciously at his watch. In the past few minutes he had been reacquainted with

Alicia and already had an uncomfortable feeling. He'd seen his grandmother for the first time in over thirty years, and before him lay the body of a man whom, if he passed on the street, he might not have recognized as his own father. David looked back toward the door. Alicia had gone. David gave a sigh of relief and turned to Jean. "Thank God I don't have to say anything else to Alicia tonight, because frankly, I would find it difficult to be civil after her last comment. Are you ready to go?"

David took once last glance down at the body of his father. He contemplated saying some inspirational verse or verbally sharing some deep personal father-son memory pulled from the recesses of his mind, but words eluded him. There was no sentimental journey for him. Glancing over his shoulder, he reached for Edna's arm. "Are you okay, Grandma?"

She scanned the room. Her voice came haltingly and fearful. "I don't see Alicia."

"She asked if we could take you home. It's a good chance to get reacquainted. Is that okay?"

Moist, red eyes, sunk deeply in their sockets, gazed at David. She nodded, supporting herself on David's arm.

"Ready?"

With just a sliver of smile, Edna turned and stepped unsteadily to the door.

"Thank you." David nodded to the funeral home attendant who waited by the door, most likely anxious to have them leave so he could lock up for the evening. David looked at his watch. "I'm sorry. I didn't realize it was so late."

"It's quite all right, Sir." The dark suited man held the glass door open.

Jean hurried ahead and opened the front door of their Mustang convertible. "This probably isn't the best car for you Grandma. It's a little difficult to get in and out of."

David assisted her into the front seat, supporting most of her weight as he lowered her down onto the black leather seat.

"It's just fine, dear. It's so nice of you to take me home." Grandma held on for an extra moment to David's arm before he was allowed to withdraw it and close the door.

With Grandma situated and buckled in, Jean went around the driver's side and climbed into the back seat.

David looked across the front seat. "I don't know the way to your house, Grandma, so you're going to have to show me." He reached across and patted her hand, as much to gain her attention as to show emotion. "Are you still living in that rambler in Kennewick?"

Grandma sat grinning and humming.

He studied her face. Perhaps her hearing was weak. He raised his voice slightly. "Grandma, do you still live in Kennewick?"

"Oh, my Lord, no, dear. I sold that place. I moved to Richland two years ago."

"Okay. Why don't you give me your address and I can find it from there." David looked in the rear view mirror and caught a glimpse of Jean's broad smile and her attempt to stifle her amusement.

"I'll show you the way."

David tensed, sensing things wouldn't be that simple. "I guess we turn right out of here and head to Richland?" He pulled the car onto the marked street with arrows indicating south.

"I'll show you, dear. It's a little way down the road."

David turned his attention to driving in the unfamiliar city, which always made him uncomfortable. The long day was wearing on him and his patience was growing thin.

Grandma shifted in her seat. "It's so nice having you both here."

Leaning forward, Jean put her hand on Edna's shoulder. "I'm so glad to meet you, too, after all these years. I'm sorry I never got the chance to meet Larry."

Grandma's attention elsewhere, David was forced to keep her focused on directing him to her home.

Edna looked around, seemingly confused. "Turn left at the next light."

David obeyed, continuing a few blocks. His hands gripped the wheel a little tighter. "Where to now, Grandma?" His voice came harsher and sharper than he intended.

Grandma's eyes darted around. "No, wait, this isn't right, I don't know where we are. Did you pass Columbia Drive yet?"

David took a deep breath and pulled the car into a parking lot. He sensed Jean's calm-down-and-breathe gaze burning through the back of his car seat. "How about you give me your address. We have a gadget which will lead us right there."

"3971 Morningside Avenue."

Removing the GPS from the window mount, David handed it over the seat to Jean. A twinge of pain stabbed at his temples. A head-ache was one thing he didn't need on top of everything else.

Edna straightened. "Oh, wait, dear. There's the turn. Turn right at the Market Place. I know where we are now."

The tension in David's shoulders and neck muscles eased as Grandma directed him into the drive for the townhouse units where she lived.

"It's the last unit on the left. That's my white Buick parked there."

David raised his eyebrows. He hadn't considered the possibility she was still driving. He studied the well-dented metal shed that lay dead ahead a few feet, speculating how the dents got there as he pulled alongside her car. "So, this is your house. It looks nice, Grandma."

"It's a lovely home. Would you like to see it?"

David checked at the clock on the dash. "It's late, and we've had a long day, between work and the long drive over. How about we see it tomorrow?" He got out and walked to the passenger door to assist his grandmother. "Alicia needs to be at the funeral home early tomorrow. If it's okay, we'll be by a little before noon to pick you up to take you to the service. Is that going to allow us enough time to get there by twelve-thirty?"

"Of course, dear. Why don't you stay here tonight?"

"I'm sorry, we've already reserved and paid for a hotel." David walked to the front door of the townhouse. Grandma fumbled with her key in the door. "I wish you would stay. It would be so nice to have my grandson stay with me."

"I'm sorry, Grandma, maybe another time. Are you going to be all right alone tonight?"

"I'll be fine. Thank you, dear." Edna hugged David goodbye.

Saddened by his grandmother's drawn, aged face, David returned the hug, then watched as she shuffled inside and closed the door.

# Chapter 5

The next day, driving from the hotel to his grandmother's house, David mulled over Alicia's request. "Don't you think it's odd I'm picking up Grandma, not Alicia or Lorraine? You know I don't mind, it's just that I'm a stranger to her, compared to Larry's family."

"I don't know." Jean looked over at David. "Maybe they don't feel they have the time to share in your grandmother's grief when they're so overwhelmed themselves."

"Maybe." David shrugged, unconvinced. "But Alicia sounded like Grandma was a bother to her and her family, and based on Grandma's comment, she doesn't exactly consider them family, either." He pulled the car into the drive, hopped out and strode to the door. Grandma stepped out like a newborn fawn on gangly legs. She clutched a tan, old-fashioned, vinyl purse to her chest as she steadied herself.

"Hi, Grandma. It looks like you're ready to go." David's heart ached as he glanced at the fragile woman, who had just lost her last child. She had outlived her only sister, her spouse, and now both of her children. The thought of losing all his loved ones made his gut churn. He tried to imagine the emptiness she must be feeling.

In spite of the warmth of the day, Grandma wore a heavy brown tweed coat, showing many years of wear. Her brown slip-on shoes were beyond well-worn. Her hair, strewn on top of her head, was a beautician's nightmare of long fine white hair held tight with loosely held bobbie pins.

Jean walked over and leaned into David. "She can't go to her own son's funeral looking like this."

David looked at his watch. "I don't know what we can do about it now." Regret gripped him. "I wish we had come earlier. Maybe we could have helped her clean up a bit." He shook his head. He doubted Grandma was aware of her appearance or would have accepted help anyway. He remembered her being strong-willed, and even with her advanced age, it was apparent she maintained this trait. He reminisced on the once young, prim and proper, always tidy, school teacher, who never would have allowed herself to look so unkempt.

"Do you need any help?" Noticing her eyes were less red than the previous night, he guessed she had slept fairly well. Still, he imagined the deep-set wrinkles were etched by a lifetime of tears and sadness as well as good times.

Grandma's eyes shined and she flashed a brief smile. "I'm just fine, dear. You look so handsome in that navy blue suit."

David reached out, took her free arm, and lowered her onto the car seat. With the GPS loaded with the address of the funeral home, David backed the car out of the drive.

Grandma looked out the window as David drove. "Do you know where we're going?"

"Yes, Grandma. I have the address this time."

"I see. I wasn't too sure about that. No one has told me anything about where it is we're going."

David turned and studied her face. "We're going to Mueller's Funeral Home, the same place we were last night."

"Oh yes, I almost forgot. The funeral home. Are we going to visit Bernice?"

Glancing in the rearview mirror at Jean, David raised his brows with a slight shake of his head and eyes narrowed in concern. "No, Grandma, we're going to Larry's funeral."

"Larry? Yes, that's right, he's dead too." Her voice drifted off. "Today's his funeral you know? Is he going to be buried next to Bernice?"

Uncertain of the disposition of the urn, an uneasy burning speared his eyes. David tried to blink it away. "I don't know where they made plans to bury him. Maybe next to Bernice."

"Oh, I wondered about that."

Arriving only a few minutes behind schedule, David scoured the near empty lot for a close parking space. He offered Edna an arm to exit the car. Once inside, he glanced around the lobby, searching for Alicia's familiar face or even Kora-Lee's. Though he wasn't sure he would even recognize her, he imagined he could make an educated guess on her appearance.

After a few moments, an attendant in his crisp black suit and tie strode up. "Are you Larry's son?"

"Yes, I'm David." Extending his hand, he introduced Edna and Jean. "I don't see the rest of Larry's family." David noticed the reluctance from the emotionless, dark-haired, middle-aged man, as he straightened his horn-rimmed glasses before motioning them down the hall.

"Your room is this way."

David grabbed hold of his grandmother's arm and followed the attendant into a small sitting room facing what apparently was the chapel. "What's this?" David glanced around the room lined with sturdy wooden chairs with deep red corduroy cushions, all of which were empty. A wall of large windows looked into the chapel area, slowly filling with people. A modest selection of recently added colorful bouquets joined the previous night's assortment of white and purple flowers gracing the stairs and circling the podium. "Where are the rest of the family members?"

The attendant shifted his weight. "This is the private grieving room the widow and the Pearson family selected for your comfort. The rest of the family members will be entering the main chapel shortly, where they'll be seated with the other guests."

David shook his head in disbelief, swallowing his first thought. Knowing he was putting an innocent man on the spot, he prodded the attendant nonetheless. "Is there a reason we're not all seated together?"

"Mrs. Pearson thought you would be more comfortable in a private room, separate from the immediate family." Light reflected off the drops of perspiration on his forehead and the attendant swiped at his forehead with a white handkerchief from his pocket.

David held his tongue, but allowed his mind free reign. *Yeah, right! This was done for our sake.* He asked the attendant to explain to Kora-Lee and her daughters, his concern. "I think we should all be seated together. We're all Larry's family, especially Larry's mother." David patted Edna's arm.

The attendant hustled out to relay the message. It didn't matter, David knew what the response would be the moment the attendant departed. A slight twinge of remorse stabbed at his conscience for putting the attendant in the position to try to reason with a group of people who obviously couldn't be reasoned with.

Returning, the attendant motioned David over. "I'm sorry, Mr. Bryant, Mrs. Pearson prefers the existing arrangements. Please, if there's anything else I can do, let me know."

It wasn't the attendant's fault. There was no point in pushing the awkward situation further. David extended his hand and thanked him for his help.

"I'm feeling faint." Edna turned and reached for David's hand. "I don't think I can make it." Her knees buckled.

David caught her under the arms just as she collapsed to the floor. He called for Jean's assistance. "See if you can get some water for her, and maybe a wet cloth."

With quick assistance from the attendant, David dabbed at Edna's forehead while Jean bent over her with a glass of water. "Are you doing okay?" David awkwardly helped her to a seated position. "Let's get your coat off, it's too warm in here to be wearing a coat." Removing the coat, David's mouth gaped at the sight of the stains sprinkled across the front of her cream-colored floral dress. He also became aware of the run on her mismatched knee high hose which showed underneath the torn hem of the dress. Seeing her appearance, he couldn't help wondering how adequately his grandmother's needs were being met by her supposed loving and caring son and his family.

After a minute or so, color returned to Edna's cheeks. Looking around, her eyes widened. "Where is everyone else?"

David could almost fathom Kora-Lee seating him away from the crowd as if he were a bum in a swanky restaurant. But the thought of Larry's own mother being asked to sit apart from the rest of the mourners, especially Kora-Lee and her daughters, pissed him off. He motioned for Jean, who steadied the chair as David eased Grandma in place. "We have our own separate room so you can grieve in private, Grandma. I thought it would be less stress for you than sitting with the rest of the guests."

Grandma nodded, seemingly satisfied with the answer, but David boiled at the inane dealings of the whole thing, briefly wishing he hadn't come. Then he looked at his grandmother weeping and alone. He leaned toward Jean. "I wonder what would have happened to Grandma if we hadn't come. Don't these people have a conscience?"

His father was dead, he should feel some emotion, yet how could he? He had only seen him twice since he was five years old. He didn't feel like he had lost anyone special to him, because he hadn't. Funny, Grandma considered family the bloodline, regardless of whether there was any emotional contact involved. Whereas, David considered family the people who were there for you, emotionally and physically, whether blood or not. His grandmother had apparently tried to forge a relationship with Kora-Lee and her granddaughters, but from the looks of the sorry arrangements here, it was obvious the only concrete relationship forged was forced by his father's marriage to Kora-Lee. Now, with Larry gone, their blatant disregard toward her was clear. Any family relationship that may have been carved by the passing of time seemed severely splintered now. Grandma's last child had died. It was the cruelest and most difficult obstacle for a parent to face. Her closest relatives geographically, and by association, did not appear capable of showing compassion. He couldn't recall crying since he was a small child, and no tears would fall today. Not for his dad. The only grief revealed would be for the tragedy faced by the old woman next to him. Overwhelmed, he patted Grandma's cold hand. "Do you need a Kleenex?" He handed a box of tissue to her.

"It's not right," David told Jean. "I know Larry was her son, but with my limited exposure how his family is treating Grandma and us, it's hard to imagine him as a caring man." The thought of how this other family could be so dysfunctional boggled his mind. Larry certainly hadn't been a role model to Nathan or David. He never gave their mother or them a second thought, or even child support, once he returned to the states.

The minister strode in from the side vestibule, interrupting David's thoughts. Impeccably dressed in the appropriate garb for the occasion, black suit and tie, pressed white shirt and shiny patent leather shoes, he addressed the small gathering from the podium. In the front row, David spied Lorraine, Kora-Lee, and Alicia seated next to a young girl, probably the daughter she mentioned. Larry's granddaughter, Edna's great-granddaughter. Buried in his thoughts, he hadn't seen them enter the chapel.

"We are gathered here to pay our final respects to Larry Jacob Pearson and we pray for his wife and family who will sorely miss him."

David listened to the minister's words which came loud and clear across the speakers on the wall of their small grieving room. The minister spouted well-rehearsed lines of the expected norm for the occasion, bowed his head in prayer over a small brass urn which undoubtedly held Larry's remains, then invited Alicia to the front.

She strode to the podium with the stature, allure and attire of a model walking a cat-walk. Prim, proper, and poised, she faced the audience with confidence. Pausing, she brushed back her deep auburn hair from her face before starting. She began with some trivial stories of her life with her father, and told those gathered how much he would be missed by his wife and daughters. After Alicia finished her part of the eulogy, Lorraine took the microphone. She shared stories of being Daddy's oldest daughter, and his pride and joy, and all the related hoopla of him being a wonderful father.

There was no acknowledgement of David, Nathan, or Edna. No sign of respect of Larry's mother left alone without her son, her last child. David had already decided he didn't wish to associate himself with this family. He shook his head and squeezed Jean's hand, inwardly grateful for the love and respect of his own family.

Grandma sobbed openly with deep breaths into a wrinkled flowered handkerchief. "Larry was all I had, he took care of me, and he was the only one who really loved me since Bernice died. Now he's gone, too. What am I going to do?"

For all of the negative thoughts which had passed through David's head in the previous few minutes, Edna's words relayed what David had failed to recognize. Larry was her son. He loved her, in his own way, and she loved him. Maybe that was enough. David put his arm around his grandmother but turned to face his wife, keeping his voice low. "To hell with Kora-Lee, and I'm not sure what to make of her daughters. They may have been Larry's family, but they have made it clear they don't want to be part of my life and I wonder if they intend to be part of Grandma's life."

Jean acknowledged, placing her hand on his leg.

Tuning out the continuing drivel from Lorraine, David took a deep breath. With his arm around the frail old woman's shoulders, he said, "I know, Grandma, I'm sorry he's gone. You still have Nathan and me. And we love you. We're your family now, and we'll be here for you." A pang of resentment pierced him for the position and responsibility in which he now found himself. He didn't need the stress. He was already overwhelmed with six-day work weeks and still finishing the basement and clearing the acreage of his new home.

The minister concluded the ceremony by thanking the congregation for their support of Larry's loved ones. After inviting everyone to the reception downstairs, he turned and disappeared from view.

"We'll help you through this, we promise." Jean took Grandma's arm and led her out into the hall.

The attendant greeted them by the door. David caught an attempt at a smile from the man. "Don't forget the reception in the hall downstairs."

David shook his head. He had no intention of being ignored by Larry's family any longer. He looked over at his Grandmother. "I think Larry's mother has had enough for one day."

Edna stopped in her tracks. "Oh, no, dear. My friends have all come to the funeral. We need to go to the reception."

David took a deep breath before conceding. Edna's presence at the reception was appropriate and necessary, though he doubted his patience for being civil to Alicia and the others after the way he and Edna had been shunned the past hour. Nodding at the attendant, he followed him down the hall where they were directed to a flight of stairs. David thanked the attendant and escorted his grandmother to the hall laid out with long cafeteria-style, tan tables covered with white cotton tablecloths and lined with tan upholstered folding chairs. "Come on, Grandma. Let's find a place to sit, and then I can get you something to eat, if you like." David steered Grandma toward a nearby table and helped her get settled. "Would you like something to drink?"

She nodded. "Are there sandwiches or crackers? I haven't eaten anything today."

Jean scooted a chair closer and sat down next to Edna. "I'll sit with Grandma while you get a small plate for her and you."

David headed toward the end of the short refreshment line. He scanned the crowd for Edna's supposed family, in a small way, hoping to at least speak with Lorraine after all these years. A pleasant-looking middle-aged plus woman approached. He refocused his attention.

"Hi, I'm Barbara. You must be David. Your grandmother was so excited when she called me last night to tell me you had come."

David extended his hand.

Barbara took his hand in both of hers with a warm relaxed smile showing genuine care and concern.

"I'm so pleased to meet you at last. I've known your grandmother through garden club and church for over ten years. I can't tell you how much it means to her to have you here. She's shared so many stories about you and your twin brother."

The comment surprised David. After all these years, his grandmother had still spoken of him and Nathan. "Really?"

Barbara gestured toward the moving line. David swept his arm out, motioning her ahead of him. He examined the assorted tea-sized sandwiches, egg salad, and either tuna or chicken salad, dressed with olives and pimento. Nothing looked appetizing. He selected a few for his grandmother, took a spoonful of fruit salad, and a bit of macaroni salad, and grabbed a clear plastic cup of non-alcoholic punch. He'd come back and get some much-needed coffee for himself in a few minutes and stop for a burger or sub sandwich on the way home, when he was more in the mood for eating. He headed back to the table where his grandmother was seated.

Barbara glanced in the direction Edna was seated. "I'm so thankful you are here to help her through this. It's a relief for me. I won't have to worry so much about what will happen to her now." Barbara must have thought herself too forward and presumptuous. She paused before continuing on. "You will be keeping in touch and watching out for her, won't you?"

He closed his eyes. His mind spun a whirlwind of thoughts before he drew a deep breath, realizing the commitment he faced with his answer. He nodded. "Of course."

Barbara smiled her approval and carried her plate to the table to join Jean and Edna. Setting the plate down for his grandmother,

David waited for Barbara to take a seat before introducing her to Jean. He looked forward to chatting with Barbara further.

"Come on, let's offer our condolences to Kora-Lee." Jean grabbed David's arm.

"Why?" He pulled away, disgusted by the whole charade being played by Kora-Lee's grieving family, and their cold-hearted treatment of their own grandmother.

"Because it's the right thing to do." Jean turned to Barbara and Edna. "Excuse us for just a few minutes. We'll be right back."

Nudged on, David followed Jean. "Let me get myself some coffee first." He grabbed a Styrofoam cup and poured a cup of java with a splash of cream, before unwillingly weaving through the crowd to where Kora-Lee stood. He watched curiously as Kora-Lee, dressed in all black, accepted condolences from friends while dabbing at her heavily blushed face with a tissue.

Jean pushed on, unfazed. "Hello. I'm Jean, David's wife. We're so sorry for your loss."

Kora-Lee turned, her dark brown eyes wide, her jaw dropped in unsuspecting surprise. She stood motionless for a beat before speaking. Her words of gratitude seemed disingenuous. Obviously uncomfortable around them, Kora-Lee glanced around the room, focused her gaze elsewhere, and excused herself to chat with other mourners. With a jerk of the head, she dismissed them.

Alicia stepped forward with more grace, and certainly more manners, than her mother. "We're glad you could make it." She put her hand on a young girl's shoulder, and beamed down. "This is my daughter, Lacey."

David and Jean took turns shaking hands with the composed dark haired girl of around ten. Lacey resembled her mother in many ways, but there were obvious characteristics from her father's side. "We're pleased to meet you, Lacey." David recognized Lorraine standing next to Alicia. Lorraine smiled and extended her hand. "Hi, remember me? Lorraine."

David studied the two sisters standing side by side. The contrast in height and features became apparent. Lorraine was several inches shorter, had a tawnier complexion, and a smaller nose, like her mother's. It was hard to picture them as sisters. However, Jean and her sister looked nothing alike, either. "Hi, it's been a long time. I'm sorry about your dad. But then, he was my dad too."

Lorraine wore a pasted-on smile and offered words of appreciation though hollow of much emotion. Not knowing her, David withheld judgement and accepted her words with his own fake smile. Talking with the strangers who were his stepsisters was uncomfortable, and forced, just as he expected. "Well, I'm glad I could be here to pay my respects and help Grandma Edna through this. I hate to leave her alone during such a difficult time." David glanced back to where he had left his grandmother. "I'd like to stay and chat, but Grandma could use the company." David pointed in the direction where Edna was seated. "I'm sure she'd appreciate you stopping by when you have a moment, to see how she's doing." He shook his sisters' hands, then taking Jean's hand, he guided her back to his grandmother. Nearing the table, David saw Edna sitting alone and looking around, unconsciously pushing the fruit salad around with her fork. He hurried back and sat down. "Where's Barbara?"

"She had to get home to her husband. He's quite ill. Wasn't it nice of her to come?"

David patted her shoulder. "Yes, it was, Grandma. I was hoping to talk to her some more, though."

"She said she would get your phone number from me and call you sometime next week."

A few more friendly faces emerged from the otherwise aloof, if not hostile, crowd. David and Jean introduced themselves to Grandma's neighbors, Fred and Marge.

"Hi, your grandmother's told us all about you. We're so pleased she has people who care about her." Fred glanced at Edna before continuing. "I'm not sure how much you know about her situation."

"Not much. If today's experience is any indication, I can imagine." David looked around the respectable crowd of people. He guessed they were there primarily to support Kora-Lee and her girls. Grandma sat mostly ignored. David didn't mind being shunned by these people, but neither Larry's spouse nor his loving children even approached Edna with a kind word or caring hug.

The hand had been dealt in a game David was still trying to understand. There was nothing left to do but finish out the play.

After all, Edna was family, and family always takes care of family. David motioned to Jean then stood to leave. Pulling back his grandmother's chair he took her arm. "Come on Grandma. Let's take you home."

# Chapter 6

Back at Grandma's house, David took the keys, unlocked the door, and held it open for her. Stepping inside, the stench of urine abruptly announced a pet in the home. A pet that most likely did not get out or get its box cleaned. David wrinkled his nose and glanced at Jean. Grandma's small, black, stringy-haired mix of cocker and terrier, yapped and trotted to the door. It looked and smelled sorely in need of a bath. After seeing Grandma's appearance, David doubted she managed to bathe herself often, let alone the dog.

"Hi, Missy. I'm home. Did you miss me?" Grandma bent down and massaged the dog's fur by his neck with a playful pat.

"That's the most disgusting dog I've ever seen." David scrunched his face, his nasal passages burned from the overpowering odor of ammonia.

Jean shook her head and looked around. "This place looks terrible." She took in a deep breath before walking toward the living room. David led Grandma across the stained, gold-green shag carpet to her dirty, shredded, cat scratching post of a sofa, an obvious breeding ground for bacteria. He didn't see the cat, but the odor was tell-tale.

The semi-closed dingy blinds allowed little light into the room. Under these circumstances, it was almost more light than David cared for. He thought back to thirty years earlier when he had last seen his grandmother's home. Surely this was the same sofa. It looked at least that old. He would bet it hadn't been cleaned since. With trepidation, David glanced around at the dust-covered blinds and the cobwebbed ceiling. He walked over to the windows, hesitating before he drew the blinds the rest of the way open. With the brightness of the sun illuminating the room, David looked closely at the cobwebs and behind the curtains. His eyes widened at the small black specks darkening the corner. His skin tingled and he brushed away imaginary crawly things on his arms. "Good God." He covered his mouth at the sight, studying the black specks, then closed his eyes momentarily in denial of hundreds of tiny moving arachnids. He looked back at Edna seated on the sofa with Jean, and wondered how she could live in such horrendous conditions. David gestured with his head for Jean to come.

"What?" Jean went to the window leaving Edna still playing with the disheveled dog. Her eyes followed David's gaze. She drew back, shaking her head. "Tell me that's not what I think it is."

Totally baffled by the situation, David watched his grandmother fumble with a Chap Stick laying amidst magazines, coffee cups, even pink foam curlers wrapped with hair, scattered across the dark pressed wood coffee table. He took in the clutter of the room. Ragged outdated issues of Better Homes and Garden, Sunset, Flowers and Garden, and other magazines and papers littered the floor. An accumulation of old baskets of faded, yellow and red reed, possibly hand-made, along with shoe boxes of yarns and fabrics holding dozens of half-finished sewing projects sprung up like weeds in an unkempt yard. Beaded Christmas ornaments flowed over odd sized boxes and trays on the hearth of the soot-stained, over-sized, rock fireplace. The living room furniture was a strange melding of the gold ratty sofa, oversized brown chair, cheap end tables, and beautiful mahogany antique pieces. He walked over to a curved mahogany dresser along one wall.

Watching him, Edna smiled. "The furniture belonged to my mother and father." She walked over to the dresser which sat to the left of the smoke-stained rock fireplace and practically caressed an ornate wooden mantle clock. "This clock was a wedding gift for my parents in eighteen-ninety-one. Look, it still runs perfectly."

David looked at the clock, which read eleven forty-two. He listened for the steady beat of the pendulum, ticking time, not quite accurately. "It's beautiful, Grandma." He thought back to his last visit and envisioned a younger woman in control of an orderly home. He recalled a neat, unpretentious, home with everything in its place, a true showcase for her talents of needlepoint and sewing.

"Is this what happens when people get old? They stop caring about their homes?" David watched Jean swipe the top of the dust covered mahogany dresser with her hand.

"I don't think so. It's more likely her eyesight is failing and maybe something else more serious. Who knows? It's obvious though, she's not able to care for herself, let alone the house. She probably doesn't even realize how dirty it is. I don't understand how Alicia and Grandma's friends can see how she's living and just ignore it." Jean glanced around the room.

"I could use some water." Edna sat wiping her eyes.

"I'll get it." Jean excused herself and headed for the kitchen. David suspected she welcomed the escape from the spiders which had always terrified her. When she returned a few moments later, she handed Edna a glass. Edna accepted it with eager gulps. With a sideways glance, Jean whispered to David, discreetly updating the situation. "I can't leave this place in this condition and feel good about myself. How could Larry allow her to live like this? Hasn't anyone else noticed how dirty it is? There's a pile from the dog in the corner of the kitchen."

Jean led David into the filthy kitchen, reeking from dog poop. The light green Formica counters were cluttered with food scraps, some, atop white Styrofoam meat trays. David looked at the gold and brown stain covered, kitchen carpet and held his breath. He didn't have to guess what the stains were from. He noticed the dog dish, alive with flies, rejected even by the dog, filled with dried table scraps from only God knows when.

"How long do you think it will take to make this place presentable?" David looked at his watch. "I know it needs a lot more work than we can do today, but maybe we can at least clean the kitchen and bathrooms and remove the spider's nests."

Jean sighed. "Let's see what we can get done in a couple of hours. I'll call home and let the girls and Marie know we'll be a little late, and then I'll get started on the kitchen. You see if you can find a vacuum." Jean looked under the sink. She pulled out a well-worn sponge and can of cleanser, shook it, and frowned at the hollow sound. Spying the laundry room, she opened the cupboards. "Maybe there are more supplies in here."

"Grandma's going to wonder where you are."

"Tell her I'm making a cup of tea, and ask if she'd like one, too." Jean returned empty handed of supplies.

David leaned in, kissed his wife, then walked out to join his grandmother. Stopping to use the bathroom on the way, the brown stained porcelain bowl, and grime covered sink disturbed him all the more. He scrunched his face at the sight. How could anyone live in a home only two years and have it fall to such frightful condition? Rejoining his grandmother on the sofa, Missy plodded over and jumped into her waiting lap. Looking up with a raised lip, the dog snarled at David.

"Missy is a sweet dog, and she's so protective of me. She always barks to let me know if someone is at the door, or if I don't hear the phone." Edna's tremulous hand stroked the mangy dog. "I used to have a cat, too." She cast her eyes downward. "She was a wonderful companion, but she died."

Relieved at least there was only one pet to battle over odors and cleanliness, David resisted the urge to comment, choosing to change the subject to something hopefully productive. "Where do you keep your vacuum Grandma? Jean thought maybe we could spend a few minutes helping you out while we're here."

"Oh, you. Don't start sounding like Barbara. That's not necessary. I can clean when you're gone. Where is Jean? I want to show both of you my home. Larry sold it to me when he was in real estate."

David's mouth fell open. How could a man consider selling a two-story home to his elderly mother? It should have been obvious that by ninety, taking the stairs would begin to present a challenge to most people. Was this man so hell-bent on making a real estate commission that he'd sell a home which wasn't suitable for a senior citizen, especially his own mother, to make a buck?

Grandma pushed herself off the sofa and headed toward the kitchen, calling for Jean.

Hearing her name, Jean appeared in the hallway. Grandma led her visitors down the still darkened hallway, pointing out her needlepoint hangings of orange oriental poppies, vibrant purple pansies, and roses in shades of red and pink scattered across the once white walls. Jean flicked on the light switch to better see the meticulously crafted pieces of artwork. Fine quality detailed works showed the patience and persistence of Grandma's younger years.

"My friend Barbara loves these pink and red roses." Edna pointed to a gold painted framed needlepoint. "I promised it to her when I'm gone." She removed the picture from the small nail and turned it over, revealing the shaky, sprawled, black letters of

Barbara's name and a date penned on the paper backing. "You make sure she gets this when I'm gone." Edna showed off beautiful moss green oriental silk hangings woven with intricate flowers in vibrant hues of orange and red which hung in the dining room. "Larry brought those back for me from Korea." Her voice lowered before she continued. "When he returned with his new pregnant wife and her young daughter."

David wondered if he would ever understand the relationship between his grandmother and Kora-Lee and Larry's step daughters.

Edna moved slowly, gripping the stair rail as she climbed the first flight of stairs to the landing. Halfway up, she stopped. Her chest heaved heavily. She bent down over a small corner table and picked up a black fluted vase shaped like a tall cylinder. "I grew these and dried them myself."

David's eyes swept over an assortment of dried flowers that filled the dusty vases and chipped garage sale pots, now broken and faded by time, suiting the surrounding décor and the resident of the home.

The upstairs held Grandma's bedroom with a full wall of mirrored closet doors, a large white and gold dresser, a neatly made bed covered with a white and yellow spread, and a small wooden clothes drying rack, with several personal unmentionables hanging from it. David rolled his eyes as he followed her into the master bath. Edna's bathroom was equally appalling to the one downstairs with a mirror bearing the spray of many washings and teeth brushings. A blackened sink had not seen cleanser for some time. Edna pushed open the door to the guest-room. David turned to catch a glimpse of Jean's wide eyes. The double bed lay draped in a red crushed-velvet bedspread. Red glass lamps with dingy yellowed shades sporting gold tassels, flanked the bed on small, mismatched, dark wood grained, night stands. The gaudy room lacked only plastic beads to complete the look of college dwellings of the late sixties.

"This is my craft room." Edna creaked open the door to the last room. Clutter buried most of the room. Clearly the keepsake room, bookshelves and file cabinets bulged with fabric, yarn, and patterns. David glanced at the vintage treadle sewing machine and table covered with a visible layer of dust and wondered how many years it had gone unused.

"Well, what do you think?" Grandma's smile relayed her pride.

"It's very nice." David and Jean nodded their heads, then, dutifully followed her back down the stairs.

Jean veered off at the bottom of the stairs. "I think I'll duck into the kitchen and get back to the cleaning I started. Holler if Grandma gets suspicious."

David walked across the living room and joined his grandmother by the window and a gold painted metal plant stand. "Your African violets are incredible." Bending over to examine the plants, David noticed a half dozen of the largest pink and purple African violets he had ever seen, stretching nearly two feet across. "I've never seen African violets as big and healthy as these." He wondered how she could take such good care of plants when her house looked like a tornado had swooshed through it.

"I've taken a dozen clippings from this one plant. My garden club is always telling me they've never seen anything like them." Edna's eyes sparkled as her fingers stroked the velvety leaves. "I have a green thumb, if I do say so myself. I'm a master gardener, you know."

Though her home was beyond dirty, Edna's stance and confident tone conveyed her pride in her abode and her many talents. David glanced at the sofa cushion. A few swipes with his hand failed to dislodge the dog hair coating the gold velour. A large pillow wedge and blankets sat piled at the end of the sofa.

"Are you still able to manage the stairs okay, Grandma?"

"Of course I am. I just took them, didn't I?" Her words hissed like venom.

He suspected she had been using the sofa as a bed, but there was no point in pursuing the issue. Instead, he turned his gaze to the faces in the framed photos on the octagonal end table, next to the sofa. Facial characteristics helped identify the spirits from the past. There was Granddad Jacob as a young soldier, and another of Larry in his uniform looking about the age David remembered him when his parents divorced. A black and white eight by ten photo of a beautiful young woman sat next to the others, most likely high school graduation from the look of the sweater and simple, curled-under hairstyle. Edna, perhaps. He doubted it. His mind flashed back to Bernice. This picture may well be the last formal picture ever taken of the woman who would have been his aunt had she not died so tragically in a car accident at twenty-one.

A sensation of light breathing tickled David's neck. The presence of Edna watching him caused him to turn away from the shrine to her family. "They're beautiful pictures, Grandma." There was no point in drawing her into the past. Not with the memory of burying her last child still fresh in her mind. He needed a brief reprieve and Jean had been noticeably absent for some time. "I'm going to get some water, Grandma. May I get you some?" David walked down the hall.

"I couldn't find her vacuum, so I tried to sweep the dining room carpet." Jean held up an old worn corn stalk broom and pointed to the metal dust pan piled with dirt. "I don't mind helping clean the house, but … I'm not taking care of the spiders." Jean grabbed a dingy dish towel from the counter and wrapped it around the bristles of the broom. Picking up a rubber band from the counter, she wrapped it around the broom handle holding the towel in place and held it out to David. "Here."

It was Jean's turn to keep Grandma busy while David dealt with the icky task of destroying the minute arachnids. Showing interest in the contents of the china cabinet, Jean lured Grandma into the dining room. "I see you have some beautiful carvings." Jean stood in front of the over-sized cabinet.

"Oh, yes. Larry brought me some of these from Japan and Korea, others I picked up when I took Alicia with me to travel throughout Asia, after she graduated from high school." Edna opened the glass cupboard, lovingly gazing upon a jade dragon figurine as she withdrew it.

David watched to make sure Grandma was fully involved in her show and tell, then cringing, he headed for the living room curtains. Lifting the broom handle high and pulling the curtains back, the spiders nests were gathered onto the towel and taken out the back door to be disposed of. After half a dozen trips outside, David brushed away the creepy sensation and some remnants of silky web. He exhaled a massive sigh of relief and took a final glance at the arachnid-free walls and ceiling. He'd done his part.

Over the next hour, they swapped roles keeping Grandma out of the way and entertained while the other cleaned. With the kitchen sinks scoured and scraped, the toilets scrubbed, the cupboards wiped down, and dog scraps and messes wiped up, David reminded Jean the day was getting late. "We've got to get going. The girls are waiting and Marie has to be home for the weekend for her own family."

At the door, David paused. His left brain screamed of the responsibility which lie in his future, but his right brain fought back with a twinge of guilt as he hugged Edna goodbye. The kiss on his grandmother's cheek betrayed her emotions. David wiped her salty tear off his lips. "We'll see you soon." David took her gnarled hand, freckled with the spots of age, and held it for moment. His head hurt facing the reality the past twenty-four hours was only the beginning of how his life was going to change. Attending his father's funeral pushed him into the position of assuming some responsibility for his grandmother. He didn't know to what degree. For the moment, he had no desire to pursue a relationship with Alicia or Lorraine, but he knew his relationship with his grandmother somehow was just beginning.

# Chapter 7

For the first few weeks after Larry's funeral David called his grandmother weekly. After all, she was family, and it was the right thing to do. But as the calendar flipped into fall and the rituals of everyday life with his hectic work schedule and family responsibilities, the once-weekly calls stretched out. Eventually the calls became another required task to squeeze into his life, more out of obligation than love. From the sound of things, Grandma was in good hands with her friends from the garden club, especially Barbara, who dropped by often. David was sure there wasn't much to worry about. Once in a while he wondered how she was doing and reminded himself he needed to call more often, but he had a life and a job and family. If Grandma needed anything, she knew she could call him.

Before he knew it, Christmas had come and gone, with all the confusion of shopping, decorations, commitments, sports and family drama. David's only private time in the evening found him in front of the computer keeping up to date on the news, the economy, and checking his modest investments. The promise of keeping in touch with Edna had become a faded vow until one evening the shrill ring of the phone drew David's attention from the screen. Surely, Jean or one of the girls would get it. The continued ringing reminded David he was home alone. Turning away from his computer, he retrieved the telephone from the bookshelf in the den.

"I'm so lonely. I miss Larry so much." Grandma's tired voice caused a stab of guilt. David regretted his neglect and imagined his grandmother's grief. He wondered what his life would be like if Jean, Rachel and Emily, even Nathan, were dead. His chest tightened at the thought.

"Alicia's been by to check on me. She even brought me a

lovely spinach and noodle casserole. It's much more than I can eat by myself, though."

David wrinkled his face at the mention of the spinach casserole. A sarcastic comment came to mind. He squelched it. "Alicia's been by? That's nice. Does she visit often?" His interest was piqued, perhaps he had misjudged her. Maybe the whole seating arrangement at the funeral was all Kora-Lee's doing. Maybe there was hope his stepsisters would maintain contact with the woman they had called Grandma for nearly forty years. He inhaled a calming breath, at least Alicia was there to see to some of Grandma's needs.

"She's been by a few times. It's so nice when she brings Lacey with her. Lacey reminds me so much of my Bernice. But, Alicia makes me so angry trying to convince me Larry wanted to be cremated. I know that's a lie. When am I going to see you again?"

David flinched at the sorrow in her voice and the question he couldn't evade. He mumbled a feeble excuse of his busy work schedule and promised to try to visit sometime soon. Saddened, and draped in guilt not wholly deserved, David said a reluctant goodbye, promising to call her again soon.

Over dinner that evening, Rachel came up with an idea. "Since Grandma wasn't around when we were little, we can send her pictures of us growing up."

"Let's make a scrapbook. I can do the lettering with my gel pens and decorate the pages with stickers." Emily eagerly got into the plan.

Jean nodded. "That's a good idea."

"Can we go to the craft store tomorrow after school?"

David grinned as he waited for Jean's reaction, knowing Emily took advantage of every excuse to hit the craft store.

The next evening Jean pulled out her file boxes of old photos. She called to Emily and Rachel. "If you're done with your homework we can get started." Arms loaded with boxes and supplies, Jean plopped down on the floor of the living room. "Care to join us dear?"

David shifted in his recliner and looked up from reading the newspaper. He sat silent for a moment or two, finally shrugging, he set the paper aside on the end table.

"Look at this." Rachel held a photo. "I sure was cute as a baby, much cuter than Emily with her bald head."

"Yeah, well, you weren't so cute here." Emily rebounded with a photo in hand of Rachel when she was about seven years old.

Rachel reached across, failing to snatch the photo from her sister's quick hand. Between laughs and ribbing, photos best suited to providing a window on the past were selected and cropped to various shapes and sizes with a variety of zig-zagged borders.

"Let's include some from our vacation to Yellowstone and to Disneyworld." David scanned the group of pictures he had in hand. Rachel took charge, laying them out with the glue stick in hand. Emily manned the glitter pens and displayed her talent with lettering across the pages. Everyone rummaged through Emily's sticker box for stickers to accent the mounted photos on the array of patterned paper.

"What do you think, Dad?" Emily presented the book to David for his approval.

David smiled, impressed with his family's efforts. The few hours of sorting old pictures of his childhood, his wedding, and photos of Rachel and Emily growing up had been a good idea. It would give Grandma a glimpse into the lives of the family she hadn't witnessed growing up. "It's very nice. I'm sure Grandma will like it. I'll mail it tomorrow."

# Chapter 8

The parcel delighted Edna when the postman arrived at her door. At seeing the return address, her eyes widened. Excited, she scurried to the table and sat down to open the box. The beeping of the microwave announced her tea was ready, but she ignored it with a new priority at hand. With brown paper torn aside and the treasure removed from the white box, Edna ran her fingers over the yellow album cover decorated with childlike drawings of people. Edna traced the large black lettering that read *OUR FAMILY*. She flipped the pages, pausing, lingering, and studying the photos, allowing her mind to place herself into key events. She pondered what her life might have been like had she been there to share the moments with her grandson and his family. Tears formed, she brushed them aside along with the imaginary life. Her clock chimed two o'clock. Edna startled at the sound, not realizing how quickly the day had gone by while she was lost in the precious images of a past of which she should have been a part. Her forgotten tea water had long gone cold. Edna got up and called Fred and Marge. She desperately wanted to show off the gift.

Edna waited until after dinner before tapping out the large penned numbers on the dial to call David.

"Grandma? What are you doing up so late? Is everything okay?" David sounded drowsy across the phone line.

"I wanted to wait until after dinner hour." Edna glanced outside. It couldn't be that late could it? "What time is it there? Are you in a different time zone?"

"No, Grandma, we're the same time, but it's almost ten at

night."

Flustered, Edna stammered. "I'm sorry, I only wanted to thank you for the lovely gift. It was so nice to receive the photos of your family."

"I'm glad you like them. The girls had fun picking out the pictures of them which weren't too embarrassing."

Edna caressed the album in her lap. "I'll call you in a few days, dear."

"No. That's okay. I'm going to be up a while yet."

Edna wasn't sure if David was just being polite, but she was eager to talk about all the events she had missed. "It looks like you and Jean had a lovely wedding, dear." Edna ached for all the years lost. Her thoughts returned to the present. "When will I see you again and meet my grandchildren?"

"I'm sorry. I've been putting in a lot of overtime, plus it's basketball season. Emily has games most weekends and I'm one of the coaches."

"I know you're busy, I understand." She forced a smile and attempted to hide the disappointment in her voice.

"Maybe we can all make it this weekend. I don't think Emily has a game on Saturday."

Her heart quickened its pace. "If you're sure it's not too much trouble?"

"No, Grandma, It's not too much trouble. You're a very important part of my life right now. I have to talk to Jean, but I think we can come over this weekend. I'll let you know Friday night. Okay?"

Edna wiped a lone tear as she hung up the phone. She called to Missy who tramped down the hall and begged at her feet. Edna bent over, and with long slow strokes pet her only companion. "David and his family are coming this weekend. Isn't that wonderful?"

# Chapter 9

David rummaged through his tools in the garage. He tossed selected screw drivers, wrenches, and pliers in a plastic bucket. Once stashed in the back of the car, he returned to the house, eager to hit the road. "How's everyone doing?" He peered into the kitchen where Jean was busy gathering an assortment of rags and cleaning supplies.

"I'm about done." Jean walked to the stairway and called to Rachel and Emily. "Are you girls ready?"

"We've been waiting to meet Grandma." Rachel tramped down the stairs. "Hurry up, Emily. Don't forget the CD player and your CD's." Rachel headed out the door with her music and coat in hand.

"Are we leaving or what?" David posed by the door momentarily before heading toward the car with the overnight bags.

"Someone has to check the doors." Jean hurried through the house, pausing at the bottom of the stairs, calling out. "We're leaving, Emily. Dad's waiting."

Emily ran down the stairs and flew out the door. Jean checked her purse, loaded her arms with her cleaning supplies, and with the rest of the family in the car, took a deep breath and walked out the door to the garage.

"Everyone have everything?" David waited for a moment. Last minute forgotten items were inevitable with a family of women. He studied faces as all parties in turn nodded their heads. Armed with enough repair and cleaning supplies for every possible situation, David turned the key in the ignition, and the family headed out to visit Edna and attack the condition of her home.

"The kitchen and bathrooms have to be a priority." Before the car even left the neighborhood, Jean had pulled out a pen and paper and busied herself with one of her famous lists of chores - sinks, toilets, tub, cupboards, and floors. "Did you remember the vacuum?"

David nodded. "I also brought the shampooer. I'll fix the leaky faucet and see if there are any other repairs, then hopefully I can convince Grandma to let me shampoo her carpet."

With the plan roughed out, they sat back and enjoyed the drive away from the drizzle and traffic of the Seattle suburbs to the dry, less hectic, side of the mountains.

"Remember," Jean glanced over the back seat and looked at her daughters. "I warned you what the house looked like, so I don't want to hear any remarks, even out of Grandma's earshot. If we all pitch in and put in a full day today and a few hours' tomorrow, we can head home early afternoon, stop for dinner someplace, and still have a relaxing Sunday evening. You guys can catch up on some of your homework if you need to. Hopefully we can make Grandma's house a little more livable."

Emily's head swayed to the music. She pulled the ear bud from her ear. "We can do the vacuuming and dusting."

"We'll see, I think it'll be better if you just keep Grandma busy and talking so your dad and I can clean."

Rachel unplugged her earpiece. "I don't understand why she doesn't want you cleaning. I'd love it if someone cleaned for me."

David shook his head with a grin. "From the looks of your room, I'm not sure you know what cleaning is." David looked in the rear view mirror to see Rachel scrunch her face before responding. "Ha ha ha, very funny."

Out of the corner of his eye, David saw Jean grin and shake her head. "You're not old Rachel, older people are generally too proud to have others clean for them. We'll have to play things by ear when we get there and see how it goes. Let's stop on the way and eat so we don't have to worry about eating there, if you know what I mean." David looked over at Jean. "I'm thinking fast food, or deli. We need to get there and get as much done as we can this weekend."

After a brief lunch stop, and with the heat of the afternoon taking charge, David and his family arrived at Grandma's condo unit. David glanced at the carport as he pulled up beside her car. The door to the tool shed at the end of the carport had what appeared to be a new dent. "It looks like Grandma forgot to stop in time and ran her Buick into the shed. Again. I wonder if I should ask her about it."

Jean shook her head. "Not today. But we probably should express our concerns about her driving."

David agreed. "Okay, let's try to work until six or so, then we can take Grandma out to dinner before we call it a night, and head to the hotel. Leave everything in the car until we've visited a while. We don't want it to look like we only came to clean."

David led his family through the gate and into the small front courtyard littered with old lawn chairs, a rusty metal table, and a makeshift clothesline. Missy's yapping announced their arrival as Grandma opened the door and they stepped inside. David stiffened at the odors that hung in the stagnant air. In his months of absence, David had allowed himself to forget the condition of his grandmother's home. He couldn't comprehend how Alicia or her friends, who supposedly loved and cared about Grandma, had not taken steps to improve her life. Maybe they tried to clean and Grandma resisted? That was certainly plausible, based on his brief experience with her. David knew he would have to at least try to keep his grandmother's home from being either a health hazard nor a dangerous situation and, hopefully go the step beyond and restore a resemblance of clean.

"We made it." David embraced his grandmother.

Rachel and Emily walked up beside their dad. He put his arm around Rachel. "Grandma, this is Rachel. She's sixteen." He looked across to Emily and put his hand on her head. "And Emily is thirteen."

Grandma's smile lit her whole face, in spite of her moist eyes. She hugged each of the girls. "Gracious, look at how big you girls are. I had no idea how lovely you were."

Jean nodded and winked at Rachel.

Missy's constant yapping made talking nearly impossible. Emily squatted down to pet the mutt with a loving hand. David watched as she wrinkled her face and pulled back. No doubt the dog was still sorely in need of a bath. "Emily, how are you and Rachel at bathing dogs?"

Jean pointed the girls toward the living room then leaned in toward David. "It's going to be like opening Pandora's box."

"Come on Grandma, let's go sit down." Emily led the way, with Missy plodding behind.

David followed Jean into the dimly lit kitchen. Crumbs and scraps of food had invited pests. The stench of urine from the carpet crept into his nose and muddled his other senses. Scraps of food littered the carpet, uneaten, was ground under foot as Edna apparently didn't see well enough to pick up any remains. David took a deep breath. He hated to upset Grandma, but the home needed some serious TLC. The trick was how to do it without upsetting her. "Why don't you get started, while I chat with Grandma a while. I'll find a way to get one of the girls to help you."

"Would you girls like something to eat?" Edna sat between the girls on the sofa as David entered.

Rachel bent down and stroked Missy. "We're fine, we just had lunch."

"Oh, you shouldn't have done that. I would have made you something. Do you like Missy? She's such a wonderful pet."

At the mention of the dog, David fought back a look of disgust. He watched Rachel pet the dog, make a face, and wipe her hand on her jeans. He chuckled under his breath.

"Goodness." Grandma looked around, confused. "Where's Jean? Is she all right?"

"She's just freshening up after the long drive and then was going to start some tea. You stay seated and I'll check on her." Raised brows focused on Emily, he reminded his daughters of their role in keeping their grandmother occupied. "Why don't you guys tell Grandma what you've been up to with school and sports."

"Sports? Gracious, I admire young girls who play sports. I was quite an athlete myself., but it wasn't so popular in my day for young girls to play sports." Grandma grinned and positioned herself to listen to Emily.

David nodded then hurried down the hall. Grabbing a cup of water, he opened the microwave and set the timer for sixty seconds. "I told Grandma you were making her some tea."

Jean had already brought in the bucket of cleaning supplies and looked up from scouring the sink. "It's a beautiful day. Why don't you have her show you the yard? That way I can at least run the vacuum."

It was the perfect diversion. David rummaged in the canisters for a tea bag, steeped the bag for a minute or so and carried the cup into the living room.

He handed her the cup. "Here you go."

Grandma looked at the cup. "Is there sugar in it? I always have one teaspoon of sugar with my tea. Not two, just one."

Emily started to giggle. David shot a glance at her and returned to the kitchen for the sugar and quickly back to Grandma. "Jean's making herself a cup, then she'll join us." He handed Grandma her tea and went to the window. "It's such a nice day and we haven't seen your yard yet, Grandma. I remember how nice it always was when Nathan and I were younger. Why don't we take a walk outside and you can show us your plants? Jean will be out in a few minutes."

Grandma set the tea cup down. "Oh." She brought her hand to her face. "I am a master gardener, you know." She pushed herself off the sofa and walked to the side door which opened into her small back yard. David and the girls followed her outside as Jean entered the room.

"Are you coming, dear?" Grandma turned and looked at Jean.

Jean suddenly sneezed and brought her hands to her eyes. "I wish I could. But I think my allergies are acting up today."

Grandma looked disappointed. She shrugged, and turned away. David knew he'd have to stretch out the tour of the yard as long as possible.

The small garden, probably once well maintained, now lay overgrown with ground cover climbing over other plants and bushes in need of pruning. The sweetness of cherry and apple blossoms hung in the humid air. With the late winter weather, most plants were dead or dormant. David could see though every square foot of her small backyard was planted with bushes, trees, ground cover, climbing roses and other plants he didn't have a clue about.

"What's this?" David leaned over some purple and green leaves with small purple flowers.

"That's Ajuga, it grows like a weed, anywhere you put it. Would you like some? I have so much of it."

"We have a bank that would be great for it. Do you have a shovel?"

"There's one in my shed, dear."

"How about this?" David pointed out a large bush with whitish pink flowers.

"That's a viburnum." His grandmother's eyes twinkled as she gently touched the plant. David heard the sound of the vacuum start up. He knew Grandma's hearing wasn't the best, but still, he steered her toward the farthest part of the yard toward some trees growing along the six foot, battered, crooked, wood fence separating her small yard from the condo unit behind her. "These are my fruit trees." Edna pointed to the larger one. "This is a mulberry tree."

"What's a mulberry tree? I've never eaten a mulberry before." Rachel walked over and studied the tree, fingering the leaves.

Edna spun around and laughed. "Well dear, I'm afraid you won't be eating any today either. The magpies tend to favor the fruit and it's so difficult for me to pick it. I just keep the tree for the birds." Edna turned and headed to the opposite corner pointing to a smaller tree beginning to bud with early growth, in anticipation of spring. "This is my cherry tree." Edna pulled a low branch down and frowned. "I've tried everything I could think of, but the starlings and robins always beat me to this, too." She ambled up and down the two sides of her sixty-foot or so, by twenty-foot yard pointing out all the trees and flowers.

Fascinated by her wealth of knowledge regarding plants, David still remembered the pride she had in her garden at her old house, the last time he had seen her. It overflowed with a showcase of flowers and bushes and an overabundance of grapes draped across sturdy old wooden pergolas. It amazed him how Grandma could name each and every one of her assortment of unique plants, none of which he remembered even minutes later. The hum of the vacuum still echoed from inside the house. Grandma showed no awareness of its sound, but she slowed her step and her breathing was labored.

"Your yard looks nice, Grandma. I like these. What are they?" Emily bent down and fingered a delicate rose colored blossom tinged with green.

Grandma bent down, her smile as delicate as the bloom. "That's a hellebore. It's my favorite. I bought the plant at a garden show."

David straightened and turned in the direction of the house. The vacuum cleaner fell silent. David waited a minute or so, then motioned to Emily. "It is beautiful, Grandma. Let's go finish your tea. We can dig the Ajuga later."

Inside, Grandma cozied herself back onto the living room sofa. Jean was still breathing heavy from her mad dash running the vacuum around both levels of the house. David noticed the ground-in food and crumbs were gone. The room looked more presentable, though the persistent odor still permeated the place, burning his nasal passages.

"Jean, didn't you say the girls needed some supplies for school?" He looked with pleading sad eyes toward Jean.

Taking her cue, Jean smiled and nodded at her daughter. "Rachel, wasn't there something you needed?"

Rachel jumped up. "Oh yeah, I need some poster board."

Jean grabbed her purse. She walked over to Grandma. "Is there anything you need at the store while we're here? The girls need a few things for school. How about you join us so David can fix your leaky sink?"

Grandma looked down at her worn, slip-on, once-white canvas shoes. "I could use some new shoes. What about you dear, aren't you coming?" Edna stared at David with hands on her hips.

"No, I want to get the sink fixed. It'll only take a minute, but maybe I'll see if there's anything else that needs a quick repair. You guys take your time. I'll be fine."

Grandma eyed him skeptically, but seemed eager to get out of the house. She grabbed her purse and navy blue quilted coat with a ripped hem, and shuffled after Jean to the door.

Jean whispered to David who was at the door to say goodbye. "We'll be back in a couple hours. Will that do?" He held the door as the girls eagerly escaped to the fresh air. With everyone in place, Jean backed the car out and pulled away.

With Missy safely out of the way at Fred and Mabel's for a few hours, David maneuvered the upright yellow shampooer filled with not only water and shampoo, but also a healthy dose of scented pet urine deodorizer. After nearly an hour and a half of strenuous pushing and pulling, lifting and scrubbing, Missy's odor diminished markedly and David inhaled the clean spring breeze smell, as promised. He straightened his back and relaxed his shoulders surveying his effort, wondering how long the improvement would last. Cleaning Grandma's house would certainly be an ongoing struggle. There had to be other options that didn't involve bi-monthly trips across the state. A cleaning service was the obvious answer, but even that wouldn't be without problems of its own. David could already imagine his grandmother's protests. With the last of the attachments by the door and the empty soap and disinfectant bottles in the outside trash bin, David wiped his forehead with his sleeve. He glanced over at the still unrepaired leaky faucet and trudged to the living room sofa for a much-needed breather. The sound of a car pulling into the driveway startled him just as he was dozing off.

"The place smells and looks great." Jean's welcome voice validated his efforts.

David forced his aching body off the sofa and greeted his family at the door.

Jean held up a grocery bag and lowered her voice to David. "I picked up a few things so we can make breakfast here tomorrow."

Emily followed, carrying a bag from a discount shoe store and set it down by the table. She inhaled deeply. "It smells a lot better, Dad."

David watched as Grandma entered and looked around without much emotion. Oblivious to the efforts directed at her carpeting, she eyed the kitchen and asked if the sink had been fixed.

The faucet was an easy fix. A rubber washer was replaced, and a few bolts tightened. The carpet needed several hours to dry and David's stomach craved real food. He looked at the wall clock and figured it would be a good time for an early dinner. Everyone piled into the car.

"Is there any place in particular where you'd like to go for dinner, Grandma?" David sat posed behind the steering wheel awaiting a clue on his destination.

"There's a lovely place where I go with Barbara sometimes. They have the best mashed potatoes."

"That sounds great, just tell me the name and which direction to go."

Sitting next to David, Grandma grinned as she peered out the window. David reached across the seat and took her hand. "Grandma, can you tell me where the restaurant is?"

Grandma shot a glance to David. "Of course I know where it is. I've eaten there many times. It's on Columbia Drive."

David smiled at her response. He turned the car onto Columbia Drive, knowing at least there would be plenty of eating spots from which to choose, should Grandma's memory, and source of directions, fail him. Luckily, she spied the big green lettering of the restaurant sign not too far down the street on the right.

Grandma had a hearty appetite, finishing her huge mound of mashed potatoes smothered in extra gravy as requested. Though she did justice to her meal, a lone biscuit remained and Grandma insisted on a doggy bag. David cringed, knowing full well where the biscuit would end up.

No sooner did they get home than she pulled out part of the biscuit and tossed it on the carpet for the dog. David knew Missy would turn up her nose and walk away without touching it. "Grandma, you can't be feeding the dog off the rug. Put the food in a dish. Besides, it isn't good to feed animals food intended for people, it could be bad for them."

"I know. Mother always told me not to feed my Boston Bull puppy anything but dog food." Grandma spoke slowly. "One day when I was in first grade and Mother was out, I gave him part of Mother's home baked doughnut. My poor puppy choked and died. I felt so bad. Daddy never stopped teasing her about how dry her doughnuts were."

David didn't know whether to be serious over the death of her dog or laugh over the comment on the doughnuts. "Well, then you know what I mean." He hoped he'd made his point while he attempted to hold back his laughter at her story pulled so easily from over eighty years earlier.

"I won't feed Missy any more scraps." Edna cast her gaze downward, avoiding David's stare.

"It's getting late. We're going to head to our hotel now. We'll be back in the morning."

"Oh, you. Do you have to leave? I thought you were spending the night here." Grandma rubbed her hands together.

"Maybe another time. We thought it would be better with the girls to get a hotel since you have only one bed." David was thankful for the built in easy excuse.

"I've hardly had a chance to talk with my granddaughters." She reached out and motioned for the girls to come closer.

"We'll see you tomorrow, Grandma." Emily stepped forward and hugged Grandma.

"I wish you could stay."

"We'll be by in the morning and have breakfast together." David ignored his grandmother's pout as they headed for the door and a much needed good night's sleep.

Grandma was already seated at the dining table eating a piece of toast when David and his family arrived the next morning. David joined his grandmother while the girls followed their mom into the kitchen. "I thought Jean and the girls could treat you and make breakfast for us this morning so we have a chance to talk."

"Oh. I don't know about that." Grandma looked toward her kitchen and started to stand. "They won't know where anything is."

"They'll be fine, Grandma. Let's you and I go into the living room and relax. We'll let the ladies wait on us."

David's remark brought a smile to Grandma. She hobbled behind him down the hall. to the living room. "Come, Grandma, sit down." David plopped onto the grimy sofa suddenly aware of a new odor. He wished he had thought to shampoo the sofa and love seat too. Maybe next time.

"Grandma, Jean and I have been thinking about how much you have to do by yourself with Larry gone. Most people your age need a little help. You, however, are doing remarkably well getting around as you do." David justified his forthcoming white lie as incentive for his grandmother. "We use a cleaning service, even though we're able to care for our home." David studied his grandmother, hoping his lie would encourage her to give a housekeeper a chance. "There are other things we'd rather do with our time, so we have a lady come in once a week for the regular cleaning. We'd love to pay for someone to clean for you."

Grandma's resistance didn't surprise him. Her voice rose as she squinted at him. "Oh you, I don't need a cleaning service. And you can't trust other people to come into your home. I'm perfectly able to clean my own home. I just don't like to. I can do my own laundry, too. I've cared for myself all these years."

David winced at her comment. Her clothes were stained and carried the odor of dirty water. David had seen and smelled the dish cloths and towels which had been put into drawers, stiff, and dingy, from air drying. While shampooing, he had surveyed the small clothes drying rack in Edna's bedroom displaying towels and undergarments apparently washed by hand and put out to dry. "At least think about it."

The aroma of bacon floated into the room. "It smells like breakfast is ready. I hope you're hungry, Jean makes a great breakfast."

Emily came in all smiles, standing like a doorman at a high class hotel. "Breakfast is served, and I made the pancakes."

Edna came alive at the table surrounded by her newly found family. She barely stopped talking to eat. But as the morning wore on, the reality of the approaching work and school week loomed over them.

"Grandma." David looked at his watch. "It's late. We need to leave soon so we can get home by evening. The kids have school tomorrow."

Rachel and Emily rose and gathered plates and silverware from the table. Jean washed the dishes with the soap purchased during their prior shopping excursion. New sponges, scouring pads and sink cleanser were stashed under the sink. It may have been a futile move, but David hoped they would get at least some use. In a matter of twenty minutes, counters were wiped, and leftovers wrapped and stowed in the fridge with a reminder to Edna to eat the leftovers within the next few days.

"You girls be good, and come see me again, okay?" She hugged each of them before turning to David. "Are you sure you can't stay?"

Her look of despair caused a stitch of sadness for David. "We have to get going. I'll see you in a few weeks." He reached out to embrace Grandma. She clung to him like a drowning victim clutching a lifeline. Smiling weakly, she dabbed a tear as David and his family turned and walked out the door.

# Chapter 10

Monday afternoon David sat at his desk reviewing charts from test data. Still tired from the full weekend and long drive, his mind wandered. He couldn't shake the image of his grandmother's living conditions etched in his mind. Surely, there was something he could do to improve her situation, without constantly traveling across the state to do the work himself. He needed his weekends for more than driving and doing chores for his grandmother. Maybe it was selfish, but good God, he hadn't asked for all of this, and he was busy enough before Grandma's situation. There was no way he could take time off work to go to eastern Washington. Not with the tight scheduling he faced. David looked at his watch and forced himself to focus on the task at hand. Tomorrow's scheduled test flight was in the morning and people were waiting for his input. With the revised plan signed off, he delivered it to the test director and pushed his way out the door. Driving home, he mulled over the situation considering the few options available to him. Grandma was adamant about not having strangers in her home, but David had to do something.

Jean was in the loft, busy on the computer when he arrived home.

He pulled up a chair. "I've been thinking about what to do about Grandma's house. It seems wrong nobody seems to notice how she's living except us. No one else seems to care."

Jean glanced up from her work and faced David. "Maybe she scares them off. You've seen how she can be. Even we had to do our cleaning behind her back."

"You're probably right. Alicia is at least a familiar face. If we could convince Grandma to let her come in and clean, then her concern over having strangers in would no longer be valid."

Jean lifted her open palms in shrug. "It's worth a try, but Alicia hasn't exactly been overly involved in Grandma's life since Larry died. Besides, it sounds like your grandmother isn't particularly on good terms with her or the rest of the family. What are you going to say to her to convince her to go and clean, even if Grandma agrees to it?"

Shaking his head, David winced. "I don't know. I get the feeling she won't do a whole lot without there being something in it for her. And I don't feel right asking Grandma's friends to help out any more than they already do. I'm sure they do plenty for her already. There really isn't anyone else. It's worth a try for our peace of mind, isn't it?" David pushed his desk chair back and went downstairs to grab a beer. Grandma's circumstances had become major stress on him. His neck and shoulders tightened every time he thought about it. Ideally, Alicia wouldn't have to be coerced to assist in their grandmother's care, but his dealings with that family thus far were a galaxy away from how he had perceived caring and concerned relatives to be. He had to deal with the situation as it presented itself, and Alicia was the only one he could approach. There was no other alternative which Grandma would even consider. Prepared to offer a bribe, if necessary, and with resolve, he thrust his doubts aside and walked to the kitchen. Taking a deep breath, he blew out his frustrations, and picked up the phone.

The phone was answered right away. Alicia's eagerness to chat seemed like a good sign, so David jumped right in and explained his plan.

"I don't know why you think Grandma will let me clean her house for her. I've tried before. I took a shampooer over once about a year ago and tried to clean her carpet. All she did was nag about how I was doing it wrong and how it was going to make the place feel damp. Anyway, she's still pissed over Larry being dissected as she called it, and cremated."

Alicia's explanation certainly was believable. But David's patience was seeping away. "Look, I know it's tough. But doesn't it bother you she's living in such conditions? Jean and I just spent our whole weekend cleaning and driving. It would sure help me out, not to mention improve Grandma's environment."

"I don't think she minds the mess. I think she likes things that way."

Hearing her resistance, David found himself counting mentally. "Do you think it's good to allow her to live like that?" He pictured Alicia rolling her eyes during the silence before her reluctant reply.

"Well, I can see if she'll let me." She paused. "I'll try."

A swell of relief washed over him. It was a near-perfect solution to ease his concerns over Grandma's house, and perhaps it would renew the damaged relationship between his grandmother and Alicia. He hung up the phone and grabbed another beer from the fridge before retreating to the living room and joining Jean on the sofa. He shrugged, "I'm not going to place any bets, but at least she said she would try. We'll see what happens." Grabbing the remote off the coffee table, he notched up the volume and tuned to the six o'clock news. He took a swig of the cold ale, allowing his frustration to ooze away. Still, he couldn't brush aside the nagging sense a storm was brewing off on the horizon.

# Chapter 11

Edna didn't wait until the usual Sunday to hear from David. Instead, she called sobbing on Thursday evening a few weeks after their past visit. "Someone stole my silver set." She struggled with the words through her anger.

"What kind of silver are you talking about? A tea set?"

"No. My silverware. It was real silver. Eight place settings, plus serving pieces. They were in a lovely wooden case." Edna pursed her lips. She couldn't believe David didn't understand.

"I'm sure it will show up. Where did you last see it? Maybe I can help you figure out what happened to it."

Edna scowled. She hated David's condescending tone. "It was hidden in the living room. You remember my sofa end tables are like cabinets, with doors. It was inside one of them. It's been there ever since I moved into this home."

"Is it possible you moved it?"

"No." Her hands shook. She raised her voice. David obviously wasn't hearing her. "I paid over two-thousand dollars for it. I'm sure someone stole it."

"Okay, Grandma. Did anyone else know where you put it?"

Edna thought for a moment, she had told only two people where the silverware was kept. "Only Barbara and Alicia."

"Well, I'm sure neither one of them would have stolen anything from you. Is anything else missing?"

Frustrated by David's persistence in questioning her, Edna took a deep breath. She emphasized the words. "Nothing else is missing, only my silverware. I know Barbara would never steal from me, she's my dearest friend. She even takes me to church with her." Her eyebrows raised at the thought which flashed in her mind. She had doubted Alicia's character in the past, but believed the girl's bad habits were behind her. Besides, she had been the only one in Larry's family who had called and visited her since Larry died. Buried bitterness and distrust resurfaced like a small tremor in the wake of a larger quake, spreading throughout her body. She shuddered at the thought, but it was the only explanation. She whispered, "I think Alicia stole it."

"Grandma, Alicia wouldn't steal from you. She loves you. Why would she do anything so spiteful?"

David's naiveté didn't surprise her. "You don't understand. You don't know her the way I do." Edna paused, remembering Alicia's rebellious years. She didn't like to gossip ... however, David was family. He needed to know the truth. "She probably stole it for drug money."

"What makes you think that? She doesn't seem like someone who would get involved in drugs. Plus, she's a mom who I'm sure cares about Lacey. She wouldn't risk doing something so mean. I'm sure there's another explanation."

Edna shook her head. David didn't know about Alicia's troubled past. "She used to be quite a handful for Larry and Kora-Lee, she was even in trouble with the law." Edna didn't want to share too many details, although she felt compelled to warn David. "Just be sure you never loan her money. She's borrowed money from me, and I've never seen a cent. Believe me, it's just a matter of time before she asks you for money."

"Grandma. When was the last time Alicia came by to see you?"

"I don't know when it was ... last week sometime. That's when she stole it. She came by with a vacuum cleaner and said she wanted to do some cleaning for me. I didn't want her to, but she insisted. I just don't know what got into her. I should have known she was up to something."

"I'm sure there's another explanation. I'll come over during the weekend again and you and I can look around. I'm sure it will show up."

"We'll just see about that." Edna stewed. "I'm not going to have Alicia in my house ever again." She banged the phone down. No one could convince her the silverware had been misplaced. She knew it had been stolen.

# Chapter 12

Hanging up the phone, David buried his face in his hands to squelch a scream. His inner turmoil was rising to the surface. He chuckled at the obvious irony of the situation as he went to the living room to tell Jean the latest breaking disaster story.

"You're never going to believe this." He sat back in his recliner kicking up the foot rest. "Grandma apparently had some real silver flatware. Worth around two grand, she says it's been stolen. And, here's the clincher, she says Alicia stole it."

The last bit of story brought Jean's head bolt upright, facing him, eyes staring unbelieving. "What? Are you serious? Do you really think Alicia would do something like that?"

"Grandma's serious. I'm not so sure. She probably moved it and forgot where she put it. You know how we've found things in odd places." Through a forced smile, David sighed, "I know what I'm doing this weekend."

David heard the phone ringing. He ignored it. Grandma had just called yesterday. He was exhausted. He needed at least a few days' break. From the loft over the kitchen and dining area, he heard Jean's voice on the phone downstairs. Her words were short and terse. She yelled up to him to grab the extension, warning it was Alicia, and she was mad.

He clutched his head, took a few deep breaths, and picked up the receiver on the desk offering his stepsister his best forced warm welcoming greeting.

Alicia didn't bother to acknowledge. She started right into her hissing. "That's the last time I clean house for that woman. I never should have listened to you. Now Grandma is accusing me of stealing."

Stunned, David absorbed Alicia's angry words. Jean came upstairs and stood next to the desk to listen to the conversation. David focused on calming Alicia down. "I'm sorry. Grandma called me, too, last night. I didn't know she was so suspicious."

"She called you and told you about her silver? Great. I can only imagine what kind of shit she spewed about me. I don't know who the hell you think you are, waltzing in to her life, telling me what I need to do, and now you just sit at home in your own little world, while Grandma tells everyone she knows, that I'm a thief."

Defenses now on high alert, fanned by the venom in Alicia's voice, David chose his words carefully. "Hold it, Alicia. I don't know why you're mad at me. I only started looking out for Grandma because it was obvious the rest of her family stopped giving a damn about her. You can't seriously think her living conditions are acceptable."

"What the hell do you know about me and my family? You weren't around to see how Grandma treated Mom and Lorraine and me, how much she belittled Dad for marrying a woman who was with child, as she put it. Don't pretend to know about how we treated her. Even though you and Nathan were never around, all we ever heard growing up from Grandma Edna was how precious her twin grandsons were."

The pot had been stirred, the aftermath now unavoidable. David's anger boiled over. "Whoa. Don't put that on me. As you said, I wasn't around. Remember, we didn't get to see our dad while we were growing up. Your mother made sure of that. And, from what I saw, and the vibes I got at the funeral, your mother still resents us."

"You don't have a clue. Grandma always thought you and Nathan were better than Lorraine and me because you were her only *real* grandchildren. She never considered us as her grandchildren. Maybe that's why we find it hard after so many years to consider her family."

David slunk down in his office chair. He couldn't fault Alicia's fury. "I'm sorry, Alicia. I can't help how she treated you and Lorraine, or what she said about me and Nathan. All I know is, right now, at her age, she needs someone to make sure she's not living in a sty. If you and your family don't care enough to correct that, someone needs to."

"Well, I guess that proves Grandma was right. You're so much better than the rest of us. Have fun with her. It won't be long before you see what she is really like."

David flinched and pulled the phone from his ear as the sound of the phone slamming down reverberated in his ear. End of discussion. He turned to Jean. He knew she'd heard enough to piece it together.

Jean shrugged. "Well, it sounds like she's not volunteering to plan Edna's next surprise party."

David laughed. "It's funny, though." He paused at Jean's look of confusion about the situation. "She never said she didn't take the silver."

# Chapter 13

David and Jean pulled into Grandma's driveway before noon the following weekend. Upon opening the house door, her eyes widened and she stammered. "Is it that time already?"

"We're a bit early. It's good to see you." David offered a welcoming embrace. His grandmother held on until David laughed and hinted she should save some of the hugging for their farewell. Edna waved them in. Stepping inside, David immediately noticed the odor from the dog had diminished since he had shampooed the carpet on his last visit. Still, the stagnant hot air was stifling upon entering the dining room. Why were old people afraid of fresh air? Missy bounded down the hall. David glared at the dog and walked into the living room, ignoring the annoying yapping. He cracked open a few windows to allow the breeze from outside to air the place out. Eyeing the mangy, black haired creature plodding after him, he looked around the room for dog messes.

"You mentioned you had a few chores for me." David nosed around the house for possible spots where his grandmother might have stashed her silver. Not sure he entirely trusted Alicia, he didn't believe she would steal from her grandmother. Besides, after hearing Alicia's side of the story, it sounded like there was plenty of resentment from both sides.

"I'm so glad you came. I need to do some shopping for dinner tonight. You are staying for dinner and spending the night, aren't you?"

David and Jean exchanged glances. "No, Grandma. We can't. The girls are home and we need to get back to them and get our own chores done. We can't spend the night this time."

Grandma frowned, furrowing her brow. "I wish you could stay. You have to eat anyway."

"I'm sorry, next time. Jean can help you make a shopping list." He winked at Jean before continuing. "I can do a few repairs before we go to the store." He rummaged on the card table and handed Jean a pen and paper, his eyes pleading. A pencil drawing caught his eye. He studied the youngster's depiction of three females holding hands. Two had long jet black straight hair, and one with short white hair. The artists signature, Lacey, was carefully written in cursive across the bottom. "This is a nice picture from Lacey. Is it new?"

Grandma's frown shifted immediately. Her eyes sparkled as she scampered to David's side. "Oh, yes. We colored together when Alicia was vacuuming my carpet. Lacey is such a nice young girl. She reminds me so much of Bernice at that age."

Convinced Alicia had no role in the missing silver, David knew he and Jean had to find it today to put the whole misunderstanding to rest. He headed for the kitchen and shuddered at the sight which had become the norm, counters covered with crumbs, spilled food, and the dog dish filled with old table scraps. David groaned, afraid of what he would find when he opened the door of the harvest gold refrigerator straight from the '70's. Leftovers sat on plates and in bowls, uncovered and dried up, resembling some ancient find from an archeological dig. He wrinkled his nose at the foul odor, but sighed a small relief. There was no green fuzz growing, yet.

David glanced around to make sure his grandmother wasn't watching and removed a few plates and bowls. He tossed the contents in the garbage and studied the empty matching gold dishwasher. He guessed, in spite of the appliance, Grandma probably washed dishes by hand, so he quickly grabbed the dish soap and scouring pad. With the few bowls washed and dried, he returned them to the cabinet. Sure, she'd miss the food, and accuse someone of doing something behind her back, probably stealing it, but it was the lesser of the evils. He couldn't risk her eating anything that might make her sick. He brushed aside a few jars, checking for hidden spoiled goods. Instead he spied Grandma's reading glasses sitting out of place next to the mayo and ketchup. Removing them, he chuckled and put them on the counter. "Are you missing your glasses, Grandma?"

She wandered in, spying the glasses on the counter, she picked them up.

David grinned at her. "I found them in the fridge. You must have accidently put them in there with some of the food." Noticing her scrunched expression and furrowed brow, he knew he was in trouble. Nonetheless, he forged ahead. "Do you think you might have misplaced your silverware accidentally, too?"

"Oh, you. I would remember. It's a big box, not like these glasses. Anyway, I've already called my insurance man."

David saw her face redden before she stomped off. He returned to the refrigerator and pulled open the produce drawer. A plastic bag of dark green mush, once a member of the lettuce family, lay at the bottom in a wet slimy puddle. He pulled it out with his thumb and forefinger and tossed it in the garbage under the sink, leaving a trail of the slime across floor.

"Damn." David watched the slime meld into the brown indoor-outdoor carpeting knowing full well pulling up the dirty and germy carpet would have to be one of his next projects. Disgusted, he picked up a wet dish rag from the sink. He flinched at the rancid smell and feel of it as he carried it at arm's length to the washer and called Jean for help.

"I think it's time to do a load of laundry again. Do you mind gathering some of Grandma's clothing and towels while I'm gone? I'll wipe down the fridge, and then take her to the store." David pulled a rag from the drawer. He cringed at the stiffness and odor of the replacement rag, and returned to the laundry room once again, allowing the lid of the washing machine to slam down. Grabbing several paper towels from the roll, David wet them, made a futile attempt to wipe the carpeting, and returned to the refrigerator.

"What are you doing?" Edna stood in the doorway with her hands on her hips. She stepped over to the trash can and peered in. "Why are you throwing away perfectly good food?"

David felt like he did when he was six and pulled a chair over to the counter to sneak his favorite gingersnaps from the big white ceramic cookie jar.

"Just a bit of lettuce that has gone bad, that's all. See." He gathered the white plastic liner and lifted it out of the garbage can.

Grandma scowled. She walked over to the refrigerator and nosed around inside.

He rolled his shoulders to ease the increasing tension. With the bag full, David escaped outside and dumped the evidence of his crime in the dumpster.

Once inside, Grandma faced him at the entrance to the kitchen, her hands on her hips. "I guess I'll have to buy more produce, too. Can we stop at the Public Market?"

David glanced up at his grandmother. "Where?"

"The Public Market. I always prefer to buy my produce there. Mother always bought her produce at the outdoor market. It's much fresher."

He dreaded making another stop for produce, but then decided it was simpler than trying to convince Grandma the produce at the store was plenty fresh. "Sure, Grandma, if you like." Grabbing his keys, he mumbled to himself. "Just what she needs, more produce to spoil in her refrigerator."

"Okay, I have to get my purse. A young lady never goes anywhere without her purse." She hobbled off toward the dining room, returning with the battered tan purse she carried everywhere.

"Aren't you coming?" Edna looked back at Jean.

"No, I think I'll do some reading, and relax while you're gone, if that's okay?"

Edna sulked. "You know I don't like having strangers alone in my house. Look what happened with Alicia." She looked over at David and started to protest.

"Jean's had a long week Grandma. If it's okay with you, let's let her stay." David noticed her hesitation as she studied Jean.

"You are David's wife, I trust you. You can stay if you like, dear."

With Grandma out of the way, David knew Jean could scout the house for places the missing silver might have been stashed. He hoped when he returned they would be able to put that mystery behind them. He shooed Grandma out the door and turned back to Jean. "Good luck finding the silverware."

"I hate to snoop, but we can't accuse Alicia of stealing something that hasn't been stolen."

"I know. Sorry you're missing out on your girls' night out."

Jean shrugged. "Just bring me a cold Coke when you come back. I have a feeling I'm going to need it."

David kissed Jean on the forehead and turned to see his Grandmother waiting stern faced by the car her arms crossed at her chest.

Insistent on pushing her own cart, David flinched as Edna maneuvered it, steering like an insecure six-year-old on her first two-wheeler, veering one direction, over correcting, and then, nearly running into the produce tables. Remembering the shed at the end of the carport, he imagined her ability to drive a car was severely deficient by now, also. He dropped the question as casually as possible "Are you still driving, Grandma?"

She shot an accusatory glance his way. "Of course I am. How else do you think I can get around? I certainly can't walk now, can I? And, I'm not going to ask my friends to drive me everywhere I need to go." She cocked her head, rolled her eyes like a teenager, and wheeled her cart around the corner.

Not having any choice for the time being, David forced his agreement. It was a touchy subject, but for everyone's sake, another situation which he would have to address soon. A bite of bitterness gnawed at him. He hadn't asked for all of this responsibility and now Alicia made it sound like he wanted to take charge. Hell, if others only gave a modicum of awareness, he wouldn't have to do everything.

Grandma stopped at every display of produce, holding each specimen close to her eyes, rolling it over in her hand, and sniffing it. "I miss not being able to buy fresh produce every day." She reached the array of plump fresh berries, plopped one of each into her mouth, and, seeing David watching her, smirked like a playful chimp stealing a banana. She lifted a green plastic basket of red morsels and grinned as if they were precious stones.

David's mouth watered at the sweet scent. His stomach growled its realization it needed nourishment.

"I remember when I used to make jam every year. Have I showed you the freezer full of jam I have in my shed?" Grandma snatched another berry.

The thought of a freezer full of homemade jam sent a shudder up David's spine. He wondered how many years' worth had accumulated and mentally added another item on his growing list of things to check. He shook his head as Grandma put plastic bags holding lettuce, onions, and apples into the cart. Apparently, she had forgotten about the produce stand, which was fine with him, though he suspected most of this week's produce purchases would be next visits spoils.

Grandma leaned in close, eyes squinting at the price signs. "I remember when lettuce was ten-cents a pound. Now look at the price of things."

David walked beside his grandmother, reaching out periodically to help her steer the wobbly cart around the corners and through the aisles filled with late Saturday afternoon shoppers.

"It's been so long since I've had such a leisurely time shopping. I enjoy it so much."

David glanced at his watch. He found no enjoyment strolling through the aisles of the grocery store for over half an hour and still being only halfway through. Rounding the corner, the smell of hot bread spilled over the back counter where bakers busily prepared the "guaranteed fresh every hour," bread. Edna walked over to the center display. "When I'm feeling stronger, I want to start baking again. I used to make bread and cinnamon rolls every month, I'm an excellent cook, you know? There's nothing like fresh home-baked bread and rolls."

David agreed. Edging the cart quickly away from temptation, he wheeled quickly down the next aisle. Stopping, he reached for some toilet tissue knowing she was down to two rolls.

"Oh no dear." Edna's quick frown stopped David. "I have plenty of tissue."

"I checked under the sink and you're about out. You might as well buy the things you need for a few weeks while you're here since it's hard for you to get to the store these days."

"Oh you." Grandma gathered her brow and pouted as she started down the aisle again. David grabbed the package of tissue, and catching up with her, placed it in the bottom of the cart. "Is there anything else you need?"

"Oh, I almost forgot. I have to get baking powder, Mother is having the Rebekahs over for tea this evening. She's been a member for so many years you know, ever since Father became a member of the Independent Order of Oddfellows. Have you ever been to one of their meetings?"

Though David had heard of the Oddfellows, he had never heard of the Rebekahs. He guessed the group was the woman's equivalent of the men's fraternity. He turned around and studied his grandmother's face, wondering how many years in the past her mind was.

Grandma continued pushing the cart. "Mother is going to make her baking powder biscuits with her homemade raspberry jam. She asked me to pick-up some baking powder."

"I don't think your mother needs baking powder." David said with hopes of bringing Grandma back to the present day.

Edna huffed and glared at him. "Of course, she does. How would you know?"

David followed her down the aisle, nervously checking his watch again, predicting a longer day than expected, he sighed. "Let's go get some baking powder, Grandma." Searching up and down several aisles, uncertain where to find it or even what it might look like, he finally spied the red can. Grabbing one, he handed it to her. "Here you go, one can of baking powder."

"What's this? What do I need baking powder for? I have some already and I don't do much baking these days." Grandma waved him off like a pesky gnat.

David took a deep breath, reminding himself her age allowed for erratic behavior. He sighed. "Of course, I don't know what I was thinking," and placed the can back on the shelf.

As he pushed the cart to the car, David wondered about the planned stop at the Public Market. His grandmother hadn't mentioned it during the past hour. He was certainly not going to bring it up if she didn't. He hurried the groceries into the car, settled Grandma into the seat, and headed back to her home. As he expected, the whole idea of the stop at the Public Market was long gone from her mind. With a sigh of relief, he managed the quick drive to her home and pulled the car into the driveway.

Jean greeted them at the front door, as David carried in the bags of groceries. "I peeked inside every drawer, cupboard and closet. There's no sign of the silverware. I managed to find some white vinyl LP's from Betty Crocker and broods of dust bunnies, but there are no real silver place settings in this house."

Looking over his shoulder to the clanging in the kitchen, David shrugged. "Maybe there is no silverware. It might be something she's remembering from years ago." He shook his head. "I don't know what to think at this point."

Jean nodded to the back door. "I changed her bed and washed her mohair sweater in the sink. It's outside drying. Don't forget to remind me to bring it in before we go home this evening or we'll be in trouble."

Grandma shuffled out from the kitchen. "You are staying for dinner, aren't you?"

David and Jean exchanged glances. "Sorry Grandma, we need to get home. Jean can help you get dinner started if you like, before we leave."

Her eyes cast downward. "I wish you could stay."

# Chapter 14

"I can't find my sweater anywhere. Someone has stolen it." Grandma's distraught tone accosted David and Jean when they returned two weeks later.

"Why would anyone want to steal your sweater, Grandma?" David stole a glance to Jean thinking yet another imaginary theft.

"It's not here, it's been missing for weeks. I've looked everywhere. Who would take my favorite sweater?"

Without warning, Jean bolted from the room. David heard the rear screen door bang open and closed. Moments later she returned. With a slight twist of her body, Jean showed David the sweater hidden behind her back.

David nodded his understanding and ushered Grandma to the sofa. "Why don't you sit down while Jean and I look around to see if we can find it?" He joined Jean in the hall.

Jean whispered. "I left it outside drying the last time we were here. Tell her I'm looking for it. We'll just have to make up a story about finding it."

A few minutes later, Jean reappeared with a wide smile and the sweater draped over her arm. "It was in your bedroom closet."

Grandma's eyes narrowed. She snatched the sweater away and began caressing it, first with her fingers, then by rubbing it next to her cheek like a small child with a favorite blanket. She stopped and sniffed the sweater. Her moist eyes glared.

"Someone has washed it. This is a mohair sweater, it has to be washed by hand. Who would do this?" She started to cry.

Jean sat down next to her. "I'm sure it's okay." Jean patted her hand. "May I see your sweater? It looks like it was washed very gently. I'm sure it was hand washed. It smells exactly like the soap I use at home for hand washing." Jean brought the sweater to her nose and breathed deeply to convince Grandma.

"No." Grandma snatched her sweater away again. "It's ruined, feel it. It's not soft like it was."

David reached across and gently took the sweater from his grandmother and studied it. "It's not ruined Grandma, it looks fine. It's clean. That's good, isn't it?" The sad irony of the situation struck. A filthy sweater covered with sweat and food stains from years of wear was preferred to the clean, fresh smelling garment. He guessed it was probably the fresh smell that gave it away, because she obviously hadn't seen the dirt that had covered the sweater.

Jean looked at David and held her hands out questioningly. She mouthed the words. "Should I tell her?"

David shook his head, his finger to his lips. Confessing would only upset her more.

"Do you know how much I paid for this sweater? Edna's eyes glared as the sharp words spit off her tongue. "Twelve dollars. Now I'll have to buy another."

It seemed absurd, but his grandmother's grief was real. David attempted to calm her to no avail. There was no need for Jean to feel guilty about her good intention. At least Grandma would be wearing something clean and fresh for a change. That is, if she would still wear it now. It was best to drop the subject and wait until she forgot about it. And with Grandma's ever diminishing memory, David expected it would be soon.

# Chapter 15

Edna trudged into the kitchen and opened the refrigerator, revealing near empty shelves. David hadn't been by for a month, and Barbara had gone to visit her daughter somewhere out of state, Edna couldn't recall where. She didn't feel hungry but she knew she had to eat something. The produce bin held a few leaves of aging lettuce, a mushy tomato and a few withered peaches. She closed it and contemplated her prospects for dinner, shrugging off the idea of settling for canned soup. She could never get used to the taste of canned soup, not after having made her own for so many years, while her children were growing. Perhaps eggs and bacon, she thought. Yes, that would be perfect, and not too much trouble.

She had promised David she wouldn't drive anymore after he asked about the dented storage shed. Surely, he would understand the urgency though. With Barbara gone, and Marge not doing well, she hated to bother Fred. Confident, and with a sense of smugness, Edna grabbed her tan handbag and keys and sauntered to the car. She turned the car onto Columbia Drive for the three-mile jaunt to the market. At the sound of the siren, Edna stiffened in panic. Uncertain where the sound was coming from, she shot a glance in the rear-view mirror. Catching the glare of the burning sun, she squinted. A white car with flashing blue lights had pulled up behind her. Edna's heart raced as she steered the car off the road to the shoulder. An officer marched to her side of the car and motioned for her to roll the window down. Her hands trembled as she clutched the window knob, finally getting it to cooperate.

"May I see your license?" He snapped at her with an outstretched hand awaiting her license.

Edna fumbled for her wallet. Unable to retrieve the small laminated card, she attempted to hand the wallet over to him.

"I'm sorry. You will have to remove your license yourself."

Flustered, Edna struggled to free the license. The glassine window held it tight, refusing to release the precious authorization to drive, as if not wanting to reveal its hidden secret.

"Do you realize you could have hurt or even killed someone when you ran that stop sign?"

His words rang out like bullets, shattering her confidence. She knew there was a stop sign on the corner, how could she have missed it? "I would never hurt anyone. I just didn't see the sign." Edna finally freed the license with shaky hands, and handed it over to the stern-faced officer with arms crossed. Her eyes welled up as she reached for a tissue from her purse. She dabbed her eyes as the officer examined her license.

His eyes narrowed. He shook his head, handing the license back. "Do you realize your license expired over three years ago, Mrs. Pearson? I can't let you continue to drive until you pass a driver's exam and get your license renewed."

His glare forced Edna to look away.

"If I were you, I'd consider parking the car for good."

Edna pouted. She knew he was going to make a fuss about her age, and the expired license, but what did he know? After all, she had driven for over seventy years and had done just fine. "I didn't remember about my license, but I'm perfectly capable of driving." She used her most convincing tone while watching him scribble out the citation on his clipboard before turning it toward her.

"Sign here."

Edna took the clipboard and stared at it.

The officer pointed to a line at the bottom.

Edna's unsteady hand relayed her frustration as she inked her name on the line. Waving off the officer, she returned her focus to starting the car again.

"You don't understand, Mrs. Pearson. You can't drive. I can take you home, or you can use my car phone to call someone to get you."

"But the market is less than two blocks away." Her hands still trembled as she stuffed her wallet and the ticket, inside her purse.

"Doesn't matter if it's a half a block. You can't drive. Do I make myself clear?"

Her temples throbbed. "Just take me to the market. I'll call my neighbor from there."

The officer helped her into the squad car. "Be sure to have someone move your car as soon as possible. Remember, no driving until your license is renewed. You probably want to consider finding another way to get to the market. Perhaps you've been driving long enough."

Arriving at the market, Edna needed to free herself from the tension engulfing her within the squad car. She knew it was proper to thank the man, but she scowled as she opened the door and stepped unsteadily out. She stomped toward the wide glass doors of the grocery store, stopped part way, and looked back staring as the officer pulled away. She pooh-poohed the idea of calling Fred to get a ride home and somehow arrange to get her car home. The whole idea was absurd. With the officer out of sight, she turned around, and trudged back in the direction of her car, without the bacon and eggs.

Edna stewed all the way home. Safely in her driveway, she mumbled about the nonsense of having to take a driving test. Imagine, she had been driving for longer than that young officer's father had been alive, probably, even longer than his granddad.

Fred had offered to drive her to the Richland branch of the Department of Motor Vehicles the following Tuesday, for her driver's exam. Though she still resented the idea, she knew better than to arrive for her test alone. Her anger and resentment still fresh, Edna climbed into the passenger seat of her Buick. She fumbled for the seat restraint after Fred reminded her it would be required before even starting the vehicle for the exam. Menacing clouds loomed overhead and light rainfall danced across the windshield.

By the time they pulled up to the red brick, single story building with the American flag fluttering in the gusty wind, dark clouds blanketed the sky. Fred followed Edna inside and took a seat in the back of the room. Edna approached the counter and pulled off a ticket, relieved there were few other customers. She sat with Fred, clutching her purse, and checking the clock, until her number was called only ten minutes later. Her heart fluttered with all the nervousness of a teenage girl applying for a license for the first time. The female Department of Motor Vehicles clerk behind the counter spoke only to bark orders. She never looked up, only pointed to the vision testing machine. Edna placed her forehead against the bar, bumping the glasses she was not used to wearing. Flustered, she pushed herself to focus on the blurry characters she knew were the key to her being able to drive in the future. She stuttered the letters to the woman who glowered at her. The clerk mumbled she had passed, though barely, and moved her along to the next attendant. Edna sighed, her neck muscles loosened. A middle aged woman with no hint of pleasantry, dressed in a light brown uniform, approached. She ordered Edna to move her car to the front parking spot and wait for her to come out and begin the test.

Palms sweaty, Edna pulled the car in front of the building. She shuddered at the thought of driving in the constant rain, but there was nothing she could do now. She gripped the steering wheel, ready to show everyone she was still capable of driving.

The examiner marched over to the driver side window and motioned for Edna to roll it down. She proceeded to follow orders, turning on her indicators and lights, and stepping on the brakes. The unsmiling female with eyes of steel, walked around studying the lights and checking the tires. Edna's stomach churned watching the woman maneuver around the car, finally opening the passenger door and slamming it behind her, sending a spray of water across the seat.

Reaching across, the examiner fastened her seat belt and faced Edna. "Is your seat belt secure?"

Edna tugged on it, smug, she had it in place.

"If you are ready, you may start the car." The snappy abrupt tone relayed indifference and impatience. There was no concern for the examinee, it was just a job, all business.

Edna puzzled over the nonsense. "Imagine, after over seventy years of driving you make me take a driving test. I never needed an exam to drive when I first started driving." The car lurched forward.

"Pull into the street and head toward Riverside Boulevard."

Startled, Edna glanced across the seat. She couldn't remember where Riverside was. She turned the car right and studied the cars speeding past. She recalled when she was a young girl and there weren't many cars. Mostly she and her mother used streetcars, or the bus, when they went downtown to shop.

"Turn right, here, Mrs. Pearson. We're heading to Riverside, remember? Now, turn left at the next intersection."

The woman's constant shifting in the passenger seat made Edna nervous. She kept shouting out orders to turn right, turn left, and make sudden stops.

"Mrs. Pearson, you need to pick up your speed a bit, stay with the flow of traffic."

Edna shot a glance across the seat. She seethed at the condescending tone.

"Okay, Mrs. Pearson, I need you to turn right at the next light, then pull into the outdoor market down a few blocks on the left. Park the car in one of the diagonal parking spots behind the stand."

Edna didn't like how fast the orders were flying. She didn't understand. It wasn't right to put her through all of this. "You're making me nervous." Her fingers clenched the wheel. A dull thud banged in her chest. "I'm perfectly capable of driving. I just don't know where all these cars came from."

"The traffic is fairly light, Mrs. Pearson. Are you sure you're comfortable driving?"

"Don't tell me about the traffic. There are cars everywhere. The last time I came to Seattle there were hardly any cars."

"We're not in Seattle, Mrs. Pearson, We're in Richland."

Confused, Edna glanced over at her passenger. The woman was staring at her, mouth agape. Flustered, Edna returned her gaze to the road. "I don't understand. I recognize the old stores and the outdoor market." Her mind was in a haze. She just wanted to be done with all this nonsense.

"Watch out. There's a stop sign." A loud voice screeched from next to her.

The shriek startled Edna. A loud horn blasted. Panicked, Edna slammed on the brakes. She lunged forward, restrained by the seat belt shoulder strap. The car skidded to a stop sideways on the slippery street. Her pulse raced and her breathing was shallow. A black shiny car swooshed by in front of her. She blinked momentarily from the glare. Her mind grew muddled.

Edna gazed in awe at the black shiny metal which reflected the sunlight as it bumped along the street. Her eyes widened. She had never seen a car before. Everyone on the street was running out for a look. Soon the whole street was lined with people.

"Isn't it pretty? See the lights, like little chandeliers, hanging from the side?" Edna giggled like all six-year-olds do, as the car with its little wheels tried to get through the crowd which had poured into the middle of the cobblestone street. Sometimes, in wet weather, Edna had seen the horse drawn carriages lose their footing and slip on the smooth stones.

"Mrs. Pearson. Are you okay? Are you hurt?"

Dazed, Edna turned and studied the face of the woman next to her. She smiled and clambered down from the trolley she was riding in, and hurried over to the sidewalk. "Come on, we have to hurry." Edna looked down the street. She could see people gathering at the outdoor market. She was surprised by the cement walkways though. They weren't made from wooden planks that went *squish* on rainy days. They weren't even covered with an awning, like most of the sidewalks she and Mother followed on their way to the Public Market downtown.

"Mrs. Pearson, stop. You can't walk away like that." A stern faced woman scurried alongside.

Edna dashed along the street. She wanted to see the Indians who had slept on the sidewalks the night before. Early in the morning the market always came alive with the Indians selling brightly woven, colored, handmade, blankets and baskets. Edna loved to watch as the Indian women wove the reeds of different colors in and out and wrapped them around to make such beautiful and useful baskets. A firm grip took hold of her arm. Edna turned and pleaded. "Please can't we buy one? I like the baskets so much."

"What are you talking about, Mrs. Pearson? We need to get back to your car. We can't leave it in the middle of the street."

Edna yanked away and wandered down the street against protests, and melted into the crowd. The damp crisp air chilled her, and she tightened the red scarf which her mother crocheted, around her neck. She was thankful Mother was with her to keep her from becoming lost in the maze of sellers and buyers.

"Mrs. Pearson, please, we have to go back." Edna ignored the urging tone at her side. She wondered who the bothersome woman was, suddenly realizing her mother was nowhere in sight. She puzzled over where her mother had gone.

The market was buzzing with activity and the air filled with the sweet aroma of fresh sweet melons, spicy herbs and bouquets of flowers. She squeezed through the people gathered in front of the first few stalls. The Farmer's Market was one of her favorite places. She especially loved going in the mornings when the farmers backed their wagons up to the wooden stalls and unloaded their produce and dairy goods. Edna liked to browse but Mother kept insisting they get going. She turned around to face the impatient tone, not at all like her mother's.

"Mrs. Pearson, please. We have to get back in the car. It's blocking the street."

A large hand encompassed hers, a comforting arm wrapped around her shoulder and led her from the produce stand. She blinked and studied the uniform of the gray haired woman. "Where's Mother? What happened to Mother?"

"Mrs. Pearson, your mother's not here."

The firmness of the voice startled Edna. She didn't understand why this unfamiliar woman appeared so angry.

"I think that's enough for today. We need to get back."

Edna turned with questioning eyes. "Where are we going?"

"Mrs. Pearson, you're disoriented. We need to get back to the DMV."

Edna brought her hands to her warm cheeks then rubbed her sweaty palms on her coat. She looked around at the crowd, which had gathered, gawking at her, shaking their heads. The woman led her down the street to a big white car parked in the middle of the road.

The woman opened the door and helped her into the passenger seat. "I don't think you should drive." Climbing behind the steering wheel the strange woman drove her back to a large brick building with a sign, "Department of Motor Vehicles."

"Come on inside. Is there still someone waiting here who can take you home?" The woman's voice softened. She approached and offered her arm.

Edna pulled away and frowned.

Shaking her head, the examiner delivered her message. "We can't give you a drivers' license in your condition. Have your friend take your car home, Mrs. Pearson, sell it."

Edna didn't understand what had just happened. What did the woman mean, *her condition?* She shuddered at the thought she was losing her driver's license. Imagine, being told she couldn't drive anymore. What was she going to do? Edna scowled. Too proud to admit her failing, she crossed her arms. "I don't want to drive any more anyway." She was so mad she could chew coal.

# Chapter 16

As the flowers faded on the fruit trees, and blossoms on the perennials alternately bloomed and wilted, Edna could scarcely believe it was approaching a year since Larry's death. Her bills and paperwork piled up, and with it, her frustrations. Things she normally handled with no apprehension were now the bane of her days, causing increasing angst. Surveying the disarray in her living room, an avalanche of white envelopes and magazines covered the card table like drifts of snow after a blizzard. She had always managed without difficulty in her younger years. When she was married, she had taken responsibility for all the financial affairs, writing every expense and cash entry into a small accountant's ledger. Even in these past few years when things had become more taxing, Larry helped out when things became overwhelming. Now, without him, she had no one to handle her financial affairs.

Edna walked to the brass pole light, flipped the switch on, took a deep breath, and sat down. How did everything pile up so quickly? She pushed aside coupons for pizza, dry cleaning, windshield repair, and gutter cleaning, shaking her head at the absurdity and waste of getting so much mail she didn't want or need. She sorted through the bills and pushed the occupant mail to the side. Her fingers fumbled with the contents of a white envelope with green bars at the bottom and a label printed in red, reading, FINAL NOTICE. Unfolding it, her eyes strained to scan the fine print of the correspondence from the electric company for a clue. The pace of her heart raced as she read "Services will be disconnected." She didn't understand, she had always paid her bills on time. Indignant, she struggled to contain her frustration, though she couldn't control her quivering body. Her left arm brushed against the pile of junk mail, sending a flurry of envelopes and advertisements floating to the floor. "It's not fair." She picked up a few more envelopes and ripped them open, studying the contents, confused by the columns of numbers and rows of type. How come everyone was making things so complicated? Frustrated, she conceded defeat. She needed to be rescued from the paper work which buried her, but didn't know who she could trust to handle such a responsibility. Her breathing quickened. She stood and walked to the phone, pausing, before dialing Barbara's number.

Hot tea and Barbara's favorite brand of peanut butter cookies were waiting when she arrived.

"I appreciate your help, Barbara. I know it takes time away from Robert." Edna pulled out her check book and recent bank statement, handing them to Barbara. "I don't understand how they can cut off my power. I paid the bill."

Barbara flipped through the cancelled checks and studied the letter from the power company. "It looks like you paid only $10.71 Edna, not the $70.71 you owed."

Edna snatched the bill. "Let me see that. How can my electric bill be so high?"

Barbara laughed. "Everything is much more expensive these days. I'll call the power company and get this squared away. Let's look at the rest of your bills while I am here and make sure everything else is okay."

With Barbara's help, the useless mail was tossed, checks written and signed, and envelopes stuffed, sealed, and stamped. Edna watched the clutter on the table disappear.

Barbara reached across the table and took Edna's hands in hers. "You know I don't mind helping you, but you need to find someone who can help you with your bills on a regular basis."

Edna tightened the grip on her friend's hand, frightened of the reality bearing down. She had to face the fact she wasn't getting any younger and her chores were taking on a difficulty she could never have anticipated. "You're right, dear." Silently, she cursed the circumstances that had left her old and alone. With a sense of defeat, Edna admitted it was time to find someone to handle her affairs on a permanent basis. "I just don't know who I can trust." Edna looked down.

"You could ask Alicia." Barbara gazed across the table.

Her mouth dry, Edna's voice came scarcely above a whisper. "I can't trust her, even if she were willing. Besides, Alicia's not family. She's Kora-Lee's daughter."

Barbara eyed Edna with a questioning look. "I don't understand why you don't think you can trust her. You used to be close to Alicia. What happened?"

Edna frowned. Barbara was a dear friend, but she didn't like to share too much of her personal affairs with others. Conceding, she explained how her silverware set had disappeared. "I think Alicia stole it."

"I can't believe that. Have you asked her about it?"

Scowling, Edna raised her voice to Barbara, which she seldom did. "I'm certainly not going to ask her. She would just deny it anyway."

"What about David? He's been helping you this past year. Perhaps he wouldn't mind."

Edna had debated for some time about burdening David with her financial affairs, but there was no other person with whom she felt comfortable. "Yes, that's what I need to do." Even as she felt her independence ebbing away, a wave of relief swept over her.

# Chapter 17

Edna's mid-week phone call to David started right off with the crisis of the week.

"Someone stole my egg beater."

David was growing accustomed to a new calamity each week. Missing items topped the list, in addition to the never-discovered silverware. David chuckled. Remembering her glasses stashed in the refrigerator, he guessed the other missing items had found some new, totally bizarre, temporary location. He would have taken her more seriously, if the ongoing list of missing items were things of value, not merely scissors, casserole dishes, or old tennis shoes. "Are you sure you didn't put it somewhere else, Grandma?"

"No. I always put it in the third drawer by the pantry. It's not there. Someone stole it."

David inhaled deeply, a reminder to be patient in light of her increasing age and signs of dementia which he knew he would have to address. Soon. "Why would anyone break in, and steal your egg beater? I'm sure it will show up. We all forget where we put things sometimes."

"Oh, you. You think I misplaced it, don't you? But my silverware never showed up either."

Noticing the tremor in her voice, David didn't want to upset her any further so he gave in. "It's okay, Grandma, we can replace it easy enough. I'll check your doors and locks the next time I visit, okay?"

"I want you to call the police."

His neck muscles tightened like the overstretched strings on a guitar. "Why don't we wait until I can check things out first? I love you. I'll call you in a few days."

"You don't believe me." Grandma sighed loudly. "You'll see."

Before he could respond, the line went dead.

The next evening, an unfamiliar number from eastern Washington appeared on the caller ID. David stiffened, took a breath and picked up the receiver. "Mr. Bryant, this is Officer Schwartz with the Richland Police Department. Edna Pearson gave us your name and number. She called yesterday to report a burglary. This is her third phone call to us in the past few weeks. Our visits to her home have shown some damage to the door frame and window, nothing substantial enough to support a break-in. But we thought you should know in case you want to do some upgrades and make her feel more secure."

David thanked the officer and hung up, already tired from the next trip he faced, now only days away instead of several weeks as he had hoped.

Weary from not nearly enough sleep and frustration flowing like molten lava, David waved goodbye and headed out the following Saturday. After so many trips, his mind and body were on auto-pilot. Arriving shortly before noon, he greeted his grandmother. "How are you doing, Grandma?"

Edna started right in on the most recent burglary, immediately pointing out the side window. "See." She struggled to slide the window open. "It's off the track." She showed David where the wood was chipped away on the outside. "Someone tried to break in."

"Are you sure it hasn't been like this for a while, Grandma? Maybe you didn't notice it before."

"No. It just happened when I told the police about it last week. I told you on the phone. You never believe me. The officers were so nice to come right out and take a full report from me."

David forced the glass back into position on its old metal frame, wiped the frame with a rag sprayed with WD-40, then grabbed his screwdriver. With the latch tightened, David stepped back. "Now it won't be so easy to break in. I'll buy a wooden dowel to place on the window frame for extra security, and replace the dead-bolt lock on the door." Leaving the window open a bit for ventilation, David went to the back door. The small kitchen reminded him of a sauna filled with men wearing old sweat socks. Dark rings spotted the carpeting. He suspected the once wet areas now lay as host to mold and mildew. He opened the window behind the sink and checked the lock on the rear entry door.

Grandma smiled as she surveyed David's handiwork. "Thank you. I feel much safer now."

"Grandma, what do you think about pulling up your kitchen carpet? It's damp from your leaky faucet, and frankly, it smells like Missy has used it more than once." At the mention of Missy's name, the dog ambled around the corner. David forced a weak smile for his grandmother's sake, and then gently shooed the dog away.

Grandma hesitated. "I like the carpet. It's much more comfortable to walk on."

Hesitant to upset his grandmother further, David nonetheless pushed on. "Let's at least see what's under the carpet. It would be much easier to clean a linoleum floor than shampoo a carpet." David pried the dark brown molding away from the wall.

Grandma stood outside the kitchen, arms crossed. "Oh, my, are you going to be able to fix it if I don't like it?"

"Don't worry, Grandma. I'll make sure you're happy." David held his breath as he peeled back mildew infested, urine drenched carpeting from the floor, leaving remnant black particles of its rubber backing stuck to the flooring beneath. He blew out a slight breath at the sight of the buried linoleum. "What do you think, Grandma? I think it looks pretty good. Why don't you come over and take a closer look?" Standing, arms crossed, David exhaled, and studied the newly exposed outrageous gold, and brown toned, geometric, design. It was dirty, though only slightly worn.

Grandma bent down a bit to see what he had uncovered. A smile replaced her pout. "It's just what I would have selected for myself."

David smiled at the comment. From her gold velour sofa, to the tweed brown dining room carpet, he didn't doubt this floor was to her liking. "Good. Let's hope the rest of the floor is okay and we don't have any surprises." He continued to pull the carpet up, stopping to get a small red hand truck from his pickup. He moved the refrigerator to the center of the room and freed the last few feet of carpet. "Well, Grandma, it looks great, doesn't it? The room sure looks brighter."

With Grandma's blessing, he hoisted the old carpeting onto the hand truck, and with a great deal of relief, he flung the carpet into the dumpster outside. With a well-worn scrub brush, a bucket of water and ammonia, and a hefty serving of elbow grease, David put yet one more dreaded chore behind him.

Taking a breather in the living room after his exhaustive task, David noticed the large mess of papers spread across the table. "Are you doing okay with your monthly bills, Grandma?"

She hesitated. "Nathan and you are the only family left. It's too bad Nathan isn't around."

"I can help you, you know that. What do you need me to do?"

Though she looked away, David saw her face redden while she explained how difficult it had become to pay her bills.

"I need someone to handle my finances for me. I get confused by the bills lately."

"I don't mind helping, but have you asked Alicia? You know her a lot better and she lives closer so it would be much easier on you."

Grandma shifted in her seat. "You know I don't trust Alicia."

"It's just, I'm so far away. We would have to mail the bills back and forth for you to sign them, unless they're mailed to me and I am designated as power of attorney."

"I could do that. I already have a living will. I can name you a power of attorney for my health care matters, too."

David sighed. His voice betraying his brain's unyielding protest. "Okay."

Grandma's mouth turned up slightly. "Are you sure it's not too much trouble?"

"You're family, Grandma. You remember how much you and Granddad did for Nathan and me when we were little. It's my turn now, to help you."

Rummaging around on the card table for a pen, his grandmother made out a list of her monthly bills. "Let's see, there's home owner's association dues, phone, electric, and medical bills. Make sure you pay these. Of course, there will be more."

"The easiest way to pay bills will be to have them sent directly to me. What do you think?"

Grandma looked up. "Yes, we could do that. But I want to know whenever you pay a bill. Be sure to call me and tell me how much it was for. I need to record the expenses." She reached for her tan handbag, perched atop the bundle of current bills, and searched for the checkbook. "I guess you'll need this."

"Do you have any extra checks? This book won't last long."

Grandma walked to the closet and rummaged for another box. With it in hand, she clutched it like a treasure chest for a moment before turning it over to David. "Don't forget to let me know when you pay the bills. It will be such a relief not having to worry about the paperwork." Her face relaxed.

David sighed. His grandmother's weak smile erased any doubt of him taking on another chore though his senses told him things weren't going to be all that simple.

# Chapter 18

The last rays of daylight filtered through the large windows of the loft where David sat at his desk. Overwhelmed, he poured over the bills and bank statements his grandmother gave him a few weeks earlier. His grandmother kept remarkable records, especially for her age, but her method of organization was unconventional. To ease his task, he created a spreadsheet to keep track of the monthly expenses based on her past year's records. Hopefully, he could identify her financial stability based on her current retirement income. He fumbled through the musty wooden trunk she sent home with him, along with two crumpled shoe boxes of cancelled checks and old bank statements. Her most important papers, as she considered them, were kept in a nine by twelve, worn, purple and pink cloth handbag, with round plastic handles. David saw it often, laying on the card table in the living room, amidst her paper work. He rummaged through the handbag and found old passbook savings accounts, her ancient social security card, now sandwiched in yellow laminate, and oodles of lists. She had lists of all her debtors and their addresses, lists of funeral arrangements to be made when the time came, and a list of dates and names of everyone to whom she had ever loaned money. With one exception, the list of debtors consisted of everyone in Larry's family.

Jean came up the stairs with a cold glass of cola, setting it on the corner of the desk. She shook her head as she turned on the desk lamp. "We have a light. Why don't you use it? You're straining your eyes."

David mumbled he could see just fine, picked up the glass and gulped down his cold caffeine-free drink. He didn't need the caffeine. The stress of dealing with Grandma's affairs was plenty enough to keep him up at night. "Can you believe Grandma has loaned money to everyone in Larry's family, including Larry? Here's a promissory note from almost twenty years ago. She loaned him twenty-thousand dollars. I remember her saying she had paid for Lorraine's college."

Jean leaned in and looked over his shoulder. "That's probably what it was for."

David shook his head. "She loaned Lorraine and Alicia each a few thousand dollars too. It looks like the only debt ever repaid in full, was the money she loaned to Alicia's ex-husband."

Jean walked around behind his chair and began to knead his neck.

"That feels good." David stopped staring at the expenses he had totaled for a moment and turned to Jean. His tension eased somewhat, he tipped his head back and rolled his shoulders. "I can't figure how come her expenses last year were so much higher than this year. I guess I should go through the cancelled checks and see if anything jumps out. Maybe there were some unusual medical expenses like hearing-aids or hospital bills."

"You should take a break." Jean rested her hand on David's shoulder.

"Not yet." David patted her hand, maintaining his focus. "I don't understand how come she has so many different accounts at different banks. Must be the mentality of the Depression era." He laid the statements out across the desk. "She must have thought her money was safer if it were placed in different banks."

Jean glanced at the statements "I guess. Or, she simply forgot she opened some accounts, and just kept opening new ones. How else do you explain four different accounts at Bank One?"

David conceded the possibility and continued to study the previous year's bank statements. He noticed, on two separate months, check numbers were written out of sequence. One check for over nine-hundred dollars, and one for thirteen-hundred dollars.

He retrieved the cancelled checks corresponding to the statements from the shoe boxes. Thankfully, in spite of the unique filing system, the checks were at least grouped by month. The name of the payee, in both cases, was Alicia Sykes. "What do you make of this?" David held the check out to Jean.

"It is interesting, isn't it? Maybe Grandma gave her the money for a gift, or, it's part of another loan she didn't write down."

"They're odd amounts for a gift." David squinted and cocked his head. "If they're a loan, why would the check numbers be so out of sequence? Grandma didn't continue the sequence from these books 'til months after these checks were written." David turned them over to study the bank endorsement. "These checks were cashed the same day they were written." David laid the checks out next to several other cancelled checks. Grabbing his reading glasses, he compared the signatures. "Do these signatures look the same to you?"

Jean adjusted the desk lamp, shining more light on the blue checks. She bent down to study the penmanship. "Not really, the writing isn't as shaky and unsteady." She looked up. "You don't think Alicia forged these checks?"

"I don't know what else to think at this time. It doesn't make sense Grandma wrote one check and put the book away to use another book, does it? I think I need to keep checking her past statements."

He couldn't fathom Alicia stealing from her own grandmother. Surely there was another explanation. He again checked the amounts against Grandma's list of loans. No notation was made of the odd large amounts. "I don't know what to do about this." David leaned back in his brown vinyl desk chair and stretched. "Do you think I should ask Grandma?" He looked toward Jean for a clue as to his next move. He wasn't prepared to confront Alicia, but he couldn't ignore what he had found.

Jean pulled up a chair, studied the front of the check, and then turned it over to view the endorsement. "Look at this. It looks like the check and the endorsement are both written with the same blue pen, doesn't it?"

David picked up the second check, studied it carefully, and compared it to the one Jean held. "You're right. There's no point in upsetting her. I think we already have the answer." He paused. "Remember when Grandma's silverware was stolen? She thought Alicia may have been responsible. Kind of makes you wonder now, doesn't it?" David sat staring at the checks, talking to himself more than to Jean. "I don't understand how Alicia could do something like that." His chest tightened in anger. "I should have insisted Grandma put away her personal papers in a safer place."

Jean rubbed David's shoulders. "It wasn't your fault. Alicia wrote these checks long before you became involved in her affairs. Besides, we had no reason to suspect her of anything like this."

Pushing the checks aside, David gathered the rest of the statements. Perhaps his grandma was correct in distrusting Alicia. David brought his hands to his temples as if attempting to keep his head from exploding. "What kind of hatred makes someone do something like this, especially to a family member? Getting involved with her family has caused me nothing but grief."

"If you hadn't gotten involved, where would your grandmother be now? Who would be taking care of her?"

David sighed. Jean was right. There was no one to step up and care enough for his grandmother except him, and for the time being, his absent brother. With his resolution strengthened, David took a deep breath before returning to his search for further discrepancies.

# Chapter 19

With Rachel's high school graduation approaching, it was time to invite Grandma to spend the weekend with her new family. David called with an invitation to attend the up-coming baccalaureate ceremony.

"It's been a long time since I've been to a graduation or formal church celebration." Grandma's excitement danced across the line, spanning the distance between them.

The following weekend, David arrived to find his grandmother's brown, brocade, overnight bag positioned by the door, a welcome sign of her enthusiasm.

"It looks like you're all ready to go." He cast a glance at her once again forlorn appearance. Her navy blue knit pants, as well as her blue and red floral pullover, had seen better days. Jean would definitely need to do some mending and perhaps they would do some shopping, before bringing Grandma home after the weekend.

Missy yapped, running to the door. David still cringed at the sight of the mangy dog. He stepped inside to the faint aroma of bacon grease, grimacing at the thought of Grandma cooking on the stove, and the thought of hot grease. "Grandma, are you sure you should still be using the stove? Your eyes aren't as sharp as they used to be." He had wavered over broaching the subject, but the recent call from the Tri-City Fire Department regarding the smoke detector, concerned him enough to worry about her, and her neighbors. "I heard you accidentally set off the smoke detector the other day." Grandma's glare cautioned David. He would back off for now, rather than risk resentment before the four-hour car trip with her.

"Oh, you. I can see just fine. Besides, I don't use the stove much anyway."

Watching her disappear into the kitchen, David shook his head. Moments later, pans clanged, and cupboard doors closed, a likely attempt to disguise or hide evidence of her morning breakfast, most likely, cooked on the stove. She startled when David appeared in the kitchen.

"Is there anything I can help you with before we go?" David took in the sight of food crumbs and fresh spills on the counter. He poked his head into the laundry room and checked for fresh dog piles. He made a mental note to again address his concern over her cooking, when they returned on Sunday.

David secured the lock on the rear door, and pulled the blinds halfway. Missy continued her incessant barking at the empty dish by the door. David groaned. "What about Missy? Do you have someone taking care of her?'

Edna shuffled into the kitchen. "Fred has a key. He's going to stop by later and pick her up."

David found the dog food by the dryer, and quickly filled the dog bowls with nuggets and water. To save time, he'd call Fred from the road and verify information while updating Fred that Grandma was on her way. Grandma headed for the door, head held high, walking right past the suitcase. The screen door slammed behind her. David followed, picking up the small overnight case, pushed the lock button, and followed his grandmother down the driveway.

"Gracious. It's been a long time since I've been to Seattle. I grew up there, you know?"

"I know, Grandma. Maybe, we'll take a drive to your old neighborhood. Would you like that?"

Her eyes twinkled. For a moment, David imagined a little girl helping her mother in the kitchen and riding a bicycle down the once-narrow lanes of Seattle. He reached for his grandmother's frail arm and aided her into the front seat. Setting the small overnight bag in the back, he climbed in.

"That would be nice. I remember my home in Seattle, and one somewhere by a lake where I taught. I can't remember much." Her voice trailed off.

David glanced over toward his grandmother as he drove away.

She looked straight ahead watching the scenery, but a sly smile stretched across her face. "I can't wait to see your home again, dear."

"Grandma, you've never been to my house before."

"Oh." She brought her hand to her cheek. "Are you sure? I was certain I'd seen it before."

To ease her discomfort, David reached across the seat and patted her hand. "I'm sure Jean sent you pictures Grandma, and that's what you remember."

She turned. A broad smile replaced the wrinkled brow of concern on her tired face. "It's a lovely home." Her soft voice trailed off.

David drove slightly over the speed limit most of the drive, not sure how long his grandmother would be comfortable. "Let me know if you need to make any stops. There are plenty of places we can take a break."

Luckily, the drive was uneventful. With pleasant chit chat, and no more moments of confusion, David's shoulders relaxed as he pulled off the freeway exit for the final stretch home. Pulling up the long front drive to his house, David noticed his grandmother's wide eyes as she surveyed the expansive lawn and wooded acreage. He helped her out, and, grabbing her bag, led her to the front door.

"We're here." David called as he led Grandma inside where Jean stood waiting to greet them. Jean took the overnight case from David. "I just realized I haven't eaten since breakfast, and I'm starved. How long 'til dinner?" David approached the stove and took a peek inside the oven. His mouth watered as the sweet smell of basil and oregano escaped through the open door.

Jean showed Grandma the restroom to allow her to freshen up.

Edna emerged all smiles and reached over and grabbed her overnight bag. "Where's my room?"

Her directness caught David off guard and he smiled. "It's downstairs. There's only one bedroom on this floor. If the stairs are too difficult, you can stay in our room for the weekend."

"The basement is fine. I prefer not to be a bother or be in your way."

David puzzled momentarily over her words and tone wondering if he detected just a trace of martyr in it. He helped steady Grandma as she stepped cautiously down the stairs. He pointed out the features of the small mother-in-law apartment, complete with fridge, sink, stove, and microwave. David and Jean led her to the end of the hall to the bedroom. They watched as she unpacked her clothes, carefully placing them in the dresser. Then she put out her shoes, making herself quite at home.

"This is a lovely room dear, I could live in this much space. I don't need more than this to be comfortable." She walked to the window and pulled back the lace curtains. "It's nice you have enough room where someone could live, even for a long time, and not be in the way."

David glanced sideways to Jean. He didn't want to guess what she might be implying. "Yes, Grandma, it is very nice. The bathroom is right across the hall. There are fresh towels and soap, shampoo and conditioner are in the shower. Let us know if you need any help with anything." Gripping the rail the whole way, Edna stepped slowly up the stairs.

"Hi Grandma." Rachel and Emily greeted her at the top of the stairs. "I'm glad you're here and you're coming with us tomorrow."

"Where are we going?"

David led her to the sofa, reminding her of the baccalaureate service preceding Rachel's graduation.

"That's nice. I wish I had known. I didn't have a chance to get a gift."

Rachel sat down next to her. "Nobody's bringing gifts. It's just a small religious service."

The oven door clanged shut. David's stomach rumbled. "It smells like it's dinner time. I hope you're hungry, Grandma." David escorted her to the table. The girls emerged with the last utensils and sat down. David scooped a serving of cheesy noodles onto Grandma's plate.

Before pushing her plate away, she downed three healthy-sized servings. "This is wonderful, the food, and the lovely company. I haven't enjoyed a meal like this for so long." Edna grinned from ear to ear.

The next morning, David went downstairs to check on Grandma. Already dressed for the evening ceremony, her dress showed years of wear. The hem hung frayed on one side. She shuffled out of the bedroom in ratty slippers. Dismayed, he hoped he could convince her to change so Jean could get the dress washed and mended. He laid out the family's plan for the day. "We're not leaving for church until after dinner, Grandma. Why don't you put on some slacks for now? They might be more comfortable for walking in the yard."

"I'm just fine, dear." She turned and climbed the stairs, remarking how well she slept. "This is so nice. I could live in a place like this. Maybe you could build a place like this for me." She paused and fumbled for words. "Not here, of course. I wouldn't want to be in your way. It could be somewhere nearby, like next door."

David chuckled to himself.

Rachel walked in and hugged Edna. "Good morning, Grandma. After breakfast, we're making peanut butter cookies for the reception after the service. Do you want to help?"

"Mmm. Peanut butter cookies are my favorite." She clapped her hands like a young child.

David grabbed the paper and pulled up a stool at the breakfast bar to interact with the family. Edna was college educated in the late '20's, at a time when many women didn't attend college. Also, as a former teacher, Edna took a great interest in education. Her eyes brightened and she spoke excitedly, questioning Rachel. "Have you decided where you will be attending college?"

"I'm still waiting to hear. I've applied at both Western Washington and Central Washington University"

"Oh, my, will you be joining a sorority?"

"I might join a sorority. I haven't decided yet. It depends where I get accepted. Central doesn't have sororities."

"Oh, dear." Grandma shook her head and studied Rachel. "I don't care for sororities and fraternities. They encourage so much drinking. My daughter, Bernice, was killed in a car accident coming home from a fraternity party with some of her housemates. She was only twenty. They suspected the young fraternity boy driving, had been drinking." She shook her head and fell silent.

Rachel glanced at her mother. Jean rushed over. "Well, Rachel still isn't certain what she's going to do yet, Grandma. She still has a lot to decide."

Noticing the pot had stopped percolating, David poured some coffee for himself and his grandmother.

Edna looked in the cup, wrinkled her nose, and pushed it away. "Oh dear, I do prefer tea in the morning. Is that okay?"

"Certainly, Grandma." David forced the tension down, poured the coffee back into the pot, and started a cup of water in the microwave. Jean popped bread in the toaster and fried some eggs and quick sausage links. Minutes later, Emily joined the family, greeting her grandmother with a quick squeeze of the shoulders.

While David drank his coffee, he savored the rich full-bodied buttery flavor, breathing in the strong aroma. He gathered the strength he guessed he would need as he contemplated how to fill the day with activities that would keep his grandmother engaged. His plan of taking her outside proved to be a big thrill for her and used a chunk of the morning. A tour of the garden delighted her to no end. Edna continued to show an enormous amount of knowledge on the various plants and shrubs, which filled the grounds. Her face brightened when David pointed out a bank planted in Ajuga from the starts he had dug from her yard. It was thriving in the damp soil, making the bank a striking mass of purple. Mid-afternoon, Jean gathered the playing cards and shoved them back into the box after a few disastrous attempts at various games failed. "How about we get the cookies started?" Cards collected, Jean gathered the ingredients and Rachel grabbed the bowl and mixer.

Edna shuffled in. "I like my peanut butter cookies chewy, not crunchy."

"Then we'll make them chewy." Jean smiled, making room at the breakfast bar for everyone and pulling up a stool for Edna.

"I'm quite a good cook myself." Edna grinned, waiting with a fork for making the crisscrosses on the cookies and then sprinkling them with sugar.

With the room filled with the sweet scent of warm peanut butter cookies, Jean poured milk and placed the first batch of cookies on a plate.

Edna smacked her lips. "These are soft and chewy, just the way I like them."

After a quick salad and take-and-bake pizza for their dinner, it was time to get ready for Rachel's baccalaureate ceremony. Grandma sat down on the sofa. Jean wiped her hands and dashed out of the kitchen.

David joined his grandmother. His forehead wrinkled in concern. "Do you want to take a coat? It gets chilly in the evenings here." Downstairs, he retrieved her navy blue, quilted raincoat. It carried the faint scent of her home before it was cleaned. He immediately regretted he had suggested it, but carried it upstairs.

"She's not wearing that." Jean shook her head, meeting David at the top of the stairs.

"I was hoping it would look a little nicer than what she's wearing."

"Mother bought me that coat years ago." Edna had walked over and reached out for her garment before David could stop her.

Though the worn and stained coat looked old, David doubted her mother, who had passed away nearly thirty years earlier, had purchased it for her. He called to Rachel and Emily. They ran down the stairs. "Do either of you have a sweater Grandma could borrow?" He glanced at Grandma with a hint of urgency. They picked up on his pleading tone, nodded, and tromped up the stairs, retuning with a tan, loose knit, baggy cardigan. "Thanks." David carried the sweater over to Grandma. "Let's see how this fits." He held the sweater out.

"That's not my sweater." Grandma pulled away and eyed David.

"I know, but it's a bit chilly, and I'm afraid your coat will be too warm once you're inside." He shot a glance at the girls and Jean who were waiting by the door, all ready with their plate of cookies in hand.

Edna hesitated, then her face softened. She allowed David to drape the sweater around her shoulders, then help her into the sleeves. "I need my hat. Did you bring my hat?"

David scurried back downstairs and fished through the drawer of her clothes for her brown fake fur hat. He chuckled thinking the hat looked like a Russian ushanka hat. Returning upstairs, Edna placed it triumphantly on her head. She walked out the door, arm in arm with David to attend Rachel's baccalaureate.

# Chapter 20

Edna stepped slowly toward the entrance to the church. She couldn't recall if she had ever been to a baccalaureate service. The soft scent of the purple hyacinth floated on the breeze of the late spring evening. David led his grandmother by the arm down the sidewalk. Neat borders of vibrant yellow and orange zinnias and white and red geraniums lined the walkway.

"This is a pretty church, isn't it, Grandma?" Rachel reached over and took her other hand. Edna smiled as she squeezed Rachel's hand. She strutted like a peacock on show, proud and happy to be included in her great-granddaughter's event. Sunlight glistened off the arched orange and yellow stained glass windows of the old fashioned, brick church, reminding her of a structure from long ago with its pillars and arched columns. Flustered by the growing size of the crowd, Edna appreciated David was there to guide her through the sea of spring-colored pastels, and flower prints worn by the large crowd mulling around outside. She studied the smiling faces of the students wearing dress clothes for their special occasion.

Escorted through the oversize double doors into the vestibule, Edna glanced down at her clothing and smoothed her soft fabric. She smiled, feeling appropriately dressed for the day in her outfit.

"Have you ever been to a baccalaureate service, Grandma?" Rachel leaned in with a soft voice.

"Oh, gracious, no. I haven't been to any graduation ceremony in quite some time." With failing eyes, Edna strained to make out the figures outlined in the vibrant, colored glass windows. She puzzled over which Christian saints they might be. Rich chords of music bellowed from the dozens of gray pipes of a majestic organ, which dominated the space behind the altar, where the white-robed choir stood. Stepping inside the already packed church, Edna glanced around. She never imagined there would be such a crowd. David helped her into the wooden pew. The high, open ceilings filled with the strong voices of the choir, singing "Amazing Grace." Edna strived to recall the words from her youth and sang in halting words along with the choir. Her voice cracked with the dryness of age. She smiled as memories of her youth flowed through her mind.

Edna sat swaying in time to the music until it stopped and the minister instructed the congregation to be seated. He began by congratulating the new graduates, then introduced the first speaker.

"Can you hear okay, Grandma?" David looked over at her. She smiled, but sat silent, engrossed in the ceremony.

The speaker took the podium. "Too many people define themselves by what they do as a profession, rather than the type of person they are."

Edna sat poised on the edge of the pew, contemplating the inspirational words as if they were directed to her.

"When you graduate and leave here, what kind of person will you be? When you look back on your life at the end of the road, what will you see, what will you remember?" His words echoed in Edna's head. "What will you remember?" Her mind strained to remember.

Edna looked down, beaming with pride at her new, long, fitted, gray wool skirt which her mother had worked on so hard for her graduation. Mother always loved sewing for her youngest daughter. Daddy was such a dear. He bought her a new, black, felt hat with a wide rim and a silk fuchsia sash to match her mohair sweater. Edna put her hand to her head to feel the new hat atop the long blond braids wrapped around her head. Feeling so grown up in her new hat, she looked over to her father. "It's just the fleas' ankles." Smiling smugly, she looked out of the corner of her eye and saw the half dozen boys in the graduating class turn their heads to look at her. She had finally made it to her high-school graduation day. She listened eagerly for the school president to announce her name, as she sat on the edge of the long wooden bench. A lone tear trickled down her cheek, and her chest swelled over her achievement. The crowd applauded.

The thundering applause startled Edna. She gazed toward the front of the large building. Her eyes widened at the size of the crowd, her voice suddenly shrill and breaking. "Where did all these people come from?"

David looked over at her. "Grandma, these are all the graduates and their families."

"But the graduating class is only twelve. I don't remember so many people coming to watch me graduate." Edna suddenly flushed. She looked around. The fashion was not the same on these youngsters. She didn't recognize the classmates surrounding her, with short skirts, tight tops, and clunky shoes. She looked down at her mint green, flowered, double knit dress with brown slip on shoes. She touched the top of her head. There were no braids wrapped around her head, and no wide brimmed hat with its fuchsia sash, only fine, thinning hair, pinned up underneath a fur cap. "David, where have all these people come from? What am I doing here?" Her voice cracked.

David leaned over and put his arm around her. She was comforted by his smile as he hugged her. "It's okay, Grandma. It's okay. You've just forgotten where you are. It's a ceremony for Rachel's graduation, her baccalaureate."

Edna glanced over at her great-granddaughter and smiled weakly. Rachel smiled back with a broad grin. Edna bent down, and fumbled in her purse for a tissue, and dabbed her eyes. She wiped away a small tear for all the years that had passed.

# Chapter 21

Edna hurried to the door to welcome David and Jean when they arrived Saturday, before noon as promised.

"Come on in, dear. It's been so long since I've seen you."

"Sorry, we've been busy since Rachel's graduation trying to catch up on some things around the house." David placed his bucket of repair tools on the floor and embraced Edna.

"You must be hungry after your long drive." Edna released her grandson and smiled up at him.

"We're fine. We grabbed a bite on the way."

"Oh, you. You know better than to eat on the way. Let me make you something anyway, I have plenty of food here." Edna scurried to the refrigerator and began rummaging through its contents.

David peered over her shoulder. "Grandma, it looks like that's spoiled." He pulled out a small white dish. She saw him wrinkle his nose. "See, it's turning green. You can't possibly eat this." David pulled the dish out. "It needs to be tossed."

Edna frowned as David dumped the spoilage in the trash can under the sink. "That food was perfectly fine. I could have scraped off the little bit of mold. You young people are so wasteful." Edna resented David's interference. He was always after her for something when he came over. "You think I don't know how to keep up my house and you think I'm dirty." Her pulse quickened and her tear ducts welled up.

David put his arm around her shoulder. "Grandma, you're ninety-three. There's nothing wrong with needing help with some things." He walked over to the kitchen window, pushed it open, then pulled off several paper towels and began wiping down her counters.

Edna eyed him like an eagle. "You don't understand. I can clean my own house. It's just I don't much like doing it. And, I'm certainly not going to pay someone to clean it. Besides, my house is just fine as it is." Edna glanced around the kitchen, suddenly self-conscious of the cluttered counters. "You never know if you can trust strangers coming into your home. I've already had my silverware stolen." Though Edna loved having her grandson and his family in her life, she disliked the goings-on behind her back. It was insulting how her own family seemed displeased with how she lived. "You think I don't know how everyone is always cleaning things behind my back, but I've seen it."

"Grandma, you know we're only trying to help make your life safe and comfortable."

David's attempt at an explanation didn't appease her. She crossed her arms, firm in her resolve to make him understand. "I'm perfectly capable of taking care of myself and my home. You make me feel incompetent." She fought back the burning sensation in her eyes. "I have always been able to do my own chores, even when I was a young girl I had chores. I didn't care much for dusting, but Mother insisted. She also taught me to iron and darn socks when I was only eight." She deepened her voice to imitate her father, "Father always said, 'You darn a pair of socks better than anyone, including your mother.'" Edna laughed, remembering Mother's displeasure when her father said that to her.

Jean picked up a dish towel from the counter. "Grandma, how about while I'm here I help you throw in a load of laundry?"

"Oh, you," Edna frowned, "I just washed that." She snatched the dish towel from Jean. "I prefer to wash my clothes by hand like Mother did when I was a young girl. You young people today are so spoiled with modern conveniences."

"Some things don't get clean when you wash them by hand. Some things need to be washed by machine. I can help you wash a small load of undergarments and bath towels."

"It's nonsense to waste all that water and electricity when I have so few things to wash. Anyway, the washer is too confusing to use." She hobbled through the house, gathering her dish cloths and a few wash cloths. She handed the bundle to Jean. "Here, put these in the sink. I'll show you how to do the laundry."

Edna headed up the stairs with David following. She collected some undergarments from her bedroom, carefully tucking them away from sight in her arms. Returning to the kitchen, Edna pursed her lips. "See, this is all there is." She placed the items next to the sink. She turned on the faucet and reached inside the cupboard underneath the sink for her washing soap.

"Have you ever used Fels-Naptha?" She held out a large yellow bar for Jean to see. "This is the only kind of clothes soap Mother ever used." With the water still running, Edna ran the bar under the faucet for a few minutes, just enough to produce some suds, then dropped the bar into the water, and turned the knob off. She smiled as she swooshed around the soapy water and stared at the sink of rising bubbles. The smell of the soap made her nose tickle. Edna giggled and felt like she had when she was a little girl.

Hearing the sound of water running, Edna was excited to help her mother. It was Saturday, wash day. Mother smiled at her. Edna looked around the kitchen. "Where's my stool?" Edna shrugged. She couldn't understand what happened to her stool. It was always placed to the right of the big wash basin. She always used it when she helped Mother with the wash. She didn't notice the empty pot on the wood stove. Mother must have already emptied the boiling water into the heavy metal sink attached to the wall. She liked how her nose tickled from the soap shavings, and she reached up to scratch it.

Across the room was Mother's kitchen queen cupboard, with two shelves for the jars of sweet and pungent spices. Edna, remembering the stick she always used to stir the clothes, scurried over to the long drawer below the tureen, and clanged around, searching for it. "Here is the stirring stick." She proudly held out a long handled, wooden spoon for her mother to see. Then, Edna gently pushed the items around in the sink with the stick. She glanced over at her mother. "See, I can do a good job." Edna giggled with the joy of helping.

"Yes, you're doing a good job." Edna smiled at the woman who handed her a few dirty towels.

"See, everything must be washed in progression, just as you said. First the dish towels, then my undergarments, finally the other dirty clothes." Edna removed the towels and dishcloths. She wrung them out over the pot. Then she went to the laundry room, grabbed her wicker basket, and placed the damp clothing into the basket. Next, she threw in her undergarments and repeated the process. "We need to go outside now." Edna lifted the wicker basket and carried it outside to the old circle shaped clothesline, which sat on a platform above the ground.

"Do you need help hanging up the laundry?"

Startled by a male voice, Edna hesitated, uncertain who was asking to help her. "No, I prefer my way. I have never forgotten the method Mother taught me. Mother and I will remove the clothes later when they're fresh and dry. Tomorrow is ironing day."

# Chapter 22

Edna answered the knock at the door. The postman handed her a parcel. "Sign here, please."

She glanced at the return address, but couldn't decipher the writing. It was only two days from her birthday. Edna's excited hands trembled as she thanked the postman, and closed the door. Sitting down at her dining room table, she studied the package, running her fingers across the brown butcher paper. She noticed 'FRAGILE' stamped in big red letters numerous times, across the front. Edna tore open the parcel with the enthusiasm of a child, and removed the lid from the sturdy, brown box. She lifted out a dark, oak framed, eight by ten portrait. Salty tears formed, as she held the photo of Nathan in his dress blues. David must have told him her birthday was approaching. She recognized the stripes of Sergeant First Class, smiling, her heart ached to see him again.

Gazing upon the picture, the resemblance to his grandfather, Jacob, when he was in the army, was remarkable. Her thoughts drifted to how handsome Jacob had been in his army uniform. Edna had loved the military life, though the excitement of being the wife of a soldier had worn off fairly early as she faced its realities and uncertainties. Moving around was tough on the children. She was grateful they were so young when Jacob was an enlisted man. She was also thankful he had insisted on requesting a post in the states as the change was less traumatic for Bernice and Larry. Edna wondered if that was why Nathan had stayed single. Military life could be such a stress on a relationship. Edna carried the photograph into the living room. She scooted over the other framed photos on the end table, to the right of the sofa, and sat Nathan's picture among Bernice's graduation photo, and photos of Larry, and Jacob, in their uniforms. She stepped back and beamed proudly, hands on hips. Three generations of enlisted men.

The next evening as Edna prepared her dinner, Missy's yapping caught her attention. The dog ran from the living room to her. She walked down the hall hearing the phone's incessant ringing. She reached for the receiver.

"Hi, Grandma. Happy Birthday."

Edna wiped her hair away from her ear. "Gracious. You're a little early, but that's okay, dear. I expected you to call tomorrow."

"Did you get the gift I sent?"

Edna sat down on the sofa, confused. "I thought the gift was from Nathan. I didn't know you sent it, David."

"Grandma, this is Nathan."

Edna's heart skipped a beat. She brought her hand to her face. "Is it really you?" It had been over a year since Edna became reacquainted with David. Now, Nathan had surprised her with a phone call. Her heart swelled at the realization beginning today, she would get to know her other grandson.

"I'm sorry I haven't called earlier. I don't have a lot of free time to keep in touch with people like I should, especially with the time zone difference."

Edna blinked back the tears. "When will I be able to see you? It's been so long."

"I'm hoping sometime next year. I won't know for sure until it gets closer to the actual transfer. The army doesn't always give a lot of notice."

Edna sighed. She knew the routine. She remembered her own move across the United States with her two little babies. "When Jacob was ordered to Fort Monmouth, New Jersey, we were allowed only one-week notice."

"When was that?"

Smiling, Edna loved sharing her stories of life in the service. "I think it was 1935. I remember both Larry and Bernice were quite young." She reached across to the end table and picked up Nathan's photo and gazed upon it again as she listened to her grandson.

"I bet it was quite a long trip for you."

"I should say. Jacob knew our old Ford would never last through the two-week trip across the states, so we traded it, along with five-hundred dollars, for a shiny, new, blue, Chevrolet." Edna smiled at the memories of the classiest car she had ever seen.

"So what did you think of New Jersey?"

"I loved living on the east coast although Jacob was seldom home and never really adjusted to the lifestyle." Edna sighed deeply, remembering the antique stores, the dances, and socializing, with the military wives. Her head swayed as she started humming an old Bing Crosby tune that resonated through her head. "Where the Blue of the Night Meets the Gold of the Day."

Words crackled with static across the phone line. Edna stopped humming to listen to the voice and the words. "It's difficult getting used to a life so far from home, and so different. It's hard to be happy away from those you love. At some point, you just need to return home."

Edna sat stunned. She closed her eyes. The words echoed as if she heard them just yesterday. Jacob had never been happy in the military. She couldn't believe what Jacob had just said to her. She fumed. He always had to have something to complain about.

"I've requested a transfer to Washington, to Fort Lewis."

The words shocked Edna as if she'd been struck. She turned away, feeling betrayed. She knew she shouldn't have been surprised, Jacob had hinted now for over a year of his dissatisfaction living in New Jersey.

"But I like the other army wives here, and the children have friends. Especially Larry, he's finally adjusting so well with the other children." It didn't matter though. Jacob was miserable. If Edna wanted to continue to live with him, she was expected to honor his wishes. She had long questioned her decision in marrying this man, but now, there were the children. She and Jacob had agreed to stay together, and make the best of the situation, for the sake of the children.

"Grandma. Are you okay? What are you talking about?

You're not an army wife anymore and your children are both gone now."

"Bernice and Larry are gone? Where?" Edna shook her head. She brought her hands to her temples, and closed her eyes. Her heart pounded, causing a dull pain in her chest. "I don't understand. What happened, Jacob?"

"Grandma."

Edna detected frustration in the tone across the line.

"I'm not Jacob. This is Nathan."

Edna studied her surroundings. She was not in her home with the crystal prism chandelier hanging over the large mahogany table, where she had entertained so many of the ladies from the base. The surroundings seemed simple and disorganized, not at all like her. "I'm sorry, I don't understand."

"This is Nathan, your grandson. Do you remember? I called to make sure you received the photo I sent for your birthday."

Edna glanced at the color photo of the uniformed officer, in her lap. She whispered to herself. "Nathan." Then she smiled and returned her attention to her caller. "When am I going to see you again?"

"Soon, Grandma. I'm sure I'll see you by your next birthday."

"That's too long. I might not live that long." Edna's voice drifted off as she returned the phone to its cradle.

# Chapter 23

Edna couldn't remember what happened. She awoke, lying on the living room carpet. The early rays poured through the windows. She tried to move her right leg and arm to push her up but they failed her. Her heart raced and sweat formed on her forehead and dripped down her cheeks. She could taste the salty drops. Panic gripped her. No one would hear her cries for help.

She lay on the floor for some time before the phone rang. Missy yapped as she ran in circles. Edna fought to push herself to stand, or even crawl to get to the phone to answer it. She experienced no pain, only numbness down her side. Missy settled, strutted over, and lay down next to her. Edna slowly reached out her left hand and stroked the dog's black fur. She wondered how long she would lie alone like this, helpless as a baby. A short while later, the phone rang a second time. Edna waited, praying to hear someone come to check on her. She gazed at the old antique clock on the bureau, dizzy, her eyes strained in a failed attempt to make out the time. For a few minutes she concentrated on the tick tock of the wooden pendulum as it swung back and forth. Then, came the pounding. She listened, wondering if her ears were playing tricks on her. Hearing the pounding again, Edna turned her head toward the door. Her breathing relaxed, realizing someone was knocking. A man's voice came from outside. She guessed it was her neighbor, Fred.

"Edna ... are you here?"

The knock grew louder, then a key turned in the door. Edna was glad Fred had the foresight to ask for a house key in case of an emergency. He called out again as he walked in. "Edna. Are you okay?" Seeing her on the floor, Fred stooped, and awkwardly raised her to a seated position.

"Thank God you're here. I can't move." Her voice cracked as the sound labored from her parched throat.

Fred bent over to console her. "You'll be okay now; I'm calling an ambulance." Edna's muscles relaxed, knowing she wasn't alone. She sat dazed as she looked at her leg that didn't feel a part of her.

The wailing of the sirens stopped outside Edna's condo. Missy's constant yapping pushed her tension level up and she snapped at her dog, which she rarely did. "Quiet, Missy."

Fred met the emergency crew at the door and led them into the living room. One of the EMT's carefully lifted her and carried her to the sofa. They were quiet as they raised her eyelids and shined a light. They pumped the black cuff of the blood pressure monitor so tight Edna thought her arm would snap like a frail tree limb. Her heart thumped fast but unsteady like a poorly tuned engine.

"What are you doing?" Flustered, as they talked around her and passed things back and forth, Edna called out. "What's happening? Talk to me." Her words sounded strange and slurred.

"It will be okay, Mrs. Pearson, we are checking you out. Do you have any family nearby who we can call?" One of the crew looked at Edna then turned back to Fred as the other technician held his radio and called out numbers. A voice cracked across the line in response.

"David. Somebody call David." Edna's voice broke with fear.

Fred stepped in and spoke soothingly. "I'll call David and let him know what's going on and tell him you're going to the hospital."

"I don't want to go to a hospital. I just want to rest for a few days." Edna struggled to speak clearly enough to catch the attention of the emergency crew. "Why are you taking me to a hospital?" Edna's heart pounded like a drum against her chest tight from the rage swelling inside.

The lone female EMT turned her attention to Edna, speaking softly, but with authority. "I'm sorry, Mrs. Pearson; you've likely suffered a stroke. Resting in bed isn't going to do it. We need to take you in for observation, and some more tests. "Do you know how old you are, Mrs. Pearson?

How ridiculous, Edna thought, of course she knew how old she was. "Ninety-two ... no wait ... ninety-three."

"Do you know how long you were out before your neighbor arrived? Do you remember what happened?"

Too many questions all at once upset her. They didn't make any sense. How could she possibly know how long she was out? She frowned and turned her face away from the woman, and mumbled, "I don't remember what happened. You can't expect me to remember that."

Lifted onto a stretcher, she was hooked to a machine that beeped in time with her heart. The ambulance pulled out with lights flashing and sirens blaring for all the neighbors to notice. Before she knew it she was wheeled through the double doors of Good Samaritan Hospital.

"Please, someone. Call my grandson for me. Is anyone listening?" Edna stared into the hall as a dash of white coats and machines rolled by.

# Chapter 24

The nurse directed David to Room 304, bed B, the farthest from the door. He knocked before he edged in. Faint sunlight filtered through the gauze-like curtains, casting light on Grandma's distant and frightened eyes. David bent down to kiss her cool cheek. He immediately forgot about his long drive as he gazed at her, helpless, in the stark, dreary hospital room. "How are you doing, Grandma?" David winced at the beeping of the machines and the sight of the wires which snaked around her, overwhelming her frail body.

"Oh, David, I'm so glad you're here. When can I go home? When is the bus coming so I can leave this terrible place? No one tells me anything."

Her voice strained over nearly unintelligible words. David grabbed a chair by her bed and slid it over. "You had a stroke, Grandma. I just got here and haven't had a chance to talk to the doctor yet." He sat down and held her cold clammy hand. He forced a smile to avoid expressing the agony he suffered sitting in a hospital room, breathing in the stagnant, antiseptic odor. "I'll see Dr. Smith later today. Why don't you rest? I'll let you know what the doctor said after I speak with him." David stroked his grandmother's arm, and it began to warm. "I'll be back to see you in a little while." David patted her arm, turned, and walked out.

His phone call to the doctor before leaving home had allowed him time to consider the options he knew were going to be presented for his grandmother's care. Continuing to live on her own was not going to be one of them. After a short drive to the medical center, David rode the elevator to the fifth floor to search out Dr. Smith. He knocked on the open door as he announced his arrival. "Dr. Smith? I'm David, Edna Pearson's grandson."

"Come on in." Dr. Smith waved David in and motioned to a chair opposite him.

David took a seat in front of a large, cherry wood desk piled with papers and files.

Dr. Smith immediately set about discussing Grandma's situation. He fumbled through papers and scribbled more notes as he spoke. "Your grandmother has suffered another mini stroke. In and of itself, I wouldn't be worried, but I suspect she's had a number of these over the past few years. They're called Transient Ischemic Attacks, or TIA's for short. They seem to be coming more frequently. With her advanced age, I strongly suggest some sort of assisted living arrangement, or considerable home health care at a minimum. I also suspect she is suffering from early to mid-stage dementia. My best guess would be Alzheimer's Dementia, which will worsen with age."

David nodded at the doctor's direct words. He had suspected as much with her increasing forgetfulness and bizarre words and reactions. Still, his chest tightened. His worry over his grandmother's safety had grown over the past months after two visits by the local fire department for a fall, and a minor stove fire. This meeting merely confirmed earlier concerns. With this latest stroke, Edna's ability to continue to live on her own again was only a fantasy. How could he possibly find care-givers who would put up with her difficult nature? He knew he would be blasted with her full wrath if he told her she needed to move to an assisted care facility. David's gut twisted as he sank down in his seat at the thought of the upcoming confrontation. "I know my grandmother will have to accept help cooking, cleaning and bathing as doctor's orders, but I still am not looking forward to breaking the news to her."

Dr. Smith chuckled. "I understand. If you, or your grandmother, have any questions, let me know. I'll be more than happy to talk to her."

David stood and thanked him, then with a sigh, and hesitant steps, he walked to the car to return to face Grandma's fury.

Minutes later, David guardedly poked his head into his grandmother's room and studied her eyes for some indication of her mood, before he edged inside.

"David, when can I go home? I don't like it here and nobody's telling me why I'm here. I just want to go home."

"Grandma, since you've had another stroke, the doctor says you can only go home if you agree to have someone come and help take care of you."

"That's okay, dear. I'm sure Barbara can come help me out 'til I get stronger again."

David shook his head. "No, Grandma, you don't understand." He guessed his Grandma already understood his message, but was too proud, and stubborn to admit it. "He means professional help, a trained nurse or nurses' assistant. Barbara is a wonderful person, and a dear friend, but she can't do it. She isn't a trained caregiver." For all of the relief David felt knowing she would be better cared for, and less of a danger to herself or others, he recognized his grandmother's resentment. She didn't see her lack of personal hygiene and how she appeared to others, or comprehend how her home had fallen to such dreadful conditions in such a short period of time. "Your bedroom and bathtub are upstairs and you won't be allowed to take stairs by yourself any longer."

She shot a quick response even before hearing him out. "I don't need the bed, I sleep just fine on the sofa and I can wash up in the downstairs bathroom."

David took a deep breath and began counting to ten slowly in his head. "Grandma, that's not enough. Your glaucoma is worse, and it's dangerous for you to cook. You need to bathe, and the downstairs sink isn't adequate. You're going to need help." He punctuated his final words with a firm gaze.

"I don't need strangers coming to take care of me and I can wash myself with a cloth."

Responsible for her humiliation and anger, David decided to try a different approach, one which would appeal to her desire for socialization, and not make her feel helpless. "Wouldn't it be nice to have someone to help you with chores, and to talk with throughout the day?"

Her angry pout flashed her disagreement like daggers.

"I'm sorry, Grandma, you have no choice other than staying in the hospital, going to a retirement facility, or having a professional care provider come to your home."

"No. I want a second opinion. This doctor doesn't know what he's talking about." She struggled to sit up in her bed, fighting the wires and restraints that held the monitoring equipment in place.

The proud woman had been independent for most of her life. David, sitting by her bedside, stroked her forehead and long thinning hair. "You've always trusted Dr. Smith, though."

"Oh, you." Grandma's eyes squinted and her lips pursed like she'd bitten into a sour lemon. "I want another doctor's opinion."

Her command came without allowance for anything but obedience. Reluctantly, David agreed to find another doctor to meet with her the following afternoon. "Goodbye, Grandma, I love you, I'll be back to see you tomorrow." David gave her shoulder a gentle squeeze, which was about the only part of her not hindered by wires and gadgets. He waved and headed out to leave a message for Dr. Smith at his office. If Grandma wanted a second opinion that was her prerogative. Surely one of Dr. Smith's associates could offer a second opinion.

David didn't want to be deceitful, but he was entrusted with her care. He would do what was right, even if it meant upsetting her and facing her fury. If there were an option, he wouldn't hesitate to turn the job over to someone else. Alicia had managed to stay mostly absent since Larry's death, especially since her attempt at cleaning failed. With questions still looming over him about Alicia's honesty and motives, it was probably best she remain absent. And, Nathan was still out of the country. David once again, found himself at Dr. Smith's door to request an appointment with one of his associates.

Dr. Armado arrived in Grandma's room early the next morning. She shooed David out of the room with authority, "I want to talk to the doctor alone." David left, knowing full-well stories would be fabricated and embellished to portray her ability to care for herself and maneuver around the house, especially on the stairs. He also had confidence in Dr. Armado's ability to see through her fantasy. David had done all he could to lessen the risk of harm to his grandmother, or others. He had already tripped the fuse to her stove, forcing her to do all her cooking in the microwave and he set back the temperature on the hot water tank. Several neighbors and friends had emergency contact numbers. All throw rugs and footstools had been removed to avoid tripping. There was no doubt, for Edna's safety, it was time to take her living arrangements to a more controlled level.

Grandma's frantic high-pitched voice penetrated the hospital door spilling into the hall. For the doctor's sake, David opened the door and poked his head inside. "Is everything okay here, Grandma?" David approached her bedside glancing at the doctor for a sign. Dr. Armado looked back with a slight shake of his head and a shrug. David studied his grandma's tense face and knew the news hadn't been well received.

"I don't want any help. I don't need it." Sharp, bitter words spewed like hot steam released from an over-heated old jalopy.

David flinched, half expecting something to be thrown at him.

"As I explained to your grandmother," the doctor focused his gaze at David, "my recommendation is for a health care worker to come to her home at least during the day." He watched his patient out of the corner of his eye, before continuing, "The alternative is to find a full time care facility."

"Do you hear that, Grandma? You need to accept help." Sympathetic to her plight, David fought the tone of giving orders. "It's the best thing for you, Grandma." She half sat, half lay in bed, draped in a hospital issued, blue, cotton robe, her eyes brimming and blinking away tears. David's impatience softened. The fragile, defeated woman almost made him sorry for the situation he had to impose upon her. He reached for her hand. She pulled it away without a word. Her expression spoke of pain and anger. The doctor departed, leaving David alone to reconcile with Grandma and try to salvage the damage he had done to the relationship he had worked so hard to forge.

"Grandma, you know this is for the best. This way, you can still stay in your own home, and you can give me some peace of mind knowing you're safe." Her face relaxed a bit, but she refused to offer an indication of acceptance. "I'll interview some caregivers. Think of them as companions who will be there to offer friendship as well as assist you with grooming and such." David heard his condescending tone. He knew Grandma hated it. He bent down to kiss her cheek.

Edna's face reddened. She tugged at the tubing restricting her movements. "You can't know what it feels like to be old." She adjusted her hospital gown and rolled to her side facing away from David. "I will not have anyone see me naked."

# Chapter 25

After three days in the hospital, Edna ached to see her place again. The numbness in her right leg was gone, and she grinned like an eighteen-year-old moving into her first apartment. Struggling with her new stability cane, at David's insistence, Edna hobbled into the house, flipped on the light switch, and glanced around, smiling at the familiarity and independence it signified. She shivered and rubbed her arms for warmth for a moment before shuffling to the thermostat and cranking it up all the way.

"Where's Missy? Why isn't she here to greet me?" Edna nervously glanced around missing her lone faithful companion.

"Fred took her in for a few days. Why don't we get you settled and then I'll walk next door and get Missy?" David placed the small box-shaped overnight case at the foot of the stairs.

Edna immediately grasped the handrail and started up the stairs.

"Wait, Grandma, let me help you." David rushed over and grabbed her arm.

Edna frowned and pulled her arm away. "I'm perfectly capable of taking a few steps myself. I'm not an invalid. I just want to put my things away."

"Grandma, you know what the doctor said about stairs. You're not supposed to take them by yourself. Your caregivers will be here to assist you during the day and get you to bed safely. Do you understand?"

"I don't need any help, and I don't like being talked to in that tone."

"Grandma," David's voice rose. His tone firm.

She couldn't believe how stubborn he could be. She scowled.

David grabbed her suitcase with his right hand, using his left arm for support, assisted her ascent. She stopped at the landing, taking a few deep breaths she paused to study her dried flowers before continuing to the top of the stairs. Once in her room, David placed the overnight case on her chenille bedspread. Edna flipped the latch and removed her white bed jacket, camisole, and undergarments hiding them from David's view. She pulled open the top two drawers of the white and gold bureau and nestled her things inside. Grabbing her other personal items, she walked into the bathroom and set them out. "I must have forgotten my hairbrush. It isn't here." Edna stepped into the bedroom. "David, we need to call the hospital. They have my hairbrush."

David double checked the suitcase. "I'm sure we picked it up, Grandma. I remember putting it in your bag."

Edna put her hands on her hips. "It's not here. You don't believe me. Come see."

David looked around the room. "Did you put it away already?"

"Oh, you." Edna followed David to her dresser.

He opened the top drawer.

"I didn't put my hairbrush in there." She reached across to stop his intrusion into her private items.

Grimacing, David revealed the missing hairbrush. "Look, it must have gotten tangled in your clothing."

Without a word, Edna grabbed the brush and shuffled to the bathroom. Ambling out, she headed to the top of the stairs and stood dutifully, awaiting David's assistance back down.

"We only have a few minutes before your new caregiver arrives. Let me get you some tea and then I'll go get Missy."

Seated on the sofa, Edna fluffed the throw pillows. "I still don't understand how come I have to pay for services I don't want or need."

"We've been through this already, Grandma. You know you need help getting around so you don't get hurt." The microwave beeped. David patted her hand and left her to sulk until he returned with her tea.

She stirred her tea and took a sip, then scowled. David always made it too hot. Sipping her steaming but satisfying beverage, she envisioned her last bit of pride gobbled and gulped down into the belly of a big fish. She sunk into the sofa cushion as David disappeared out the door to fetch her only solace.

Moments later, the door banged closed. A high-pitched bark announced David's return. Missy rounded the corner and pounced onto Edna's lap, licking her hand. She stroked her dog, then bent down and buried her nose into her fur. Tears gathered in the corner of her eyes. "Gracious, has Missy been bathed?"

"Yes, Fred said he had her groomed."

She glared at David. "I hope he isn't expecting me to pay for that."

"No, Grandma, he did it as a welcome home gift. I'm sure he isn't expecting to be paid."

Edna cast her eyes downward in one final plea. "I don't want anyone in my home, and I don't need them. Besides, how can I afford it?" She had saved prudently for years. Her income from her teacher's retirement and social security was sufficient, but there were bills to be paid every month. She hated the thought of throwing away her hard-earned money to pay people to do things she was perfectly capable of doing herself. Somehow, she would think of a way to prove to David she didn't need help.

"Don't worry, you have enough money. I've been over your books and you will be able to live comfortably for many years." David squatted next to her and smiled. "There's nothing for you to worry about."

Missy yapped, jumped down, and trotted to the door before it chimed.

"I'm sure this will work out fine, Grandma." David headed toward the door.

Edna sat fixed and erect. She disliked David's condescending tone. They could force her to have someone come into her home, but she was not going to enjoy it. Murmuring voices came from down the hall. Edna knew they were talking about her. Agitated, she tapped her foot on the floor until David and a tall woman with greyish hair, appeared in the room.

"Grandma, this is Mabel." David's eyes narrowed, hawk-like, awaiting her response.

She forced a smile before allowing her eyes to greet Mabel, who extended her hand. Edna ignored the greeting as she looked her over. Not overly made up, but appearing professional. Judging by her large round stature, it appeared she at least knew how to cook, which was something Edna always favored.

"Hi, Mrs. Pearson- I'm pleased to meet you. I've heard so much about you."

Edna's eyes shot an accusatory glance at David. She wondered what kind of talking had been done behind her back.

Mabel quickly continued. "Your grandson has told me how knowledgeable you are and what an interesting life you've led. I really look forward to hearing some of your stories."

Still skeptical, Edna softened her gaze.

David motioned toward the living room. "You'll have lots of time to get to know each other after I show you around." He walked down the hall and showed Mabel the bathroom, then headed to the kitchen. Edna trudged along behind them feeling the part she had so often in her childhood, the tag-along little sister on Pearl's dates. She didn't appreciate being left out of the conversation and certainly didn't appreciate them talking about her. Following the perpetrators of her misery into the kitchen, Edna stood hands on hips, listening.

"Make sure she knows you're in charge of the meals and cooking." David handed Mabel a folder.

*Imagine,* Edna fumed to herself, glaring as David and Mabel swung around, caught in their plotting. It had only been a few minutes, and Edna was already a non-being in her own home.

David led Mabel upstairs. Edna knew David would scold her if she attempted the stairs and he didn't invite her to join them. She tottered shakily back to the living room with her cane, and sat down, bringing her hands to her warm flushed face. Missy trotted behind and pounced on the sofa next to her. Edna stroked her best friend and whispered how she was lucky to have the little dog, the only thing in her world that hadn't begun ordering her around.

Returning, Mabel smiled as she sat down next to Edna. "Well, the setup is workable, but the stairs and bathroom are going to be a problem. I'm sure we can handle it. We'll do just fine, won't we, Edna?"

Determined to set the ground rules early, Edna glared at this stranger in her home. Coolly she said, "I prefer Mrs. Pearson."

Remember, we talked about the stairs, Grandma?" David's eyes narrowed with a direct gaze at her.

She looked down.

"You must not take the stairs alone unless Mabel, or your other help is here. Mabel will make sure you're in bed for the night, and Sarah will be here first thing in the morning to get you dressed and make your breakfast. You can take the stairs only after Sarah arrives in the morning to help you. Do you understand?"

Edna's anger swelled, but she knew better than to say anything now.

David's tone softened. "Grandma. I've got to get going."

His comment caught Edna's attention.

"I told you I could only stay for the afternoon."

Her emotions overwhelmed her, remembering the little girl in the white lace pinafore who always said goodbye to her father when he left for the week to go to work on Vashon Island.

"I'll see you soon. I promise." He leaned down and kissed her cheek. A moment later he was gone.

At the sound of pots and pans clanging in the kitchen, Edna pushed off the sofa and stepped down the hall to see Mabel rummaging through the cupboards. "What are you doing?" Edna resented the intrusion into her home, especially her kitchen.

"I'm just going to make us some dinner. That's what I was hired to do."

"Well." Edna stormed over to the stove. "I've been quite capable of doing my own cooking for most of my life. If I need any help, I'll ask." Spying a grocery bag on the counter, she reached into the bag and pulled out some canned goods and bread. "What's this? This is not the type of bread I buy." Lettuce, onions, tomatoes, apples and broccoli spilled from plastic bags. "I prefer to buy my produce from the farmer's market. It's much fresher you know." Edna inspected the tomato, rolling it around in her hand, before placing it back on the counter.

Mabel took her hand. "Maybe next time I go to the market you should come and help me select the produce." Her smile warmed. "Do you like cornbread and chili?"

Edna sniffed the air. The strong onion and garlic scent made her stomach queasy. Chili wasn't particularly to her liking, but the fresh cornbread sounded good. She resigned herself to the fact as long as Mabel was there the house was no longer hers. Besides, she would make what she wanted once Mabel was gone.

Early the next morning, Edna woke with a sense of dread. Mabel had reminded her a different caregiver, Sarah, would be arriving at nine o'clock to make breakfast and do some laundry and cleaning. Edna didn't want a different girl. She didn't want any girl. It wasn't fair having to pay for services she didn't want or need. She pouted, pulling on a beige linen top with orange poppies and purple forget-me-nots. She grabbed the brown knit slacks with the elastic waistband from the wooden garment drying rack by the window, stepped into her slippers, grabbed her cane and walked to the stairway. She paused, recalling David's warning. Straightening her posture and her resolve, she gripped the stair rail tightly, and using the cane for balance, she stepped down. Safely reaching the kitchen, she filled a pan with water for her oatmeal.

"*Hmmpf.* I'm not going to wait until nine for my breakfast. I'm hungry now." She carried the pan to the stove and turned the front knob. She warmed some water for tea in the microwave, and waited for the water in the pan to boil. Hearing the toaster click down, Missy bounded around the corner and yapped for her morning treat. Edna hunched over and stroked the dog. A few minutes later, the water sat in the pan still unsettled, with no sign of bubbles. Edna fumbled with the knob then tried the others. She stomped. The stove was broken. Mabel must have broken it last night. Edna fumed in frustration. Now she'd have to make her mush in the microwave. She hated how it always tasted gooey and sticky cooked that way. The toast popped and Edna smiled at Missy as she tore off a corner and held it out. In begging stance, Missy greedily snapped at the toast. Edna barely had time to finish her toast and mush when the doorbell rang. She glanced at the clock. At least Sarah was prompt. Edna hid the evidence of her dishes in the dishwasher before scurrying to the door as Sarah let herself in.

"Oh, I see you are already up and about, Mrs. Pearson. I'm Sarah. I'm happy to meet you. Just to remind you though, I'll be by every morning this week to help you get dressed and assist you down the stairs."

Edna eyed her, waiting for the lecture she guessed would follow about the stairs. Instead, Sarah smiled and extended her hand. Edna looked down at the dark purple nail polish which adorned Sarah's long nails. Edna shook her head. Sarah looked barely out of school, maybe twenty-one at the most, her hair with a bad dye job, pulled back into a childish ponytail. She didn't even look professional in her tight jeans and tight fitting top. Edna stood firm in the doorway. She couldn't imagine this young girl having much experience taking care of anyone, let alone being a certified nurse assistant or whatever David had called her.

Sarah walked into the dining room and set her purse and a folder on the table. Missy bounded around barking at her ankles. Sarah squatted and patted the dog's back. "David said you had a dog. I've heard all about Tessy."

Missy eyed Sarah, took a few steps backwards, and growled.

Edna frowned. "Her name is Missy, not Tessy."

Sarah shrugged off the correction, grabbed her things, and walked into the kitchen. "Your grandson has set a schedule for cleaning, laundry, and shopping. First, let's have some breakfast." Sarah looked around. She turned the front knob on the stove, waited a few seconds, then turned it off.

Edna crossed her arms across her chest. She watched for a response from Sarah regarding the stove.

Instead, Sarah looked through the papers in her folder then smiled weakly at Edna. "Why don't you sit down in the living room while I do the cooking and look over our schedule?"

Edna didn't want breakfast. She was satisfied, but she couldn't very well tell Sarah. And she certainly didn't need a schedule. She wasn't one of the children she used to teach. She turned grudgingly, and went into the living room and sulked on the sofa. Missy jumped up next to her. Edna punched the buttons on the television remote and flipped through the blurry images dancing across the screen. She had forgotten to have David check the T.V. "The darn thing never works right." She clicked it off, sat back, and listened to Sarah banging around in the kitchen. Feeling helpless, Edna fidgeted with some magazines, and straightened the framed photos on the end table before the smell of bacon wafting into the room brought an unintended smile. David must have told Sarah how much she liked bacon. Not one to be chased away, Edna stomped back to the kitchen, and peeked in. "Is the stove working?" Edna eyed Sarah.

Not looking up, Sarah mumbled it was working just fine. Edna scowled. Someone was up to something.

Seated at the table, Sarah wrapped something around Edna's neck. "This should help keep your lovely shirt clean."

Edna looked down at the brown dish towel pinned like a bib draped down her front. She brought her hands to her face struggling to fight off the burning anger and shame that had been simmering. She wasn't a helpless toddler just learning to eat. Edna looked down at the plate that sat before her. Scrambled eggs and bacon. The bacon wasn't crispy which is how she preferred it.

She pushed the food around with her fork although she knew her mother hated it when she played with her food.

"You're not eating. Is everything all right?"

"Yes, Mother, I'm just not hungry. May I go to my room now?"

"What's the matter? I thought breakfast was your favorite meal. David said bacon was your favorite."

Edna closed her eyes to hold back the tears. Daddy hated it when she cried so Mother had encouraged her to try not to cry so easily. "I'm sorry, Mother."

Firm comforting arms draped across Edna's shoulders. "It's okay, Edna, I'm not your mother. My name is Sarah. I'm your new caregiver."

The concern in the soft voice made Edna feel better. Struggling for self-control, Edna raised her eyes from the plate. It wasn't her mother squatted next to her. Confused by the stranger, Edna's tears released like a spring downpour.

After breakfast Sarah ran around the house like it was hers. She picked up and rearranged things to her liking. But Edna was certainly not going to stand for the intrusion. Sarah walked across to the living room blinds and drew them back. Edna squinted to shield her eyes from the brightness of the day. Sarah bent over Edna's gold metal planter filled with a row of assorted African violets. "These are incredibly healthy violets, but it looks like they need a little water." Sarah removed a pot from the planter box.

Edna scurried over and snatched it away. "I can take care of my plants myself. They have to be watered from underneath, you know." Edna placed the pot back in its proper place and glared at Sarah. "You just get the water, I'll take care of the watering." She fingered the delicate purple and pink blossoms, plucking the dead ones between her thumb and forefinger, and dropped them inside the planter. Sarah returned with the water and Edna demonstrated how to correctly pour the water into the tray underneath. "This is how the watering must be done." She stared at Sarah assuring her directions were clearly understood. Though Edna didn't want to admit it, she enjoyed her day with Sarah, sharing stories about her family, her many friends, and her numerous travels especially to Thailand and Korea. Sarah listened with genuine interest. Edna should have expected it was too good to last. At eight o'clock Sarah announced it was time to get ready for bed.

"I'm not a child, and I never go to bed this early." Edna's rage spewed like steam from her tea kettle. She sat resolutely on the sofa to no avail.

Sarah approached and took her hands. "I'm sorry, but I need to leave at nine o'clock, and your grandson wants you in bed for the night before I leave." She supported Edna under the arm and helped her up the stairs.

Edna scowled with each step until they reached her bedroom.

"Okay, where are your pajamas?" Sarah looked about and headed for Edna's dresser.

Edna hurried over. "I'm perfectly capable of getting them myself."

"I'm sorry, of course." Sarah stepped back. "Your grandson wasn't sure if you were using protection at bedtime or not. Do I need to get anything for you?"

"Protection?"

"You know, for accidents in your sleep."

"Oh you." Edna's cheeks burned. How could she understand? Edna sat on the end of her bed.

"My instructions indicate tonight is your shower night." Sarah reached out and began to pull Edna's shirt over her head.

Edna jerked away. Her shirt, free of her arms, hung draped on her shoulders. Edna covered her chest with her arms. "I don't need your help. I'm not an invalid."

"It's okay, Mrs. Pearson, I'm used to this type of work. There's absolutely no need to feel self-conscious about it."

Edna planted herself firmly on the mattress. Of course she's used to it. She was not the one being undressed like a small child. She wondered how Sarah would feel if she were in her place. Sarah walked into the bathroom, leaving Edna alone, half naked on the bed. Her sweaty palms trembled as she wiped the tears from her hot cheeks.

# Chapter 26

Over the next few weeks Edna refused to let those girls think they were in charge. It was still her house, and she was still the boss. She only needed to convince David to talk with them and explain things. When David called on Sunday evening, her frustration boiled over. "I don't like it when they send different girls. Just when I get used to one girl another one takes her place."

"I know Grandma, but you have to be patient with them, they're trying their best and the reason different care-givers keep coming is because you scare them off. Also, they are not able to work seven days a week."

What did David know? He wasn't there to see what went on. "I still don't understand why I can't take care of myself. I have to show those girls how to do simple things like vacuuming. I like my carpet vacuumed all in the same direction. My dishes are never put away in the right places, and most of them don't know how to cook. My morning girl doesn't even know how to make mush. Even after I showed her, she still doesn't make it right."

"You're going to have to get used to some things not being done exactly as you like them."

Edna pouted. Why should she have to get used to things she didn't like. It was her house. She glared at the phone receiver wishing her gaze could travel across the line so David would know she was on to him. "How come my stove doesn't work for me?" Edna sat erect in her rocker, gripping the phone receiver, determined to get answers. It always worked for the girls. She knew David had done something to the stove so she couldn't use it. Though David promised to look at it when he visited the next time, she knew better. She fumed at the cruelty of aging. She wasn't a spiteful woman, but everyone was treating her like a child. She needed to stand up for her independence. David and her care workers would see she didn't need their help. She would show everyone she was independent, but David didn't understand. Unable to receive any satisfaction from him, she cut the conversation short.

Determined to show everyone she could take care of herself, Edna woke Monday morning with a renewed sense of confidence. She dressed taking particular care to pin her hair neatly. At least Mabel was coming this morning. Edna liked the way Mabel let her talk about the old days. Some of the care-givers had about talked Edna's ear off with silliness about the latest shows on television and the newest music, for which Edna had no patience.

Edna slid her feet into her slippers, and ignoring her instructions, started down the stairs. Her legs and energy feeling much stronger than since her stroke. Halfway down, her legs buckled. She tumbled to the bottom. Landing face down, a twinge of pain raced down her right side. Her head pounded. She tasted blood on her lip, and the sting of carpet burned on her cheek. She glanced the few feet toward the front door knowing it would be some time yet before Mabel came. Missy trotted to her side. Edna moved her left arm and stroked her dog's fur for a few moments. With a deep breath, Edna pushed off the ground, wincing at the pain that shot down her side. Giving up, she fell to the ground. Her mind whirled and went dark. When she opened her eyes again she couldn't understand what was happening. Her surroundings blurred in a whirl of activity.

"What are you doing? Please stop." Edna's voice broke. She looked up at the figure that loomed over her.

"It's okay. I just need to check your vital signs." The male figure bent over her and unfastened her top button.

"No, stop." Edna flung her arms about waving off his actions. Her heart pounded with increasing fierceness. She struggled to bring her arms to her chest and protect her honor.

"Calm down. It's okay. I need to see if you are injured."

His voice was soothing, but Edna knew better. A man is not to be trusted. Jacob's words echoed in her ears from long ago while he held her hands and tried to insult her virtue. *Come on Edna, we're engaged now. Damn it, you can't be a prude forever.*

"Please, God." Edna pleaded and begged as the male figure groped at her body seeking to touch her warm bosom. Numb from disbelief, she prayed silently for strength. *"I can't be true to myself and give in to the pleasures of the flesh."* Edna closed her eyes to block out the image of violence against her.

A soft hand stroked her forehead, and she opened her eyes. Someone bent over her, only it wasn't Jacob. Edna lifted her left arm to wipe away the tears, confused by the stiff gray nylon cuff that encircled her upper arm.

"Where's Jacob? Did you find him? He tried to hurt me."

"No, Mrs. Pearson, there's nobody named Jacob here. Your caregiver found you at the bottom of the stairs. I'm with the Fire Department. We are checking you out now."

Mabel squatted next to her with a cool washcloth and held it to the rug burn on her cheek. "Hi, Mrs. Pearson. Just lie still. You'll be okay."

Edna allowed the wet and cold of the compress to help mute the sting of the pain. It didn't help ease the humiliation of being nearly forced into a physical relationship against her will by the man she loved. The man whose ring she wore and vowed to marry.

Lying safely on the sofa, Missy yapped, and jumped up at her feet.

"You know you're not supposed to take the stairs alone, Mrs. Pearson." Mabel lifted Edna's head and placed a small crocheted throw pillow underneath the back of her neck.

Edna's eyes and nasal passages burned as she fought off the emotion. She had been defeated. David and the care workers had won. She closed her eyes and prayed for patience.

# Chapter 27

"Are you ready to come to our house for a few days?"

Edna looked up from her over-stuffed beige rocker surprised by David's enthusiasm. "What's the occasion this time?"

"We thought you'd enjoy spending a few days with us. Rachel has been home for school break and she's going back to school Sunday."

David grabbed Edna's cane and handed it to her. She leaned forward and pushed off her chair as David reached his arm out for support. Walking a few steps to the closet, Edna's joints cracked a bit. She winced in discomfort, but was relieved to get her legs moving.

Mabel came down the stairs carrying her brown brocade overnight bag. "Here you go, Edna. I think I have enough clothes packed for the three days."

"I can't forget my coat." Edna yanked down her winter coat, the metal hanger clanged to the floor. "I can't reach my hat." Edna fumbled with the cane as she tried to reach the shelf.

Mabel stepped in and pulled down Edna's fur hat. She helped Edna into her coat and placed the hat on her head, carefully tucking her pinned hair inside.

David picked up the overnight bag by the front door. Wishing Mabel a nice few days off with her family, he reminded her to check all the lights and doors before leaving. He closed the door behind them.

Stepping into the brisk air, Edna shivered at the thought of the impending winter. The crisp air stung her ever thinning skin. She studied the tall bare tree trunks and gold and brown poplar and alder leaves, littering the ground of the complex. Edna adjusted her hat, pulling it down further over her ears as she walked to the car, her breath leaving a hint of fog lingering.

David helped his grandmother into the passenger seat. He stretched the seat belt across her.

She shifted her weight feeling uncomfortable due to the restraint that held her chest and body tied to the seat. "I can't move with this thing. Why do I have to wear it anyway?"

Reaching across, David removed the shoulder belt, slipping it over her head, and tucking it behind her. "It's the law." David smiled, closed her car door, placed the bag and cane in the back seat and climbed in. He turned on the radio settling on a station playing the golden oldies.

"Thank you. That's much better." Edna scooted forward slightly and twisted her torso. The soft melody relaxed Edna. She looked forward to another visit to her grandson's home, although the long drive was hard on her backside sitting without moving for so long. The barren landscape spread as far as she could see, but Edna liked the warmth and dryness eastern Washington offered. It had been her home since her children were youngsters, going on sixty years now. A twinge of pain pierced her heart when she thought about her two deceased children. She turned her thoughts to her great-grandchildren. "How are Emily and Rachel doing?"

"They're fine, Grandma. They're looking forward to seeing you again. I'll be driving Rachel back to Central on your way home. You can see how much your old university has changed since you went to school there."

Edna puzzled over David's comment. "What are you talking about? I never went to school at Central. I went to the state Normal School, in Ellensburg. I told you all about that." Edna shook her head. She didn't understand how David could get things so confused.

David laughed, "Grandma, Central Washington University is in Ellensburg, it's the same college that used to be known as the normal school, back when it was only a teachers' college."

Edna turned, puckered her brow, and gazed out the window. "Imagine. Well, I should think I knew that." She smiled, looking forward to learning more about her great-granddaughters, maybe forge a closer bond than she had managed with Lorraine or Alicia, and probably never would with Lacey. Alicia hadn't been by to visit for so long.

On their arrival, they were met with the aroma of sage and rosemary that the kitchen fan blew out on the front porch. Edna's stomach growled, and she flinched in embarrassment. Jean opened the door and greeted them as Rachel and Emily raced down the stairs to greet her.

"Hi, Grandma."

"My gracious. I had forgotten how tall you young lasses were." She glanced across to David. "Goodness, they do take after their father, don't they?" Having her great-granddaughters looking like their father, pleased her, and she smiled. She looked forward to teaching them some of the skills she had learned as a young girl.

Jean motioned toward the kitchen, and Rachel and Emily rushed to assist with the last of the dinner preparation.

With Edna freshened up and rested briefly after the long drive, David pulled out a chair at the end of the table for her. "You're the guest of honor today, Grandma. You get to sit in my chair."

Scanning the table, Edna looked at Jean. "I must remember to give you my real silver sometime. I never use silver anymore and it would be much more formal for such occasions. I used to enjoy so many formal meals when I was a military wife."

"Real silver would be nice for special guests, like you. We didn't know you had found your silver."

"Oh no, dear. Barbara helped me with the insurance company forms. They were so nice and sent me a check for the one that was stolen. I bought a new set."

The girls came in with bowls of potatoes and green beans to pass around. Jean carried a white oval platter with a large roast chicken, and placed it in the center of the table.

Edna had always delighted in a well set table. She blushed as her stomach gurgled at the sight of the crisp golden bird, ready for slicing. She nodded her approval. With the family gathered around the table, Jean bowed her head and led the family in grace.

"That was lovely dear. I am not used to such habits with Larry's family." Edna's chest tightened. Her mind spun with old memories. She shook them off, refusing to acknowledge the emptiness of all the years she had missed with her grandsons. "I wish Nathan could join us. When is he coming back? I wish I could see him again."

"He hopes to be here this Christmas. To stay." David reached for a serving bowl and plopped a mound of mashed potatoes on Edna's plate. He continued to pass the potatoes around and ladled gravy into the well, Edna had formed with her spoon.

"*Mmmm.*" Edna's eyes misted as she smiled across the table at her family, filling their plates. She ate with a robust appetite, taking seconds on the potatoes and gravy, and relishing the warm biscuits with butter. "These are delicious dear. Women today don't spend so much time baking as in my generation. I wish I could see well enough to bake pies again like I did when I was younger. Mother taught me to bake when I was only seven." Edna turned her attentions to Rachel and Emily. "Do you girls help your mother bake?"

Rachel and Emily exchanged looks. "Sometimes. We made the chocolate pie today from pudding and whipped topping."

Edna frowned. "Mother insisted both of her girls learn to cook. Her lessons have served me well. These shortcuts of today I don't think much of-pre-baked pie crusts and canned fillings, they're not as good as fresh-baked. I could teach you young ladies a thing or two about baking sometime." Edna paused and looked wearily across the table to David. "I tried to teach Lorraine and Alicia how to bake like my mother taught me, but they weren't interested."

David stood and began to clear the table. He winked at Rachel, "Maybe Grandma can teach you something about cooking before you leave for school on Saturday?" He put his arm around his daughter.

"Would you teach me to make an apple pie, Grandma?"

Rachel's request surprised Edna. She had become accustomed to youngsters not being respectful of their elders these days. It was disheartening. "Of course, dear. But you know I don't see so well these days. You'll have to help me."

"Can you teach me too?" Emily peered up from rinsing dishes at the sink.

A smile stretched wide across Edna's face. She wiped the dampness from her eyes.

The next morning, Edna woke before dawn. She blinked her eyes, laboring to see through the darkened room, unable to recall where she was. She wasn't at home. Her mind cleared. She smiled. She was at David's for the weekend visiting with her grandson's family. A sharp pain tingled up her back, she wasn't used to such a firm mattress. Pushing herself up, she found soap and towels in the bathroom, washed her face, and combed and pinned her hair up. She shuffled down the hall with her cane and took a deep breath as she faced the stairs wondering how she would face them. Just as she was about to grip the hand rail, and take the first step up, she heard David's voice.

"Grandma, I thought I heard you moving around." Meeting her at the bottom he aided her assent. In the kitchen the strong rich aroma of fresh coffee greeted her. Her mouth watered as her stomach signaled its hunger.

Jean turned with a mug of coffee already in hand. "Do you want some breakfast, Grandma?"

Edna nodded. "I usually prefer tea, but coffee and toast are fine. Do you have any jam for my toast?"

David poured a cup of coffee warning his grandmother he liked his coffee quite strong.

"That's fine, dear." She took a seat as David carried her coffee over to her. She puckered her lips at the first sip. She glanced over in time to catch David's laugh as she held the cup out to him. "This is much too strong."

Enjoying a freshly brewed cup of tea instead, and buttered toast with jam, Edna's face brightened at the sight of her granddaughters bounding down the stairs.

"Do you want to make the pie this morning, Grandma?"

Edna hadn't baked in such a long time. She finished her breakfast eager to show her great-granddaughters her skills. The kitchen was a flurry of activity and dirty bowls as Edna delighted in the exchange of small talk and slicing of apples. "I like my pie a la mode. We'll need ice cream for dessert tonight." Edna warmed to the conversation of Rachel's return to college the next day. She ached once again, for the years she had missed not knowing the girls.

"Are you all packed and ready to head back to school tomorrow?" Jean carried the plates to the table as Rachel and

Emily paraded behind with their creation.

"Yeah, just about." She turned her attention to Edna as she cut the pie. "Are you looking forward to seeing your old college again, Grandma?"

Edna didn't understand. "Where are we going?"

"I'm heading back to college tomorrow, Grandma. I go to Central. Your alma mater."

Edna nodded her acknowledgement. "Yes, in my day we called it the normal school. You study hard and don't party too hard."

"Have you been back to the campus since you graduated?" Rachel spoke between bites of warm apple pie with ice cream melting down the sides.

"My Bernice went to college in Ellensburg for a time too, so I visited with her often before she died. She wanted to be a reporter. I think Ellensburg is a lovely town. I can't wait to see it again. It's been so long."

Edna awoke from a restless night and glanced out the window. The scent of hickory smoked bacon and maple syrup floated into her bedroom, reminding her of her mother's special care for her youngest daughter. Looking across the small room Edna noticed the silhouette of her suitcase on the chair. The excitement of going off to college after so much planning and saving, was finally here. She glanced at the illuminated dial of the clock on the nightstand and pulled it close to her. She couldn't understand why the numbers were blurred. She could barely make them out. The brightness of the sun through the open blinds told her it was later than it should be. Surely she was going to miss the train. Frustrated, Edna trembled as she dressed in her best dress. She hurried to the bathroom and fumbled with her hairpins and pinned her hair on top of her head. She couldn't understand how come she found it difficult to climb the stairs as she gripped the handrail firmly for support, and followed the aroma of breakfast into the kitchen.

"Good morning, Grandma. We didn't hear you awake. I see you managed to get upstairs by yourself, but we'd rather you wait for help." Jean was poised over the stove with a spatula. "Are you hungry?"

Edna didn't understand what the fuss was about with the stairs. She'd managed her way to the table. Rachel stood from where she was already eating, helped Edna with her chair, and set the plates of pancakes and bacon down in front of her.

Edna buttered her hotcakes and poured thick syrup over them. She usually loved breakfast, but after a few bites, her stomach rebelled. "We have to hurry or I'll miss the train. How come nobody woke me?" Feeling anxious, she twirled a few strands of long hair that had fallen loose from the top of her head.

"What train?" Rachel raised her eyebrows.

"The Milwaukee and Pacific. It leaves promptly at eight in the morning from Union Station for Ellensburg."

"There's no train, Grandma." Rachel cocked her head and studied Edna. "Dad's driving me back at one and taking you home after that."

Edna's heart beat faster. Her breathing quickened as panic crept in. "One o'clock? That's too late. I'll never get to my freshman orientation in time." She noticed confusion on the faces of the others who had gathered to her side.

Rachel walked over and squatted in front of Edna. Taking her hands, Rachel looked into Edna's eyes. "Grandma, what are you talking about? You're not going to any orientation."

"You don't understand." Edna heard the frantic tone in her shaking voice as she directed her anger at Rachel.

David walked into the dining room. "What's wrong, Grandma?" He pulled up the chair next to her and sat down. "You've hardly touched your breakfast. You've always loved pancakes."

Edna looked down at her plate, pushing the hotcakes around. "I'm going to miss you and Mother."

"Grandma. Your mother's long gone. I'm your grandson, not your father."

Rachel removed the plate from in front of her. Her eyes burned. Her head was still a cloud of muddled thoughts.

"It's okay, Grandma. It's been a busy weekend." Rachel led Edna by the arm into the living room and handed her some magazines.

Edna smiled. Her stomach churned in anticipation of the trip. "Are you sure we won't be late?" Bewildered by the urgent conversation, Edna sat on the sofa watching the commotion around her. David carried her brocade overnight bag out, along with a blue plastic laundry basket, and a knapsack. Her eyes widened as he approached. "Is it time to go?"

"Yes, We can leave now to take Rachel back to school. I'm sure the college has changed through the years. It should be interesting for you to see it again though."

Edna pushed herself up off the sofa. "I'm ready."

David helped her slide into her navy quilted coat. Jean and Emily offered their goodbyes and they were off. Rachel climbed in the back seat and David helped Edna into the front. She shifted uneasily in her seat, aware David was glancing over to look at her.

"We have to hurry. The president of the college has agreed to meet the other girls and me at the train station, and show us personally to our dormitories."

"Grandma, there's no meeting with the college president today. That was a long time ago. It's your great-granddaughter, Rachel, who is going to college now." David's voice sounded impatient.

Edna studied his face. Her cheeks burned fighting the growing frustration. "What do you know?" Her voice rose, exasperated. "The president always meets the incoming students."

Rachel leaned forward and tapped Edna's shoulder. "Grandma, tell me about your graduation from college."

Edna struggled against the restraint of the shoulder harness to look over her shoulder. "My graduation? Oh my gracious, I'm not sure when that was. I imagine it's been some time, hasn't it? I was a teacher you know, dear. What's all this talk about college?"

"I'm going to Central Washington. Dad says that's where you went, only it was called the normal school then."

David looked across the seat and took Edna's hand. "Why don't you tell Rachel what it was like when you went there?"

"Goodness, why didn't anyone tell me you were in college?" Edna smiled as the memories of her youth flashed like the old talkies, through her mind. She recalled her eagerness to see the dormitory room and meet her roommate. "I hadn't had a roommate since I was seven and shared a room with my sister, Pearl. She was ten years older than me and moved out shortly after. I remember my first day at the normal school. I wasn't prepared for what the dorm mother said when she introduced herself and welcomed me." Edna chuckled at the memory so clear in her mind, as if just yesterday. "She told me my roommate had come down with the measles."

Rachel laughed. "What did you do?"

"I spent a few nights sleeping on a lumpy mattress out in the hall, alone." Her voice drifted off suddenly feeling alone again. She glanced at David, forced a smile, and closed her eyes, resting her head against the back of the seat.

Rachel leaned in. "I bet the dorm rooms look a lot like they did when you went to school, Grandma. They probably haven't changed much. I can't wait for you to meet my roommate. She's really nice."

The car pulled into the large lot outside the rows of red brick buildings that formed the hub of primarily freshman dormitories. Rachel clambered out of the car and opened Edna's door. Edna's stomach churned as she stepped out and looked around at the strange surroundings. "I don't know this place. Is this the right place?"

Rachel and David urged her on. "It's been a long time. I'm sure it looks different than it did seventy years ago." Rachel pushed open the heavy wooden entry door, stepping inside. Edna and David followed. The large window at the end of the hall cast rays of light into the hallway, littered with signs announcing meetings, and posters promoting up-coming events. Rachel led the way past a small sitting room. A large television screen flashed a scene of a woman dancing in tight fitting pants and a short top. Guitars and drums banged out loud grating music. A group of young men and women sat on the overstuffed couch and floor cramming popcorn into their mouths. Edna looked around, trying to take in the surroundings, as they stepped into the elevator. The doors opened to commotion coming from the dorm rooms on both sides of her. A few students were heading down the hall, bundled warmly and carrying back packs. Edna turned to look at a boy with longish, jet black, hair and a large earring stretching his lobe. She sighed. It was not at all like she expected. She couldn't understand why there was a boy in the girl's dorm. Rachel inserted a key and turned the knob to open her dorm room. Edna glanced around the room. It was larger than hers at home, but still small for all her possessions, and those of a roommate. She wondered how everything would fit.

"Hello."

Edna studied the unfamiliar girl who appeared confused by her presence.

"Hey, Jessica." Rachel stepped inside and put her laundry basket on the bed. "Grandma, this is my roommate, Jessica."

Edna instinctively stepped back when Jessica approached to greet her. The dorm mother had assured her that her room-mate's measles were no longer contagious, but Edna was still hesitant. Slowly, she approached to meet her first roommate.

# Chapter 28

It was near quitting time, only two weeks after Grandma's visit. David's work desk stood cluttered with wiring diagrams and computer runs of mathematical formulas. In spite of his knowledge, he still found occasions where the intense thought process of his job made his head throb. The sharp ring of the phone clicked his thinking on hold. He hated interruptions. Frustrated, he snatched the phone. "Hello."

"David. It's Fred, Edna's neighbor."

David shifted in his seat. His heart skipped a beat or two. Holding his breath, he dropped all focus from his work.

"I stopped in to visit your grandmother this afternoon. She was outside weeding in the rain. She was wearing only a light short sleeve shirt, and socks, but no shoes. She got angry, and began hitting me, when I told her I'd come to take Missy out for a walk. I don't think she recognized me."

David's mind raced, recalling earlier odd behaviors his grandma had displayed. He remembered his conversation with Dr. Smith about Alzheimer's progression. "Is she okay?" His chest tightened.

"I called 911. The paramedics insisted on taking her to Good Samaritan. I thought I should call you."

Thanking Fred for his concern, David returned the phone to its cradle. He groaned, pushing aside the pile of paperwork on his desk. Pulling out his cell phone, David doodled on a yellow legal pad as he dialed the hospital. The emergency room nurse took his name and promised to try to locate Dr. Smith. David listened to the recorded message repeating over and over and over how they knew his time was valuable, while continuing to keep him on hold. His neck tensed as he made notes of the questions to ask the doctor when he finally answered. David's patience was all but exhausted when Dr. Smith finally picked up.

"Sorry to keep you waiting David. I just left your grandmother. I have her file here. She's going to be fine. She's likely suffered another mini stroke, but I don't think there's any permanent damage."

David breathed a little easier, rolling his head in a few circles, to ease some of the tension.

"I believe the real concern for us now is her Alzheimer's symptoms are progressing. She's presently very confused."

David continued to doodle on the yellow note pad. "I've noticed she's been having increased occasions where she seems to be living in the past as you warned me."

"That's one of the primary indicators. You need to know, as it progresses it's also likely she'll fail to recognize you, and other family members, and she'll possibly become violent. There are support groups for family members of patients suffering from Alzheimer's, if you're interested, I can put you in touch with them."

David cringed at the thought of gathering with others affected by Alzheimer's, sitting around sharing their depressing stories. "That's fine, I'll pass, for now."

"I know you're in the Seattle area, and it's difficult for you, but if you are able to take some time off it would be helpful for her to have a familiar face around."

David agreed, assuring the doctor he would schedule time off, and would call him to confirm an appointment time when he arrived in town.

Dr. Smith's voice softened. "When do you think you will be here? I can schedule time for you to discuss her current situation and options for her ongoing care."

David closed his eyes and allowed himself to process the not so subtle message about options for her care. "I'll try to be there tomorrow before noon."

"I'll be in my office most of the early afternoon unless something urgent comes up. Your grandmother should be able to talk to you, though I don't think she's fully aware of what's happened to her."

Thanking the doctor, David clicked the receiver, and redialed the admitting desk, tapping his pen on some papers as his call was forwarded to the third floor and then transferred to his grandma's room. "How are you doing Grandma? It's David ... DAVID, your grandson." David strained to hear the trembling voice on the line.

"David. What's happened to me? Nobody will tell me what is going on." Grandma's voice quivered through her panicked tone.

"It's okay, Grandma. You were a bit confused so Fred called the hospital, then he called me."

"How did I get here? I remember the bus ride, but I thought we were going to a restaurant."

David sighed. "No, Grandma, there was no bus ride. An ambulance took you to the hospital. How are you feeling now?"

"I'm hungry. I remember the bus, but I can't remember where we dined."

David rested his head in his palms and released his breath like a deflating balloon. His grandmother's life, once full and colorful, had been reduced to a withered remnant of her former life. "We'll talk about it when I see you tomorrow."

"When am I going to see you? I need to see you."

"Tomorrow, Grandma. I'll be there tomorrow." David hung the phone up and sat for a moment considering the heartbreaking reality of his grandmother's condition. Grandma's mind was eroding, along with her quality of life. Little by little, washing away her essence, like the ebbs and flows of the tide, and David was powerless to stop the inevitable destruction. His head spun like a whirlpool, dizzy at the overwhelming decisions he knew lay in his, and more importantly, his grandmother's, immediate future. A wave of helplessness swept over him.

Returning his focus to the drawings on his desk, David forced himself to concentrate. He cursed under his breath at the lateness of the day. He hated working under pressure, but with the necessary trip to the tri-cities looming, he had no choice except to finish nearly a day's work in the next few hours. He called Jean to let her know he would be late and would be leaving in the morning again. "I know you're busy too, but would you order some flowers for Grandma? I'm not sure of the room number, but she's on the third floor at Good Samaritan. I'll see you and the kids as soon as I can."

He wished the urgency of the job didn't require his presence, but his grandmother needed him, and his priority was to her not to some bureaucratic company. With his request for a few days of unplanned vacation completed, David dropped by his supervisors' office with the finished tasks before heading home to prepare for his trip the next day, and to address the difficult decisions he knew he would have to face.

The frequency of David's trips was clearly not going to decrease. Every other weekend was away from his family and he was racking up thousands of miles on his vehicle. David rested his elbows on the table, his chin in his hands, and looked across the dinner table. His head throbbed from the frustrations that played and replayed through his mind. He didn't need his blood pressure cuff to inform him his blood pressure was spiking. There was only one way out. "I'm sure the doctor is going to recommend assisted care. You know it's going to be a battle to get her to accept that."

Jean nodded. "You have to stop going at the pace you've been going. You need to convince her it's the best thing for her."

"Grandma's been through a lot these past two years. I hate to say it, but we both know it's only going to get worse. We have to move her closer to us. It really is the only thing left to do." David paused awaiting Jean's agreement.

"I know. This past year you've spent every day wrapped up in some detail of her life." Jean took the leftover dinner from the fridge and popped open the microwave. "I know you're only doing what you have to, but you spend more time with Edna than you do with your children."

With his resolve set, David had only to convince his grandmother moving from the part of the state where she had spent most of her past sixty plus years, was the best thing for her.

"I suppose I should call Alicia and let her know. I think I owe her that."

"How do you think she will take the news?" Jean got up removing the plates from the table.

Extending his palms up in a questioning pose, David shook his head. "I honestly don't know."

David groaned at the abrupt buzz of the alarm. He rolled over and held a pillow to his head before surrendering. He flipped the alarm off. His body ached to stay in bed. Six a.m., the same cruel time he normally got up for work. He glanced over at Jean, still motionless. The urge to wake her struck him, he pushed it aside. No reason to disturb her sleep. He rose and plodded to the shower to get ready for the long day ahead. Stepping out, finally fully awake, he smiled at the aroma of deep roast Columbia beans perking from the kitchen. Jean had risen and the java was brewing. His attitude immediately improved. Jean padded around the kitchen in her sorry pink robe and purple slippers, one size too big. He made a mental note of a gift idea for her approaching birthday. "Good morning." David kissed her and headed for the coffee pot. Removing his slice of toast from the toaster, he forced a smile. "Tell Emily goodbye for me. I plan on spending just one night there, but I'll have to see how things really are." With his thermos of coffee in hand for the long drive, and the spike of caffeine which he knew he would require, David headed out the door for what he estimated was nearing his fortieth trip. His mind whirled with all he had gone through in the past year and a half. He never would have guessed he had the emotional stamina for such a draining chore. He never even imagined he would be taking on such a chore. He had driven the route so many times his mind went into auto-pilot along with the car.

# Chapter 29

Edna woke the next day. She shifted uncomfortably in her bed. She could tell through the dim light something wasn't right. Her surroundings were unfamiliar and her mind disoriented. "What's going on? Where am I?" She called out. Her voice barely audible. Her mother must have heard her though, because she came in to check on her. Edna struggled to raise herself from her prone position to look around. "Mother? Is that you?"

Her mother took her hand. "It's okay, I'm here."

Edna closed her eyes. Her mind wandered through the many happy memories she had shared with her mother. "You've been gone a long time. Are we going to have another picnic?" Edna followed her mother through the woods as the towering trees rustled from the early spring breeze. Edna inhaled deeply the sweet scent of the pines. She smoothed the woolen blanket Mother had laid out for them. "He loves me, he loves me not." She giggled reaching for the small white daisy snuggled in the grass. Mother joined her. Aware of the comforting and reassuring hand on her shoulder, Edna listened to the sound of flowing water.

"Here, dear, drink some water."

The cool wetness on her lips quenched her. Her mother pointed across the river to the far side which was a patchwork of vibrant wildflowers in the meadow.

"Do you see the beautiful flowers, Edna? Everyone is thinking of you."

Edna smiled and inhaled the delicate scent of the dainty blossoms dancing in the wind. She turned back to her mother. She looked different somehow. Edna couldn't make sense of it. Her mind was fuzzy, her surroundings flat, like someone's feeble attempt at forging a beautiful Monet. Jumbled sounds and a voice floated in and out of her awareness. Her body tightened with agitation. Someone kept trying to interrupt Mother and her.

"Mrs. Pearson? Can you hear me? You need to drink, you'll get dehydrated."

Edna swallowed the water from the glass held to her lips. She looked around. Her left arm ached. She lifted it, and panicked at the sight of the tube and wires that ran down her arm to an electronic box that emitted rhythmic beeps and hissing sounds. "Help!" Her throat strained with each word. "Where am I?" Edna twisted about in her bed. She looked down at the soft blue cotton gown covering her wrinkled frail body.

"It's okay, Mrs. Pearson, you're fine." The woman standing next to her did not look at all like her mother.

Confused she scanned her surroundings. The field of flowers was gone. A glass vase of white daisies, purple fragrant lilacs, and bright orange tiger lilies sat on the end table. "Where am I? How come nobody will tell me what's going on?" Edna struggled to pull the covers off her.

"You're in the hospital, Mrs. Pearson. I'm your day nurse. My name is Terri."

"I don't understand." Edna's heart raced and her breathing quickened. She didn't remember being brought there. She only remembered Mother. She closed her eyes tight. Her mind reeled with confusion. She thought for a moment, then opened her eyes, and stared at the nurse. Fear gripped her. "I must have had a dream. I've been having quite a few lately." Edna's eyes widened as she examined the woman neatly dressed in pink cotton pants and a white and pink printed top.

"Tell me about your dream, Mrs. Pearson." Terri took Edna's hand and rubbed it.

Edna relaxed in the warmth of the firm loving hand. "I was in a beautiful meadow picking wildflowers with Mother. I was seventeen and had quite a crush on Kenneth. It was a glorious spring day and we spread our woolen blanket out and ate a picnic lunch."

"It sounds like a lovely picnic. I'd love to hear if you have any more dreams. I'll be back to check on you after the doctor has been by." Terri turned to leave.

"Where's David? Where's my grandson?" Edna raised her eyes to follow the nurse.

Terri paused at the door and turned. "I'm not sure. The doctor will be by sometime later today. I'm sure he'll be able to tell you more."

Edna lay impatiently, staring at the walls with the striped beige paper absent of any photos or design. She ached for the warmth and coziness of her home. Her mood brightened at the sound of a familiar voice.

"Hello Edna. How are you doing this morning?" Dr. Smith took her hand in his firm grasp. "Can you squeeze my hand?"

Perplexed, she weakly gripped the doctor's hand.

He smiled and nodded. "That's good. Do you know your name?"

Edna nodded. "Of course, I know my name. Edna Mooney."

"Mooney? Are you sure?" The doctor's eyes studied her much like one might ponder over a deep intriguing book.

Flustered, Edna strained to understand what was wrong. "No, wait. That was my maiden name. My married name is Pearson."

"How about children?"

"Two. My daughter, Bernice is dead." Edna squeezed her eyes shut. Her head pounded inside rebelling against something, maybe the present, maybe the past. "Is that right? No. Larry's dead too." Edna's voice dropped off. Tears rolled down her cheek, but she couldn't lift her hand to swipe them away. Frustration rose like an expanding wave ready to engulf her.

Dr. Smith drilled her on her grandchildren and other family members.

"My two grandsons are David and Nathan. Then there's Mother. I'm much too tired. Why are you asking me all this?" Edna pounded the bed with her fist. "I'm not senile you know."

"No, Mrs. Pearson, you're not senile. Sometimes people get a little confused when they get older. You've likely suffered another small stroke. What we call a TIA. It's nothing to worry about. Do you know why your neighbor, Fred called the hospital?"

Edna raised her eyebrows. "Fred? He called? I don't understand."

"He found you outside in the rain confused and disoriented. Do you remember?"

Edna eyed the doctor. She didn't remember seeing Fred.

"What has me concerned is you appear to be getting confused a lot more." The doctor looked down at his chart and flipped the pages.

"I'm not crazy." Edna resented the doctor's implication.

"You're not crazy. Confusion can occur with age." Dr. Smith looked over the rim of his glasses. "Do you remember how you got here?"

Edna thought for a moment. She remembered being at home and now she was in this small room. "I guess I came by bus. I remember the ride." Edna heard the sigh as the doctor pulled up a chair, moving it closer to the bed.

He leaned over and took her hand. "Your heart and other vital signs are strong, but we'll want to watch you for a day or two before we release you. I'll stop by and visit you tomorrow." Dr. Smith smiled and patted her hand with his goodbye.

# Chapter 30

David pulled his Chevy pickup into the visitor lot at Good Samaritan. Now familiar with the layout of the various floors after several visits he maneuvered through the halls with ease. He had long ago grown accustomed to the pine-like disinfectant and the smell of alcohol which assaulted him each time he walked into the hospital. Hesitantly, he stepped inside Grandma's room, relieved by the delicate scent of a large bouquet sitting on the nightstand next to her bed. His Grandma's confusing phone conversation of the previous day made him tremble in anxiety, but David was comforted her eyes widened in recognition when he walked in. His throat tightened upon noticing the wrinkles which set a little deeper in her drawn face and her drooped mouth.

"Hi, Grandma, how are you doing?" At the sight of her frailness, he forced a smile in an attempt to belie the sadness which had overtaken him.

"David, is that you? No one will tell me why I am here."

"What do you remember?" David leaned over her bed, taking her hand in his, halfway expecting to hear about her bus trip. Instead she told him how she had been visiting her mother.

"I talked to Mother for a while. I haven't seen her in some time, you know?"

"Yes, I imagine it's been a while." David squeezed the bridge of his nose. His nasal passage burned and he shut his eyes for a moment to hold back his tears. He recognized his grandmother's increasingly vivid visits with her mother as a sign of the cruelty of Alzheimer's. His research on the internet, and talks with Dr. Smith, had served him well. He had learned what to expect with each stage.

"Have you seen my new blue and white calico dress, David?" Grandma tried to sit up in her bed. She pointed to the chair next to the bed. "Mother made it for me. Don't you love the cross stitch? I'm going to wear it to the dance at school next week."

David glimpsed the hospital robe which lay across the chair and cracked a smile. "Yes, Grandma, it's a lovely dress." Glancing again at the small assortment of flowers on the night stand, he noticed the card stuck in the nearest bouquet and leaned in to read it. Alicia had sent them. His mouth fell open in utter surprise. After all this time. He wondered how she had found out Edna was in the hospital. Most likely Barbara had called her. "Has Alicia been by?" David held out the card pulled from the bouquet.

"Alicia? She and Lacey brought me some beautiful flowers. She's such a lovely girl, and Lacey is so sweet." Edna struggled to stretch her arm out to point to the stand of a large machine monitoring her vital signs. "See, Lacey brought that for me."

David spied a small "Get Well" card with butterflies and flowers drawn in vibrant colored felt tip pens, taped to the machine. Underneath the homemade card hung a small school photo of Lacey. David remembered his mother having him and Nathan print their names on the back of their school photos to send to their grandparents when they were small. He flipped the photo over and smiled at the writing on the back. "To Great-Grandmother, Love Lacey. "This is a nice picture of Lacey, isn't it, Grandma?"

"Oh yes, she looks like her mother, but I can see Larry in her too."

David puzzled over the confusing comment. But it made sense she longed for a link to her side of the family. He guessed it was only natural, wanting to see your lineage passed on even if only in physical characteristics. He nodded and smiled at his grandmother's new sense of peace. He was curiously amused by her new affection for his stepsister. If he were presented with an option of moving his grandmother closer to him, or having Alicia and Lorraine step up, he would welcome the reprieve. But he couldn't imagine this gesture was an indication of such commitment. Yet it was surprising, and he was certain, uplifting, for his grandmother. He realized too that he would need to inform Alicia of his plans to move Edna closer to him. He wondered what kind of resistance that conversation would entail. He took a few deep breaths, and smiled, remembering why he was here.

"When can I go home?" The panic rose in Grandma's voice. "Where's Missy? Is Mother taking care of her? She doesn't like Missy too well you know? She scolds her for jumping on the furniture."

"Grandma, your mother isn't ..." David suppressed his thought. "Missy is doing fine, Grandma. Barbara is taking care of her."

Grandma either ignored or didn't comprehend the reference to Barbara. Her eyes misted as she pleaded. "I want to see Missy."

David stroked his grandmother's hair. "You're going to have to be patient. Dr. Smith wants you to stay here a few more days."

Grandma protested. "I don't understand. Why am I here?" She fumbled over the words and turned her face away.

David leaned over with a slow soft voice hoping to draw her back. "Fred found you outside in the rain. He was concerned about you. Your mind is confused at times. It's called Alzheimer's. That is why you can't remember what's happened." David wished he could assure her everything would be fine, but Dr. Smith's words resounded in his head. *"Your grandmother's Alzheimer's is only going to get worse."* It had taken ninety-four years, but the disease had robbed his Grandmother of her identity and left only a frail shell of the once outgoing and intelligent woman.

"I don't understand what's happening. I want to go home. How come I can't go home?" Grandma struggled against the tightly tucked sheets attempting to climb from the bed.

"You're in the hospital. We've been through this already." David bit his lip at the sharpness in his voice and took a few deep breaths, counting to ten slowly. He wasn't sure how much more help he could offer without additional support from other family members. He wished Nathan's transfer were sooner rather than later. His head pounded and his neck and back tensed.

"No. I was just sitting in my chair for a while to rest, but now I'm in a meadow."

Grandma's voice had shifted, taken on softness and innocence. David studied her face. The look of panic had disappeared and she lay calm, relaxed. He rolled his shoulders and rubbed the back of his neck trying to relieve the tightness, wishing the whole situation would merely disappear. He didn't know who was more helpless in their present situation, he or his grandmother.

Intrigued, David tossed the blue hospital robe onto the neighboring empty bed, pulled up the orange molded chair and sat down. "What are you doing in the meadow Grandma?" He reached out for her hand.

"Mother and I went to visit Pearl for a picnic. Now we're gathering wildflowers, which I so like to do. Can you smell them?"

Her delusion fascinated David. He studied the bouquet of lilacs, lilies, and daisies. Did their scent trigger her memories? He inhaled deeply. "Yes, Grandma, I smell the wildflowers. How did you get to the meadow?" Her trips of fantasy had become more vivid to her, but this was just too weird for him.

"We took the train to Pearl and Stanley's like we always do. Then we took their car through Monahan and Issaquah down to the Raging River. We could see the mountains in the distance."

David recalled the stories Grandma had told about her sister, Pearl, and how fond she was of her older sibling. He remembered Dr. Smith saying often Alzheimer's patients' minds go back to the point in their lives when they were happiest. It was bittersweet that in her mind she was in a far better place than the reality in which she was living. David patted his grandmother's arm which lay limp by her side. Her eyes sparkled, and her face flushed with more color than he had seen for some time. The deterioration of her mind saddened him, but she was at peace, wherever she was. He smiled and stroked her thinning hair, worried her fantasies would take over to the point where all reality ceased to exist. It was a sobering possibility. It was possible she would be happier that way. Suddenly chilled at the frightening thought, he pushed it aside. Emotionally drained, David's head hurt just as it did when the pressures of difficult problems at work bore down on him. He knew the next phase in his grandmother's life. He mentally prepared himself for the possibility she might even fail to recognize him as time went on. He shuddered at the thought his grandmother could ever lose her identity that much. Grandma's eyes fluttered shut. David closed his eyes to block out the confused woman dependent on him for her well-being. Engulfed in uncertainty and indecision, he hesitated to leave her side, but he needed to get away from the desperate, yet inevitable, situation that ate away at Grandma's life and controlled his. He whispered. "Come back safely, okay Grandma?"

He turned and walked to the door.

Taking the elevator to the ground floor lobby, David fished the cell phone from his coat pocket as he strode toward his car. Dialing Dr. Smith's office, he paced nervously until the receptionist connected him to the doctor, who made time for him immediately.

"Thanks for seeing me so fast." David extended his hand as he approached Dr. Smith seated at his desk.

"Thanks for coming. I hate to be abrupt but I only have a few minutes. Your grandmother's health is only going to get worse. She's going to need an increasing level of assistance, more than she can get from the Nurses Assistants currently coming into her home. I will discharge her but I recommend you begin immediately searching for an adult care facility, unless you think you can find twenty-four-hour care for her."

David stared at the doctor unable to stifle the brief laugh. Grandma's grudging acceptance of her nurse assistants during the day was stressful enough. Considering full-time live in care was simply not an option. Assisting Edna had turned into an uphill battle. His fatigue and constant worry were taking a terrible toll on his own mental and physical well-being. Beaten up like salmon fighting the fish ladder at spawning time. The inevitable had hung over him since he first took over as Grandma's care provider. It was something that could be pushed aside-until this moment. "I don't think that's an option, she's like a five-year-old pushing everyone's limits already."

Dr. Smith's broad grin relayed his understanding. "You are fortunate. There are a number of very good retirement homes that offer the extra nursing care your grandmother requires. You might want to look at some facilities specifically for Alzheimer's patients. If she gets worse it will be to your advantage, and hers, to place her somewhere with a more controlled environment to prevent her from wandering off."

"Great." David shook his head. He hadn't considered the possibility of her wandering off. He didn't need something else to worry about.

"Let me know if you have any questions. If you plan on staying a few days to be with her and make permanent arrangements, I'll sign her discharge papers."

"Actually, doctor, if Grandma requires assisted living arrangements, I think for my sake in particular, I am going to suggest to her moving closer to me."

"I see." Dr. Smith rested his chin in his hand focusing on David's comment. "That's probably a smart idea."

"The problem right now is; I'm going to need more than a few days. Is there somewhere she can go for a few weeks until I find permanent arrangements and can make the move?"

"There are quite a few facilities in the area. Most of them will offer some sort of respite care for up to a month. You might want to check them out." The doctor picked up a pen and scribbled some names on a slip of paper before handing it to David.

Reaching for the paper, David thanked the doctor, turned and somberly walked back to his car. He sat for a few minutes with his hands on the steering wheel allowing the news to bounce around in his head. "So much to do, so little time." Jean used the line often. He suddenly knew how she felt. He started the car and headed to the golden arches for a quick burger, and then he'd go to his grandmother's house and look up some places and do some calling for respite care. Tomorrow he would head home and begin his search for permanent arrangements on the eastside of Seattle. He cringed, thinking about the outburst he would face when he broke the news to Grandma. And then, there was informing Alicia.

With new significant decisions looming, David called Nathan from the now familiar table at the fast food joint to discuss their grandmother's options.

"I know you can be involved only from a distance, but it's good to have another sounding board. Quite frankly she's driving me a bit crazy. I'm beginning to understand how Alicia and her family felt."

"I'm trying to work a transfer back. I know you've spent a lot of time helping Grandma Edna. When I get home, I'll see what I can do to lend a hand."

"Thanks, that means a lot. I only want to do what's best for her, but I have to keep my own sanity too. Right now I'm not sure how best to do that."

"What type of accommodations are you looking at?"

"An adult care facility is really the only way to go. It's obvious she can't live on her own and she is fighting everyone who comes into her home."

"Ouch, that's not going to go over well. Is it?"

"No." David paused, "But there are no other options. I'm also going to suggest she move closer to me so I can stop making myself crazy with all the driving."

"Makes a lot of sense. How is the money situation? Do you need any help from me to pay for any of her care? I can start sending a few hundred a month."

Nathan's offer caught David off guard. It took a moment to digest his brother's words. "No, thanks. Actually, her financial situation is much stronger than I had initially thought. Her income is currently covering her expenses, and she has some savings and she has dividend checks coming in which helps cover her medical costs. I think her finances are okay for now." David experienced a tiny sense of relief. Maybe when Nathan moved back to Washington he would get a break in spite of Nathan's career.

"So you still haven't heard from Lorraine or Alicia, huh?"

"I haven't heard from Alicia in a while, but Alicia and Lacey apparently stopped by and brought Grandma flowers and a card Lacey made. I need to call Alicia. I owe it to her to let her know I want to move Edna to the Seattle area. It would be so much simpler if they stepped up to offer more support, even if they aren't willing to take on the role of primary care-giver. I think Alicia initially called me to get me involved so I would take over. I always thought she had a hidden agenda." David bit his lip, feeling a twinge of guilt for his resentment toward his stepsisters, yet still unable to completely bury the fact Grandma's silverware had never been located.

"Could be. I hate to say it, but maybe getting involved with Kora-Lee and her crazy family was a dumb thing to do."

"Maybe, but where would Grandma be right now with Larry gone? Frankly, I'm glad I can help in some small way and repay her for how much she and Granddad did for us when Mom wasn't around. I just wish she wouldn't fight me every step of the way."

Saying goodbye to his brother, David gathered his tray, looking down at the over fifty-year-old logo of the McDonald's chain printed on the paper tray liner. He chuckled as the slogan from the restaurant chain during his teenage years, popped into his mind. *"You deserve a break today."* He laughed out loud drawing a few odd looks. He definitely deserved a break today, but he also knew he wasn't likely to get it. He had practiced over and over in his head alternate scenarios on how he would inform his grandmother of his intention. He sighed in surrender. It didn't matter how he worded it, there was no way to put a positive spin on this news.

The familiar antiseptic scent assaulted David when he arrived back at the hospital a few hours later. He found his way to his grandmother's room, hesitantly stepping inside the gloomy room, feeling a bit like Judas, about to betray her trust. "Hello, Grandma. How are you doing?"

His grandmother's moist eyes immediately made his task more difficult. "Oh, David, I'm so glad you're here. Nobody will tell me when I can go home."

David took a deep breath and swallowed. He pulled up the orange plastic chair next to the bed and took his grandmother's hand in his. "Grandma, the doctor says you can be discharged as soon as we find a new place for you to live."

The panic rose in Grandma's voice. "Why do I have to move? I don't want a new home."

David knew trying to convince her there were a lot of retirement homes with beautiful decor would not help calm the situation. To her any place that wasn't her house was a nursing home.

"You don't know what it's like to be old. It's not fair."

David shut his eyes momentarily. He didn't know what it was like to be old and helpless and dependent on others, to have others talk down to you, and tell you how you were expected to live your life. She was also right; life wasn't always fair. He sighed before he took her hand and spoke softly. "You're right, I don't. But I do know I want what's best for you, and I want you to be safe." David nearly pulled away feeling the tension from his grandmother's trembling hand. "Grandma, what would you think about moving closer to me?" He recoiled slightly remembering earlier attempts in approaching the subject always resulted in brutal defeat.

"Okay, dear, if you think that's best for me."

"Are you sure? You won't be able to see your friends nearly as often." David knew she had many good friends from living more than half of her life in eastern Washington. The move would be difficult for her.

"That's okay. I have family with you and Nathan, and family who cares for you is more important. If it's easier on you, I can come live near you. I don't want to be in your way though. I don't think I should move in with you. You'll have to find me my own place, maybe next door to you."

David grimaced at the thought of her moving in. He found it humorous she had interpreted the suggestion as an invitation to move in. It was best to let the details go for now and be thankful Grandma would be moving hundreds of miles closer, and he would be able to reclaim some of his life again.

"Do you think I can take Missy when I move?"

"It's hard to find a place that will allow dogs, Grandma, but I'll try."

"When will that be? I want to get out of here now."

"I'm going to need some time to find a nice place for you near my house. In the meantime ..." David paused before proceeding. "I'm going to find a temporary adult care facility for you where there are full time nurses and doctors. Until I have done that, the doctor won't sign your release papers."

Edna narrowed her eyes and frowned, glaring at David. "I don't want to go to a place like that. You think I'm losing my mind don't you?"

"No, Grandma, I don't think you're losing your mind. Some people's minds start to fail when they get older and things can get confusing. You can't live by yourself any longer. Something could happen to you."

Edna looked down. "I don't want to move from my condo. I don't care what you call the place, an adult care facility or retirement home, they're all the same. I want to live in my own home until I have to move." Edna's voice rose, she took a breath to calm herself. "It's not fair getting old and not being able to see and take care of yourself. I've never been one to depend on others. I just want to be left alone, why can't anyone understand?"

"I understand that's what you want, Grandma, but it's not safe anymore. You need to be where you can get twenty-four hour care."

"Why can't I stay at my house with the girls?" Edna glared at David.

David sighed, "Since your last fall, Dr. Smith has been concerned for your well-being. For your sake, you need full time care. I've called a few places that will allow you to stay for a short period of time. I thought we could look at one of them. Have you heard of Arbor House?"

"I think a lady who was in the Master Gardeners with me may have gone there. Though I always wondered who would put someone they loved in a place like that. At least it's here in town, so my friends can visit easily."

"Okay, then, let's go take a look at the Arbor House."

Edna's eyes glared hawk like at him. Her words came in the form of an order. "You're not selling my house."

"No Grandma, I'm not going to sell your house."

# Chapter 31

The next morning Dr. Smith came to Edna's room to meet with her and David. His instructions were clear. He would discharge her if she were placed in a respite care facility before David left for home.

"You know what that means, Grandma? We need to find a place today so we can get you moved in right away."

Edna studied David's face. Everyone was plotting for her to move. She had lived her whole life with a sense of independence. The thought of being dependent on others devastated her. She eyed David with resentment at his interference in her life. He insisted on taking her to look for a new home. A new home that wouldn't be hers. A new home that she didn't need. Resentment roiled even as she recognized there was no one else who had cared enough to assure she was taken care of, even though his involvement sometimes infuriated her. She softened her gaze, realizing if she had to depend on someone, she was happy it was her grandson, her own flesh and blood, not Alicia or her family. No. Edna could never stand for that. Too tired to argue any more, Edna grudgingly allowed the staff to get her dressed while David signed her release papers. She sat on the bed with her coat by her side, dutifully awaiting their visit to some care facility where she didn't belong.

They drove in silence the short drive to the Arbor House. She made up her mind, no matter what, she was going to convince David she didn't need to stay there. She refused to let David help her down from the pickup. "I'm perfectly capable of walking on my own."

David walked next to her, running ahead only to open the heavy glass door. He stepped inside as he held the door.

A middle aged woman approached and extended her hand. "Good afternoon. I'm Nanette, the social director, would you like to see our facility?"

Edna frowned as the woman took her hand.

"Welcome, please feel free to join us for lunch after the tour. It will give you a chance to see what it's like here before you make a decision."

The staff was friendly enough, but Edna knew it was all an act to impress the families of the elderly residents. Nanette led David and Edna down the hall. Edna couldn't help but notice the place was tastefully decorated in warm shades of peach and sage green. They had many silk and dried flower arrangements placed on tables and in large vases in the halls, which made it quite pleasant. Still, she shrugged, it wasn't as nice as her home, and she'd be forced to live with someone else's schedule.

"Here is a typical one-bedroom unit." Nanette turned the key in the door and pushed it open allowing Edna and David to enter.

David stepped in and looked around. "It looks nice doesn't it, Grandma?"

Edna didn't like the light colored beige carpet. How would it stay clean? She much preferred a darker color that didn't show the dirt. She noticed there was no kitchen. "How can I cook?"

"This is a facility for people who are unable to care completely for themselves. Our residents eat in the dining room."

"Well, I don't like this place anyway, it's much too small. I presently have three bedrooms. Besides, this is furnished. Where will I put my furniture?"

"Grandma, remember, this will be only for a short while. We can't move all of your furniture twice. You will have a furnished room only until we can move you closer to my house. Then you can have some of your own furniture."

"This carpet isn't going to work too well for Missy." Edna shot a look at Nanette.

"Missy?" The director looked puzzled.

Edna stood hands on hips as David explained about the dog.

"I'm sorry, I thought you knew. We don't allow pets."

"I can't bring Missy? What's going to happen to her?" Betrayal gripped her. She couldn't leave her dog. She needed Missy's companionship.

"Don't worry about that now, Grandma. We can talk to some of your friends. I'm sure someone would love to take her for you."

Edna's eyes burned. Everything was getting increasingly unfair. She had lost control of life. Her life.

"How about we check out our dining room? It's nearly lunch time." The director put her arm around Edna's shoulder and attempted to guide her from the room.

Edna planted herself firmly. She hadn't even moved in yet and she was already being told what to do. She scowled at the director, submitting enough for David to lead her down the hall to a round table at the edge of the dining room. Edna didn't like the formality of the room. It looked like a fancy overpriced restaurant with its white table cloths and fresh roses in crystal vases on the tables. She sat firmly and disinterested in spite of the hum of conversation almost drowned out by the soothing music from the jet black piano which gleamed majestically in the corner of the room.

A young worker approached to tell them of their choices for the day's lunch. "You may choose between a green salad and cottage cheese, and for the main dish there is either an open-faced turkey sandwich with mashed potatoes or beef stroganoff."

Edna grumbled to the worker, "I never eat stroganoff out. You never know what you'll get." She sullenly ordered the turkey. At least it came with mashed potatoes with gravy.

David pulled a menu from the napkin holder and glanced over it. "It looks quite nice and it appears there are plenty of choices on entrees."

David was trying to make things sound good and Edna didn't like his tone. She preferred not to think about it. She stewed watching the other residents with their smiling faces and school girl chatter sitting at the tables surrounding her. Within a few minutes, a young neatly dressed woman appeared, placing the two white plates carefully on the table. Edna looked over her meal which looked surprisingly appetizing, but that wasn't the point. "I don't want to eat like this every night with this many people around. I much prefer to eat on my own terms and with my own schedule." Edna stared angrily at David.

"You'll get used to it Grandma."

"Oh, you. I don't want to get used to it. I don't like to eat a big noon time meal. I prefer just a piece of toast with jam. Why can't I just eat in my room?" Edna put her fork down. Sometimes David made her so mad. She didn't want to get used to doing something differently than she had done her whole life.

"It's pretty good, don't you think Grandma?" David studied her face as he held a bite of stroganoff on his fork.

Edna knew he was over-acting to try to convince her this was where she wanted to move. "The food's okay, but it doesn't taste the same when they prepare food for such crowds. You can always tell." She fumed inside at the unfairness of it all when David didn't respond. Taking a deep breath of resignation, she sighed. "So, that's where I am now, is it?"

"Where's that, Grandma?"

"Winter."

David turned and glanced out the large windows facing the courtyard. "It's cold, Grandma, and the trees have lost their leaves, but it's still fall."

Edna shook her head. He didn't understand. How could he? He was still young. He hadn't yet seen autumn. "I'm not talking about the season." She looked down at her hands and wrung them as her voice quivered. "I'm talking about life. It's winter for me. The end. The winter of my life."

# Chapter 32

With Grandma settled at the Arbor House, David's tension immediately released like an unwound spring. He called his grandmother nearly every day. Fred and Barbara had been by to visit and ease his grandmother's sadness at leaving her home. For two weeks, David focused on finding a permanent home for his grandmother. Finally, he found what he believed to be the perfect option. Only fifteen minutes from his own home he found a large residence owned by a geriatric doctor and his wife. They lived in the upper level, with the second level specifically designed with full handicapped access for up to six residents, and a basement apartment for up to two live-in CNA's. Even with one of the larger rooms in the home, many of Grandma's possessions would have to be left behind. David knew how much she valued her belongings. Leaving them behind would be difficult for her.

Before calling to give her the happy news of her permanent place, David planned his conversation with a sentimental remembrance of her youth. "It is a very beautiful home with a lovely view of Lake Sammamish, which isn't far from where you taught when you first became a teacher."

"I remember the lake. How large is my new home?"

David bit his lip. Now was the hard part. "It is a large home, but six people share it. You will have your own room and your own bath. The kitchen and dining and living rooms are shared by all the men and women who live there." David sensed her heartache through the silence before his grandmother's soft voice cracked across the line.

"How will I fit all of my furniture into one room?"

"Grandma, we talked about this. You will only be able to take what will fit. If there are things you want to leave to some of your friends we can make those arrangements."

"I need to go to my home David, and sort my things out. When can I do that?"

David's neck muscled tensed. He inhaled an extra-long breath, realizing she was right. It would be easier to allow her time to sort and reminisce in her home one final time. An extra trip to east of the mountains before the move was out of the question. He had no choice but to impose upon Barbara one last time.

Dialing Barbara's number, David anticipated a quick call. Surely, Barbara would be able to take Edna to select which items to bring to her new home. He was certain Edna had shared the news of her move during one of Barbara's visits. He was wrong.

After ensuring Barbara's husband, Robert, was doing well, David mentioned the reason for his current call. "I hate to ask, but I was hoping you might be able to make time during the week to take Grandma back to her place to go through her things."

"Sure, that's not a problem. Is there anything in particular she wants to get?"

David thought for a moment. "She just really needs some time to walk through the house and see what she wants to take when she moves."

Barbara's tone notched up. "You're moving her again? Where? When?"

"I'm sorry, I thought you knew her stay at Arbor House was only respite care."

"Well, yes, I guess. I thought it would be longer than a few weeks, though. Where is she moving this time?"

David breathed deeply, tipped his head back, and exhaled slowly. "She didn't tell you?" He paused long enough to know the answer, and groaned. "I found a place near me, in Issaquah. It will be a lot easier to visit and look after her than it has these past two years."

The harshness in Barbara's voice gave a firm indication of her disapproval. "You're moving her to Issaquah? How can you move her from the only place she's lived for the last half of her life? After all I've done for her, and for you? Don't you think I should have had some say?"

David visualized banging his head on the desk. He rolled his eyes and sighed in exasperation. Damn, he couldn't get the break that even the red-haired clown, from the golden arches, told him he deserved. "I'm sorry, Barbara. You've been great. I really appreciate all you've done for Grandma, and I can't tell you how much your friendship means to her. With her ongoing health issues and Alzheimer's, I need her geographically closer to me and my family."

Barbara interjected. "You're moving her just to make things easier on you. Who will she know there besides your family? Does she even understand she's leaving?"

David glanced at the clock. His heart pounded so hard and quick he thought it might burst from his chest. So much for the quick and painless phone call. "Of course, she understands. Since I'm the only family right now who is looking after her, it's up to me to do what I think is best. And honestly, other than you and occasionally Fred, she doesn't get many visitors. Alicia's only been by just recently."

"Obviously you've thought this out. I don't see how I'll be able to visit her after she moves. It's not easy on me to make that kind of trip at my age and with Robert ill."

David noticed the change in her voice, now more restrained. Of course, she was hurt, what did he expect? She had invested a great deal of her time and energy in helping Edna, especially since Larry died. She probably values Edna's friendship as much as Edna has hers. The move would leave a hole in Barbara's life too. "I'm sorry to have upset you. I understand if you don't want to help me."

As the silence lingered, David began to think Barbara had disconnected.

Finally, Barbara spoke, "I'll call you tomorrow."

David wished her and Robert a good evening and said goodbye. Since he had already been beat up, it was a good time to call Alicia and get that conversation and those licks over at the same time. He pulled out her phone number, and very slowly tapped the buttons, practicing the deep breathing exercises from his occasional yoga exercises. In and out through the nose for relaxation. The call was answered within a few rings.

"Hi, Alicia, it's David."

"This is a surprise. What's up?"

David continued his slow breathing. "I visited Grandma at Good Samaritan. She really appreciated your visit and the flowers and card. It was really nice."

"Sure. Fred called and told me he had taken her in. Said her mind is failing pretty badly."

"Yeah. That's what I'm calling about. She has Alzheimer's. It's only going to get worse. I have no choice but to move her to an adult care facility."

"Have you told Grandma?"

One deep yoga breath later David continued. "Yes, she's not thrilled, and she can't take Missy, so you can imagine how she feels about that."

"Did she throw anything at you? Because you haven't seen her really mad unless she's thrown something at you."

David's laugh loosened the tightness in his chest. One last carefree moment before the moment of indifference or as they say, all hell would break loose. He decided on the diplomatic tactful approach. "I know you and Lacey love Edna, but you also recognize, I'm the one who's been responsible for her care the past two years." Not pausing long enough to face any defensive attack, David pushed on. "I'm moving Edna to the other side of the state. Close to me." *Whew.* He'd gotten it out.

"Wow. Just like that?"

David ignored the syrupy sarcasm. He could pour it on too. "Yep, just like that. After only two years of back and forth driving once or twice a month." He shifted the phone to his other ear. "I have the address and phone number if you want. I'm sure she'd love to have you and Lacey visit." David heard fumbling on the other end of the line. "Lacey means a lot to her."

"I'm sure."

Not certain how to read Alicia's tone, David offered a half-hearted apology, but there was no regret. His decision had been made in Edna's best interest and neither Barbara nor Alicia would convince him otherwise. "I'm sorry if you're upset Alicia but right now, whether you believe it or not, I'm only doing what is best for Grandma Edna. If you want to step up and assure her bills are paid and she has visitors regularly, we can talk."

"You're really something. Mom and I spent years doing things for her. We were never good enough for her. No, it's your turn now."

Alicia's words washed away any trace of reservation in his decision.

The next evening Barbara called. "I prayed about your decision last night. I know you're only doing what you think is best for her. You're right, she needs family in her last years, and I need to focus more on caring for my husband. I'll take Edna home to sort through her things."

Relieved his grandmother would have time to sort through her belongings, reminisce, and say farewell to her home before her move across the state, David thanked Barbara for her willingness to help. He could see no downside.

# Chapter 33

Three weeks after his grandmother's move to respite care, David and Jean hooked up a small four-sided trailer to their car hoping it would be one of their last trips to the tri-cities. Arriving before noon on Saturday, they found Edna sitting up on the neatly made bed dressed in the rose and burgundy velour cardigan they had given her for Christmas. The television was on, but Grandma seemed oblivious to its blaring noise as she stared out the window.

"Hi, Grandma, how are you doing today? Today's moving day. Are you all set?" Grandma looked up. "What? Why am I moving?" Her frightened squinty eyes glistened with tears as she stared at David.

Jean approached and sat down next to her. "David and I are moving you closer to us. Won't that be nice?"

Edna glanced sideways at Jean. "Are you sure you have room for me?"

David raised his eyebrows and grinned. "We found a very nice place for you with your own room, and it's not too far from where we live. How about we start packing your clothes?" He walked over to her closet and grabbed a bunch of hangers.

Edna stood up. "Stop. What are you doing? Those are mine." She rushed toward David and reached out her trembling hand grasping for her clothes.

"Grandma, it's okay." Jean hurried after her and put her arm around her. "We're taking them to your new home." She led Edna back to her bed.

Grandma's face relaxed. "I have a new home? Where is it? How come no one told me?" Her eyes widened, but stared aimlessly.

David continued to empty the closet, flinging clothes over the back of the stuffed chair.

Sitting on her bed, Edna rocked slowly, clutching her quilt and drawing it close to her face, caressing it like a child might with a small kitten. "Did I ever show you my quilt?"

David smiled at her. Hearing the story again was well worth the feeling of comfort it would bring to Grandma.

"I made this in 1935, when the children were still young." Edna held a corner of the full-size quilt with a white background and large pastel tulips of blue, green, pink, and orange, bordered and backed with bleached muslin. "See."

Jean ran her hand across the testament of Edna's skill. Holding out the quilt, she showed David the lower right corner. He squinted at the small embroidered initials and the date commemorating the achievement. The quilt was in remarkable shape for something nearly seventy years old.

"I'm going to start another one at the next quilting bee." Suddenly solemn, she awkwardly folded her prized possession. "Will I have a place to put this in my new home?"

David's heart sunk. He winced at her words, deciding against reminding her that her new home was merely a bedroom in a care facility. He fought the pang of deceit knowing now was not the time to burden her with the emotional truth. "Yes, Grandma, we can put it on your bed." He took the quilt, refolded it and placed it in one of the boxes they had brought. Though the decision had been difficult, he knew he had made the right choice in moving her closer to him. His grandmother's mind was fading, her reality shifting, more and more, to another time, another place.

David marveled at his grandmother's excitement as he led her to the car to take her back to her home for one last time. Grandma would spend only one more night at Arbor House. The following morning, they would finish packing the remaining grooming and personal belongings that had accompanied her there. Then they would head to her new residence, two hundred miles away.

Accustomed to the disorganized manner in which Grandma lived, David still wasn't expecting the total disarray that greeted him when he walked into her house with her leading the way. He looked at Jean and rolled his eyes in the manner which annoyed him when Rachel or Emily relayed the same response. "Now what?" He shook his head.

The dining room table was piled with boxes. Chipped

mismatched dishes, rusted and burned on aluminum baking pans, marred with dents from a lifetime of baking, and grease stained and blistered plastic ware, covered the surface of the table. An assortment of glassware and canning jars sat amidst two produce boxes piled with fabric remnants, orange knits, and scratchy brown upholstery fabric woven long ago. David eyed the dozens of clothing items sewn over the decades, both as a hobby and out of necessity, during the hard times.

The temperature in Grandma's home as always was too warm and heightened the smell of the old cardboard and dusty old wares scattered about. He walked down the hall and glanced at the thermostat set at eighty, and turned it way back making a mental note to himself to call the utility companies the coming week, to shut off services.

"Barbara helped me gather some things for a yard sale before I move." Grandma's eyes looked down. Her voice trailed off.

David detected her despair. She had talked about a yard sale several times over the past year, but David dismissed the idea as a whim, hoping it would be forgotten, so he wouldn't have to deal with it.

Grandma sat down at the table and ran her hand across some of the items. "I've always liked to collect things. When I was little, I lined Mother's kitchen windowsill with jars of caterpillars, spiders, grasshoppers, bees and tadpoles. I still remember Mother getting upset with me whenever any of the contents of one of my jars got out. She really didn't like it, but she tolerated it." Grandma giggled like the little girl in her memories. "I guess it's about time to start getting rid of some of my things." She heaved a long sigh.

David had never held a yard sale or garage sale in his life. He had no intention in having one now. "Grandma, we aren't going to have time for a garage sale this weekend. I'm sorry, we have to get you moved in to your new place by tomorrow."

Grandma held out a sheet of labels upon which she had written shaky illegible prices. "I've already started gathering things to sell."

Jean strolled over and browsed at the once precious belongings, now reduced to worn and used junk. "Let's see what you have." She picked up the remains of a flower arrangement. A lone faded flower, with broken petals, stuck out from an array of dusty wheat stalks, small cattails, and ragged stems in a brown ceramic vase, now cracked and chipped.

David followed his grandmother's gaze as she watched Jean study the vase.

Grandma beamed. "I picked and dried those flowers myself. Aren't they beautiful? I really hate to sell them, but I have to start getting rid of some of my things. I'm old. I've lived longer than any of my kin. I know I can't hang on to these things forever." Her voice faded like the yellow flowers in the vase as she turned to busy herself in the china cabinet in search of more treasures.

The irony stung David like the prick of a bee. The once beautiful arrangement was now dried and withered like the woman who fashioned it. The flowers, faded like her memories, and the vessel that held the once vibrant signs of life, was now worn and broken. The heaviness in his chest caused him to pause and ponder the eventual progress of his own aging. It depressed him. But he was confident he had family who would assist him in his old age.

An assorted hodge-podge of dated magazines lay stacked at one end of the table. David picked up several and thumbed through the dog-eared pages, clipped of easy-fix recipes and elegant desserts, that most likely now bulged from inside cookbooks and overflowed files and drawers, dishes that were intended to be prepared at a later time. An overwhelming sadness gripped him knowing the time she wished for, of baking and sewing, would never again come. Whole sections were ripped from Reader's Digest. "Grandma, these magazines are no good. There are too many pages missing." He held a butchered magazine.

"I ripped out some of the stories. I want to read them when I have time."

David's heart sunk knowing someday he would find the stories of romance, perfect lives, and adversity, stuffed in some folder, stashed on a shelf, or under a table. Stories to be read when there was time. Time he knew Grandma would never have again. Her failing eyes had played a cruel trick, and shattered all ability to see, and her weakened mind crushed any ability to derive joy or understanding from the stories. One of the cruel ironies of age struck him. When you're old you have free time, only, in many cases, the time is rendered useless by failing health. He picked up a black clay urn with a chipped handle. His grandmother bustled about gathering even more useless belongings to David's eyes, but he guessed valuable finds, to her. His chest tightened. He didn't know how to break it to her that her once prized possessions were not worth anything at a garage sale. "Grandma, since we can't possibly have a garage sale this weekend it might be better to simply donate the items to a charity, like Goodwill."

"Oh no." Her resistance was strong. "We can't do that, I can't make any money that way and I need the money."

Luckily, Jean remembered all of their own donations of household items to different charitable organizations over the years. "I'm sure Goodwill Industries would gladly accept your donations and you could take the value of the goods as a tax deduction."

Grandma looked skeptical, "How much would that be?"

"As much as you'd make on a garage sale, probably more." David held his breath as he waited for her response. He knew he would wind up tossing many of the treasures as well as the clothing items and greyed and worn linens. Goodwill would still welcome what he guessed would be several pickup trucks worth of dishes, trinkets and furnishings. He would set aside items of personal remembrance and the many crates of photos and mementos.

"Okay," Grandma answered weakly. "But only if you take them to the Goodwill in town. I don't want to donate them to any other group. We should keep track of them so I have a record."

David groaned under his breath, he had forgotten how she liked to make lists. He shuddered at the thought of what he had started. He tried to imagine recording the items before him on any kind of list. He turned around to catch Grandma sneaking up the stairs. "Grandma, wait. You shouldn't be taking the stairs alone."

"I'm not." She pouted. "I was going to wait for you to help me when you were done. I need to find some things upstairs."

David fought back his irritation and took her arm.

Jean followed them upstairs. "Let me give you a hand."

Grandma led them to her craft room. "Can you pull out that old wooden army trunk?" She bent over to sort through the assorted envelopes and bulging files of papers.

A musty odor drifted through the room as she shuffled the dusty envelopes. The bright sunlight glared into the upstairs room.

A shower of dust particles danced in the air. David coughed, turning away at his allergy to dust. As Grandma straightened up with her hands full of papers, a pile of letters spilled out. David reached out, catching them. The brittleness of the paper, and faded pencil marks, warned him to handle them like the gems they were to his grandmother. He glanced at the childish scrawl on one of the faded fragile sheets. "Dear Mrs. Pearson, thank you ..."

"What are these?" David held a letter up to Grandma's failing eyes. She took the letter and stared hard. David reached across to the pole lamp laden with dust, flicked on the switch hidden underneath the yellowed shade, and tipped it so the bulb shone toward Grandma.

With a new ray of light to aid her, she studied the old paper, focusing at the keepsake from long ago, concentrating, recalling, evoking memories from the past, before a slow broad smile spread across her wrinkled face. "It's a letter from one of my students. Where did you find it? I have a whole stack of them." Her voice was animated, eager to get side-tracked deep into this world of her new finds.

David pulled the small chair out from behind the sewing table. He eased his grandmother into it and handed her the packet of letters and cards bound by brittle rubber bands that broke when he removed them. Sitting on the floor in front of her, Jean and he marveled she still had the vintage notes, the memories of her days of teaching, memories of the lives she had touched. His interest piqued, he rummaged through the trunk and lifted out a black framed certificate of recognition issued by Goodwill Industries. "For twenty-five years of faithful service," it read. David had known Grandma donated many hours and her talents to volunteer efforts. She'd talked about it many times. He had seen notes on her old calendars and photos of the dolls for which she had made dresses, but he had no idea her volunteer efforts had stretched for so many years. "You must be very proud of this." David handed her the certificate interrupting her as she thumbed through the precious letters. Edna laid the framed certificate down and moved on with her hunt for another treasure.

Jean picked the certificate up. "I didn't realize you had volunteered for twenty-five years."

Grandma placed her hands on her hips "Twenty-eight,

actually. I volunteered for three more years after I received this. They held a lovely luncheon for me and I even made a speech."

David nodded in fascination. For all of her difficult manners and stubborn ways she never ceased to amaze him with her spunk, her energy, and certainly, her once kind heart. He smiled at the old woman, proud to know someone who had obviously touched many lives in a positive and inspiring way. Leaning in, David took a banded packet of papers. "Can I help you find something?"

"No." She continued her search. "The newspaper wrote an article about me and even took my picture when they gave me this award." She beamed with pleasure before continuing, "I bet you can't guess how many dolls I dressed for Goodwill to sell." She paused only for a moment. "Several thousand. I also made hundreds of beaded Christmas tree ornaments. Did I ever show you my ornaments?"

"Yes, we've seen them, Grandma. They're very nice. Did you find what you came up here for?"

Grandma looked up surprised, lost in her thoughts, and shook her head. She reached deeper into the chest and pulled out a photo album. She ran her hand across the front of the old-fashioned album then opened it to reveal pages of black and white photos affixed to black paper pages with small red gummed corners. Straight out of the 1950's.

David studied his grandmother's determined and frustrated face. He wished he had known her better in her younger years. He couldn't help wondering how much more she might have influenced his own life and Nathan's. He longed for a chance to get to know all he could about her in the time she had left. He noticed his grandmother's eyes intently focused on the images as she slowly flipped through the pages, gazing at the photos in wide-eyed amazement. "May I see?"

Grandma smiled weakly. "These were taken so long ago. But I remember so many of these like only yesterday." Edna ran her gnarled index finger across a photo. "See? This was Larry and Kora-Lee when he came back from Korea married to her."

"And this must be Lorraine?" David pointed to a small child around five-years old.

"Yes." Edna tapped the figure of Kora-Lee. "And Kora-Lee is pregnant here with Alicia." Her eyes narrowed. "I could never understand why he married her like that, carrying another man's child."

David sighed and looked at his watch. It was apparent her happy memories were taking a turn for the worse. He pushed his chair back. "It's getting late Grandma. Are you ready to go back downstairs?"

She sighed, replacing the finds into the trunk, and closed the lid. David pushed it back into its place in the closet. At least for now.

With Grandma's arm linked in his, David led her back down the stairs. Before him, David saw a lifetime of precious belongings that to others seemed like junk. Trinkets broken, dented, used and disfigured by wear, like the very life they represented. A life lived to its fullest. He felt a twinge of guilt about his deceit and easy way out, tossing the fragments and vestiges of her lifetime. "Let me help you with these things, Grandma. We can decide what to do with them later." David looked at her glistening eyes and noticed the tears welling up. He knew he was only stalling. He would have to face the decision of what to do with these things, eventually. For now, it was important for her, or maybe for him, to let her hold on to her past for a little longer.

A knock at the door drew David's attention.

"Sorry to drop in like this, I noticed your car and trailer. I guess this is goodbye." Fred stood outside holding a wooden chest about a foot and a half across.

"That's okay it's nice to see you again. Come in." David stepped aside motioning Fred in and called out to Edna and Jean as Fred handed him the chest.

Already considering the contents, David hoisted the chest, checking the weight, onto the corner of the table. "What's this?" He forced a closed lip smile, squelching any uncontrolled vocalization.

"I just came by to return the silver which Edna had asked me to keep when she had so many visitors in and out after Larry died. She didn't want the additional worry of it being stolen. I'd forgotten all about it."

Edna shuffled to the door. "Oh, my silverware. You brought it back. I almost forgot about it."

Jean came to the door and invited Fred to sit down to visit for a few moments.

David resisted the head thump, holding back the mix of frustration and absurdity churning inside. "Thanks, I'm glad you brought it by it gives me another opportunity to thank you for all you did for Edna. I hope Marge is doing okay."

Fred's eyes welled up. He responded she was doing fine, but David suspected she wasn't doing as well as Fred was implying. David's decision to move his grandmother closer to him would no doubt also benefit Fred too. Without feeling obliged to check in on Edna, Fred could now focus all his time and energy on caring for his wife.

With hugs and handshakes exchanged and difficult goodbyes spoken, Fred walked out the door, and Edna's silverware chest lay on the dining room table.

David looked at his watch. The weekend was getting away from them. He stood by the wooden mahogany chest shaking his head. He brought his hands to his temples and smiled at Jean. "Do you want to call the insurance company and explain this, or should I? I guess I have to take back some of my doubts about Alicia too." They laughed before heading back to the living room.

"Grandma, you need to decide what you want to move to your new home. We can take your bed and one of the dressers. Remember, you are only going to have one room." David glanced over the contents of the room. Grandma's belongings ran the gamut from the tackiest of dime store trinkets to artistic porcelain hand painted vases from Korea which she purchased on a trip almost twenty years earlier, with Alicia. David scanned the shoddy living room furniture. There wouldn't be room for much. Either her recliner, or the rocker, and hopefully, the antique secretary, a place for a few of her prized possessions.

"Do you want to pick out a few of your wall hangings, Grandma?" Jean removed a gold-framed needlepoint picture of poppies.

"Oh, no. I want you to have that."

Jean turned over the needlepoint. "It has Lorraine's name on the back." She held it out to Edna.

"Oh, never mind that. I wrote that on the back years ago, Lorraine never particularly cared to have it anyway, and I want you and David to have it." She waved Jean's comment aside, removing the matching needlepoint set of a boy and girl she handed them to Jean, before shuffling to the armoire. "I want these." She picked up a photo of Nathan and David in their matching cowboy outfits. "Do you remember this?" She handed it to David.

David took the photo, with Jean looking on. "I remember that photo."

Grandma smiled. "Your mother sent that to me when you were living in California. Aren't you two cute?"

She continued to sort through the pictures and contents of the china cabinet. Her life's possessions. Tears formed, and fell, flowing freely. Jean put her arm around Grandma's shoulders. David watched as she moved through the condo. The realization stung it may very well be Grandma's last stroll through the home of which she was so proud. David returned upstairs to the guest room where he had spent a few nights, certainly more than he had cared to. He still flinched at the sight of the crushed red velour bedspread that cloaked the bed like a draped casket. He shuddered every time he stepped in the room, even knowing the carpet was clean and he had washed the sheets. He yanked open drawers of fabric and yarn, patterns and magazines. Ninety-five years of stuff. Only it wasn't stuff, it was her life. The uneasy feeling in his stomach returned. He looked at the vivid pastel drawing of poppies framed in gold. Grandma's favorite frame color. He marveled at her love of bright, vibrant, overbearing colors. It was a reflection of the personality he was certain Grandma once had. He turned off the light and looked over his shoulder knowing someday he would have to face the huge task of tossing and disposing of so many fragments of her life.

"Can I give you a hand?" Jean poked her head into the bedroom.

David turned around and shrugged. "Nah. There's nothing in this room we need to take right now." He looked at the mass of clothes draping Jean's arm. "Are these the clothes we're taking?" David scooped them up, folded them in half, laid them on the top of the biggest box and carried the bundle downstairs.

Grandma stood surveying at the half empty living room. "What about the rest of my things?"

"After you get settled we can go through a few more things, but you're not going to have room for everything."

"First I couldn't take Missy, now I have to leave some of my belongings. Are you sure I have to leave Missy with Barbara?"

"I know it's hard, Grandma. But you can't take Missy. You have to be able to care for a dog on your own."

"I can take Missy out and care for her just fine. Why is everyone treating me like I'm incompetent?"

Noticing she was visibly shaken, David put his arm around her. "We know you're not incompetent. But you do need assistance."

"You don't understand. You're not old. I just want to stay in my own home." The tears flowed.

"It's going to be okay. I've given all of your friends your new address and phone number. Barbara said she has a brother-in-law in the Seattle area. She might visit, and most importantly, Jean and I live only a few minutes away from your new home." David patted her shoulder and drew her close.

She sniffed into her hanky refusing to look at him. "What about my violets?" Grandma's voice cracked. She hurried to the plant stand.

Overwhelmed by their ongoing prolific growth, in spite of recent neglect while at Arbor House, David stared at her purple and pink African violets.

"Are we going to have room for these?" Edna reached down and lifted a pot displaying a single plant with a one-foot diameter.

David nodded. "Of course you will Grandma." A twinge of guilt stabbed at him knowing he would be keeping most of them, as Edna would not have the space, and in time they would go the way of neglect. Then again, knowing how Jean took care of plants, it was probably sentencing them to death either way. "We'll put them in the truck last."

With the pickup loaded with boxes of personal effects and a few large items, it was time to hit the road. With a last look around, David regarded the half empty house in a state of disarray. Grandma's eyes followed his gaze. His heart ached for her. "Are you ready Grandma?"

She turned away. "When will I be able to come back?'

David and Jean exchanged looks. David couldn't lie. There would be no coming back. Not for her. Her Alzheimer's dementia had slowly but steadily snatched and stolen more and more reality.

It was going to win. Grandma would never again know the freedom of living on her own and having her own home. A twinge of pain stabbed his heart. He took ahold of his grandmother's hands and urged her to look at him. "I don't think you will, Grandma."

Her eyes glistened as she blinked back tears.

He forced back his own tears, then turning the thermostat off and flicking off the last of the lights, he led Grandma outside for her last night at Arbor House, and his last night in the tri-cities.

The next morning, David and Jean shut the door, for the last time, to what had become their "usual" hotel room. With an early start, it didn't take long to get Edna's personal belongings together and loaded in the car. To their relief, Grandma appeared at ease, even happy. Before too long, they said goodbye to the staff at Arbor House and headed home, with his grandmother, this time, for good.

As always, Grandma chatted up a storm most of the drive. Despite her confusion, she knew she was going back to a place where she had spent some of the happiest years of her life.

"My sister, Pearl, lived outside of Issaquah. We had such lovely times on picnics and walking through the woods picking wildflowers."

Somehow, the trip back to the place of her childhood seemed appropriate. Grandma rambled on about her first teaching job in a one room schoolhouse on the eastern shores of Lake Sammamish. David smiled observing her animated face as she shared the memories that danced through her mind. With only occasional brief stops, after four and a half hours, David pulled the car off the freeway onto the Lake Sammamish exit. "Here's Lake Sammamish, Grandma. Does it look familiar?"

"Where's the ferry? Will we be taking the ferry across?"

The bluntness of her words caught David's attention. He looked up with raised eyebrows and smiled into the rear-view mirror at Jean. "What ferry is that?"

"The ferry. We always take the ferry across the lake."

David glanced over at his grandmother. She sat as calm as the expanse of lake that lay before them. "There is no ferry on Lake Sammamish. You're remembering the ferry on Lake Washington or Puget Sound."

"Well. You'll see. There certainly is." Grandma clipped her words and threw back her shoulders in defiance.

David dropped the subject. Grandma's new care facility was only a few minutes away and only a block off the west side of the lake. "Did I tell you the man who owns the house is a geriatric doctor, Grandma?"

Grandma's eyebrows rose in question. "What kind of doctor? I don't need a doctor, you know."

Pulling the car up the steep drive, he looked across the seat. "He's a doctor for older people. You'll have very good care, and it's a brand-new home built especially as a care facility." David was thrilled with the location of the three-story that housed the owners, Gloria and Carl, five current residents, and a live-in certified nurse's assistant. Parking the car as close to the front door as possible, David turned off the ignition and looked over at his grandmother. "Here we are."

"Where are we?" Grandma turned, her eyes wide and vacant as she gazed past David to the large white house which loomed before her. She brought her hand to her cheek. "This isn't my house."

David threw his head back against the car seat. He sighed. Any optimism he had his life was going to be simplified by the move, seemed short-lived.

# Chapter 34

With Grandma's care-facility only minutes away, it was convenient for David to stop by and visit on his way home from work. He looked forward to his visits, no longer needing to carry his white plastic bucket filled with tools and supplies ready to fix anything that might surprise him when he got to her house. Tension-free, he slid a CD in place. He allowed his mind to wander with the heavy beat of the music pulsing in the background. Pulling up to his grandmother's residence, David glanced around at the professionally maintained lawn and the pruned arborvitae which lined the long drive. He relaxed. She was safe and in clean and comfortable surroundings. Rubbing his hands up and down his arms against the coolness of the evening, he grabbed his jacket from the front seat, and strode to the front door.

He greeted Joanne, the CNA who lived in an apartment on the lower level of the home. Making his way to Edna's room, he inhaled, welcoming the fresh scent of lilacs or roses or spring breeze air-freshener. It didn't matter, it was heavenly compared to her dreary home that reeked of a mix of musty fabrics and pet odors, or the sterile antiseptic-smelling hospital environment from which she had recently come. David smiled and offered a quick nod of greeting to the two residents watching television in the living room as he passed.

"Hello, Grandma." David walked to her bed where she sat solemn, deep in her own thoughts, her own world.

"Gracious, is it that time already? Is it dinner time?"

"No, Grandma, I'm just here for a visit."

Edna looked away, her smile faded.

"How come you're not out in the living room with the others?"

"I prefer to be left alone. I don't like mixing with the old people who live here. They're simply not my type."

Though confident in his decision to move her, he wished Grandma would find some enjoyment in her new home. Having her closer to him eased a lot of his worries and allowed more time with his family. However, now that she was nearby, he and his family were the only people near enough to stop by to see her. Several of her friends had said they would make it over to visit in the future, but David's practical nature told him it wasn't something he could count on. He wondered if he called Alicia with an update, if she would bring Lacey by. He wondered too, if that would bring any joy to his grandmother's near joyless life.

After his visit, David pulled into his driveway, pushed the button on the garage door opener, and closed the door behind him as he walked into the house, shutting his mind off from the stress of the day.

He called out as he walked down the hall to change clothes. "I'm home."

Jean met him in the bedroom. "Tough day?"

David shook his head. "What else is there?" He cocked his head, seeing his wife's serious expression. "What's up?"

"Alicia called. Says it's important. She wants you to call her right away."

David tossed his blue dress shirt in the hamper and grabbed a T shirt. "Did she give you any clue what it's about?"

Jean shook her head. "She wouldn't say."

Grabbing a beer from the fridge, David walked over to the phone on the kitchen counter, sat down on a stool, and sighed. "I was thinking of calling her anyway. Might as well get it over with." He scrolled down the list of stored contacts to Alicia's phone number and hit dial. The call was answered right away. "Hi Alicia, It's David."

"David. Thanks for calling me back."

Immediately, David sensed urgency in her hoarse and panicky voice. "What's going on?"

"Lacey's sick. Her kidneys are failing."

David straightened on the kitchen stool and focused on the seriousness of the conversation. "I'm sorry. That's got to be incredibly difficult on you and your family. Is she going to be okay?"

"We have no guarantees. She needs a kidney transplant within the next few days. I was tested for compatibility, along with Mom and Lorraine. My blood type is not a compatible donor, but fortunately, Lorraine's is. Lorraine is donating one of her kidneys. Surgery is scheduled the day after tomorrow."

"That's good news. You know Jean and I wish her only the best." David's throat had gone dry, his words cracked as he spoke and his eyes welled. In spite of the tension between him and his stepsister, there could be no ill wishes for Lacey. "I'm sure Jean will be praying for her too." David heard the slow measured breathing across the line before Alicia continued.

"That's not the only reason I'm calling, though."

"What else is going on?" David glanced around, hoping to get a glimpse of Jean and motion to her.

"When I was screened and tested to see if I might be a potential match for Lacey, the blood and tissue typing discovered something odd. Further blood tests were ordered and confirm what the doctor suspected."

David shifted uncomfortably on the wooden stool. "Okay."

"I don't know a lot about what blood types can result from different combinations of blood. I do know Mom and Lorraine have type O, and I have type B negative."

"I'm sorry, Alicia. I don't have much understanding either about how all of that works. What does that indicate?"

"The doctor concluded with my B negative blood type, it was highly unlikely that my biological father could be the same as Lorraine's, especially taking into account Peter was Chinese."

David hit speaker on the phone, quickly motioning to Jean. He sucked in air. "So, what are you saying?"

"I confronted mom. She told me she and your dad had an affair while he was still married to your mother. You knew my mom was pregnant with me when she and Larry married, right? Everyone assumed Peter was both Lorraine's father and mine, but Mom always considered the possibility that Larry was my biological father." Alicia delayed before continuing. "Larry's blood type was AB negative, which is rare, but extremely unlikely in the Asian population, and can result in a B negative offspring."

David's hand hurt from clenching the phone tightly, stressed with all the earth rattling news being lobbed at him. "Wait, there's too much going on here. You're saying you're my half-sister, not my stepsister because Larry had type AB blood? Are you sure about his blood type?" David took a long swig of his beer, wishing it were something stiffer.

"That's what was on his organ donor card."

David's heart beat accelerated like a race car speeding toward the checkered flag. His thoughts whizzed out of control. He had so many questions, but he breathed deeply, taking hold of his emotions to maintain focus on the innocent child facing a life-threatening illness. "Does Grandma know?" David hesitated. "About Lacey, I mean?"

"I'll call her and tell her about Lacey. I'm still not sure how to break the other news to her."

"I'm sorry, it's a little hard for me to wrap my head around this. I have to admit, you look different enough from Lorraine, your mother must have suspected Larry was your father, not Peter?"

"I guess she did. At first, she didn't want Larry to feel compelled to marry her only because she was pregnant with his child. As I got older the lie was already in place." Alicia chuckled. "I don't think Larry could face telling Edna about his affair. You know how Grandma can be." Alicia's chuckle progressed into a laugh, slicing through some of the tension.

"You're laughing. What's so funny?"

"Don't you see? Mom wanted Larry to love her, and accept me as his daughter, even though I was not biologically his offspring. On the other hand, not being Larry's biological child is the reason Grandma Edna never accepted me or Lorraine completely as her family. I think it's ironic that as it turns out, I am her granddaughter. I wonder if that will change her opinion of me."

David mulled over Alicia's comment. He couldn't dispute it. He'd heard Edna several times say Alicia and Lorraine weren't family because they weren't blood. He too, wondered how his grandmother's view might change with this new-found development. He wondered if Edna was simply too old to comprehend how much the family unit had changed since she was a child. Now, modern families were often blended families, interracial families, adopted from not only different parents, but different countries and of differing skin tones, even same-sex couples. Was it too much to hope that at ninety-five, there was still time for Edna and her granddaughters to forge a familial relationship?

# Chapter 35

Hearing Gloria calling out to her, Edna glanced up from watching television with some of the other residents.

Gloria almost sang her announcement. "You have a phone call, dear."

Edna eyes sparked to match her smile as she pushed off the cushion, strutting toward the kitchen with her cane, proud to have a family that loved her and called her. "Gracious. David just left. Who is it? Did they say?"

"It's your granddaughter." Gloria smiled, handing Edna the receiver.

Edna hadn't heard from Rachel since she returned to school. Her hand trembled in excitement waiting to hear about school. Taking the phone, Edna greeted her caller. "Rachel?"

"No, Grandma, it's not Rachel, it's Alicia."

"Alicia?" Edna's hand gripped the phone tighter hearing the agitation in Alicia's voice. She moved to the small chair by the phone and settled into it. She hadn't heard from Alicia since David moved her to this place. She thought back to Alicia's phone call the day Larry died. Something must be up for Alicia to be calling her now, at this time. She wouldn't call if it weren't serious. Edna's chest tensed and her voice broke. "Are you okay?"

"I'm calling because Lacey's sick"

"What do you mean? What's wrong with her?"

"Her kidneys are failing quickly. Without a transplant, she will die."

Blood rushed from Edna's head and her hands shook. "Lacey? How can that be? She can't die." Edna's heart stopped for a beat or two in panic. "She was fine when I saw her."

Gloria reached for Edna's hand, bending over her with concerned eyes. "Is everything okay, Edna?"

Edna shook her head "My-great-granddaughter could die."
Edna returned her attention to Alicia. "I've never heard of a young
child needing a kidney transplant. Will she get one in time?"

"Lorraine is a perfect match and is donating one of her
kidneys to save Lacey's life."

Alicia's words soothed Edna's nervousness, but her muscles
tightened with concern. "Oh Lord. What about Lorraine? Will she
be okay?"

"Without Lorraine's kidney, there may not be enough time to
find another suitable donor. They should both be fine within a few
weeks."

Edna's hand steadied, but her mouth felt parched like desert
sand. Edna took a few sips of the water Gloria had placed next to
her. "I never imagined someone could donate a kidney while they
were alive. That's very brave of Lorraine."

Alicia agreed. "It's pretty amazing. I think Dad inspired her by
being an organ donor himself."

Edna straightened in the chair recalling her resentment when
she learned Larry was an organ donor. Unable to hold back the
tears, Edna's grief turned to pride. The bitterness of her son's death
sweetened at the realization he possibly saved another life with his
unselfish act.

"Grandma. There's something else we learned while I was
being checked as a potential donor for Lacey. I need you to listen
and to understand what I am going to tell you."

Edna's back ached from the wooden chair. She shifted to settle
herself through the directness of Alicia's words, dabbing at her
tears with a tissue. "What's that, dear?"

Alicia's tone softened. "The doctors took a lot of blood and
tissue tests for organ compatibility. I found out Peter, Mom's first
husband, Lorraine's father, is not my biological father. It turns out
Larry was my biological father."

"Oh my word. That can't possibly be right. Your mother was
extremely pregnant before Larry married her, and he had only been
divorced for two months." Edna grabbed her water glass and took
several gulps, helping still her woozy head. "Oh my, what are you
saying? Are you sure?"

"Blood typing is very accurate, very scientific. Based on his
blood type and mine, Larry was my father."

Edna's mind spun in dizzying confusion. She struggled for a clearer understanding. "Larry was your real father?"

Was it possible, after all these years of deception? Edna fought to recall the day Larry had said he was married again and his new wife had a child and was pregnant. Had he known all along that Alicia was his biological daughter? How could he not have known? Kora-Lee must have known and lied to Larry. Edna never trusted her. Nothing made any sense.

"Grandma, are you okay?"

Edna shook her head. "No. It doesn't make sense. Why didn't they tell us?" Was Alicia really her granddaughter? Edna brought her hands to her eyes. If only she'd known. Perhaps things could have been different.

# Chapter 36

David tried to dissuade his grandmother from going to the airport with him to pick up Nathan. "The walk from the parking garage to baggage claim is going to be too much for you."

"I haven't seen Nathan since he was a child. I want to go with you." Her firm teacher voice demanded agreement.

Though they had plenty of time, the walk was going to be slow and tiring for Grandma. He quickly realized he should have arranged for her to meet Nathan at his home for dinner instead of the fast paced, hectic airport.

As David eased his grandmother out of the car he noticed her moist eyes and wide grin that stretched across her crevassed pale skin. He shrugged in defeat. Hoping to simplify the slow shuffle across the parking lot and down the long hallway leading to the baggage carousel, David pointed out the rack of wheelchairs available. "How about we get you a wheelchair, Grandma?" David held his breath hoping for an affirmative response. Even before he asked, he knew the answer. Grandma's eyes cut like a laser. He wouldn't push any further. Taking hold of her frail arm he cautiously guided her through the packed crowd of travelers scurrying by. Spotting the overhead sign pointing the way, he led her toward the airline's baggage claim. "Nathan's been looking forward to finally seeing you again after all these years, Grandma."

"That's nice dear. I'm sure he's a wonderful young man, like his brother." Grandma patted David's arm.

In spite of the years of competition between him and his brother, David missed Nathan. With the distance separating them, and infrequency of calls, the relationship had waned. He was looking forward to getting reacquainted with his brother again, as well as get some relief in decision making and the future care for their Grandmother.

Edna broke David's train of thought. "I've always thought the service was a good way of life. I enjoyed the years Jacob was in the service. I wish he had stayed on. It's so nice Nathan followed in his father and his grandfather's footsteps, isn't it?"

David thought back twenty-five years, to when Nathan graduated from high school and was uncertain of the direction of his life. Now here he was a First Sergeant and career soldier. David paced nervously checking in all directions in between glances at his watch wishing he had remembered to call the airlines and check for the flight's current arrival time.

"Hey, David."

David turned toward the husky voice he detected across the congested airport. He recognized Nathan approaching with a brisk walk. David unconsciously grinned. He had to admit Nathan looked good in his uniform. Nathan also carried about twenty less pounds around the middle than he did. For a moment, David's mind flashed to the photos Grandma had shown him of his grandfather. David hadn't previously thought his brother looked that much like his father or grandfather, but seeing him now compared to the family photos, the resemblance was striking. During the past two years Nathan's hair had grayed significantly. His deep-set eyes and the prominent nose so characteristic of the Pearson family, emphasized his likeness to Larry and Jacob. David wondered if his grandmother had seen the resemblance.

"How are you doing?" David extended his right hand to his brother and slapped him on the back in greeting. He looked to his grandmother. "What do you think, Grandma?"

"Well, you're quite a handsome young soldier, aren't you?" Edna looked down suddenly with a shy and nervous voice. "I have to admit."

David started to laugh, but hesitated upon seeing his grandmother's flushed complexion.

"I've always been smitten by men in uniforms." Edna brought her hand to her lips, seemingly embarrassed by her words.

Nathan exchanged looks with his brother, his raised brows questioning. "I'm happy to finally see you again after so long." Nathan reached out to hug her.

"Not so fast young man, we just met." Grandma pulled away, instead, extending her right hand in a handshake.

David reached out and placed his hand on Nathan's shoulder. "Grandma, this is Nathan, your grandson." He studied his grandmother's expression. No sparkle in her eyes or wide grin across her face like he expected after years of waiting to be reunited with Nathan. She was lost in another place, another time. Once more, Grandma was in her own reality.

David sighed as the announcement blared confirming the carousel numbers of the incoming luggage. Travelers scurried past to be first at their carousel as the baggage rolled down the belts. Returning his focus to his brother he continued toward the baggage claim and whispered. "Remember, Grandma's not always in the same world as the rest of us."

"Can I give you a hand, Grandma?" Nathan extended his arm to link hers.

"Do you come to Dehoney's often?" Grandma gazed upon Nathan's startled face.

"Dehoney's? Grandma, we're at the airport." Nathan's eyes widened in confusion, struggling to understand.

She ignored his response and continued. "There's always plenty of action here. Look at the crowd. It's the best dance hall in the whole city of Seattle. Come on soldier, let's dance." Grandma's flushed face revealed a self-conscious grin and she giggled like a school girl.

David smiled, shrugged, and faced Nathan. "I told you about her delusions, and you do look a lot like Jacob, I'm sure she thinks you're him."

Nathan hesitated for only a moment, then shrugged too, and played along with a smile. "Okay." He handed David the duffel bag from his shoulder and took his grandmother's arms and swung her around.

She beamed through her words. "I love coming to Dehoney's." Edna swayed back and forth. "Come on," she tugged on Nathan's arm. "Let's dance."

Nathan awkwardly danced her around, side-stepping toward the baggage carousel.

David noticed the smiles and nudges of passers-by watching the soldier dance with a fragile old woman. The tension of the afternoon escaped through his laughter. "Welcome home, Nathan."

# Chapter 37

Edna took a deep breath, taken by the scent of his cologne. She looked around the big hall with crystal chandeliers. The large wooden planked floor that had been perfect for dancing had been replaced with buffed tile. Edna loved to kick and sway to "Sneak" and "Cat Whiskers." She knew all the latest tunes. The blaring sounds of the crowd hurt her ears though, and she turned to look for the wooden stage in the front of the massive hall. Music spilled into the hall but she didn't see the stage or the jazz band that normally performed. She laughed as she watched her date awkwardly step and tap in time to the fox trot and the two step waltz. His lanky arms swinging out of tune to the music.

"You're out of practice, Mr. Pearson," Edna batted her eyes coyly at her date.

Jacob was not much of a dancer; he was clumsy on his feet. Edna, however, moved with the smoothness of fine scotch as the mellow voice of Guy Lombardo wooed the women on the floor with his sensitive lyrics and soft slow sounds. She was quick and athletic as she jitterbugged across the floor to the sax of Duke Ellington. She looked over at the young soldier's flushed face, seemingly embarrassed as he looked around the crowded floor. She knew they turned heads when they were in the room. Jacob, so dapper in his army uniform, and her, quite in fashion in her red satin dress, swaying as she danced. "Do you know the Charleston, soldier?"

Her beau shook his head.

"I don't much like dancing with just one partner. But it's different when it's a man you admire and like the best."

"I like you, too, Grandma." The soldier slowed his step and escorted her off the dance floor.

It had been a good evening with her handsome beau. She gazed into his dark eyes, beaming with pride knowing she had someone who cared about her.

# Chapter 38

David studied his brother's puzzled look. Perhaps he should have been more clear on their grandmother's increasing dementia. He stepped forward, taking his grandmother's arm. "Come on, Grandma. Let's get the rest of Nathan's things and go. It's been a long evening and we can catch up on everything on the way home."

Ignoring David, she continued her gaze at the soldier on her arm. "You know, soldier, before you take me home don't you think you should offer to buy me a drink?"

David steered her to the conveyor belt spewing luggage out for the eager recipients. "The soldier can buy you a drink at home, how's that, Grandma? How does a cup of tea sound?"

As Nathan grabbed his luggage from the belt, Grandma narrowed her gaze at David. "Do you think I'd settle for tea with you when I can have a beer with that young soldier over there?" She winked and nodded at Nathan as he approached with a large bag strapped over his shoulder. "Just you wait, you'll see." She eyed David smugly. "He's the one I'm going to marry someday." She giggled again as she took her soldier by the arm and proudly strutted down the corridor.

"Grandma, I think you're a bit confused right now." Nathan led her through the crowd.

"Never you mind now." She grinned as they walked.

Determined to make his grandmother aware of her surroundings, David stepped up beside her. "Grandma, Nathan sure looks a lot like his great-granddad, Jacob, doesn't he?"

Grandma stopped walking and breathed deeply. She protested. "You don't know anything about Jacob."

Nathan patted her arm. "You'll have to tell me all about my great-granddad sometime, especially since I remind you of him." Arm and arm, they walked toward the parking garage.

# Chapter 39

Her room was nice enough, but Edna was homesick. She missed the freedom to wander around her house and stroll through her yard. The grounds around this new place were lovely. Gloria and Carl had a gardener who came by and weeded and mowed. Edna valued the few minutes here and there, the middle-aged man spent chatting with her about the shrubs and various trees planted in the back yard. The slope of the terrain though made it almost impossible for her to maneuver around, so she settled on soaking in the color and scents from the cushioned and wicker seats and wicker table positioned around the small patio area.

David had bought her an electric bed. The ability to sleep with the bed at a slight angle helped ease some of the pain that accompanied aging. On top of her bed, lay her most revered display of talent, her most precious memento of the past, her quilt. A pencil drawing of a lake, from Emily, hung in a wood frame on her wall along with the needlepoint tapestries of a young boy and girl which she made for Bernice shortly before she died. Occasionally Edna received updates from Barbara on how Missy had adjusted to her new living arrangements. Her heart ached when she thought of her little dog that was always good at showing affection. Alicia had written twice with updates on Lacey, and Lacey sent drawings which Edna cherished, tucking them inside the frame of the mirror over her dresser along with Lacey's school photo.

Gloria poked her head inside. "David will be here soon. Are you ready to go?"

"Of course." She had been ready since breakfast. "I'm ready." Edna gathered her coat and purse and shuffled to the living room to wait for David. For the most part, the residents spent their days staring at the nonsense that flashed across the television screen, or babbled about their families and how they were going to visit someday. Simon's son came by and visited quite often, but from what Edna could tell, neither Henrietta nor Gladys had many visitors. Edna was lucky. In addition to David's weekly visits, Nathan came by when he could. Once in a while, Nathan was able to join them for dinner at David's. It was nice living closer to both of her grandsons. Though she wished sometimes she could see Alicia and Lacey again.

Today the living room was calm and quiet. Though a three-story home, all Edna ever saw was the floor she lived on, which consisted of six bedrooms, all with a toilet and sink, one main bathroom with a large shower stall, as well as the common living space with a kitchen and dining area. The hardwood floor made it easy to maneuver especially with her cane and occasional walker. The white walls and large picture windows, framed in heavy champagne colored brocade drapes, held back by a thick gold cord, always left her chilled, despite the sunlight spilling in. Placing her things down, she plopped onto the plush rose colored sofa, with overstuffed sage and deep purple pillows, and gazed far off into the distance.

With effort, she pushed herself up after a few minutes and hobbled over to the window. The glare from the sun burned her eyes as she strained to see the lake she knew lay out there, before her, somewhere. But it lay beyond the scope of her failing eyes' ability to see. Even though she couldn't see it too well, David had told her the view of the lake was spectacular. Staring off in the direction of the lake, she reminisced about her teens and young adult life where she spent so many days on the shores picnicking with Pearl and her husband, Stanley. The cold seeped through the large plates of glass. Her eyes scanned a blazing palette of fall colors that streaked across the horizon, and the trees swayed against the wind. She squinted against the light and longed for her ability to see clearly again. Crossing her arms tightly across her chest, she shivered.

Edna turned, suddenly aware of Gloria heading for the door. David stepped inside. Edna shuffled past the others. Gloria retrieved the coat and scarf from the sofa.

"Is it cold outside?" Edna grabbed her red wool scarf from Gloria and wrapped it snugly around her neck.

David held her coat out and eased her arms into it. "It's nearly winter, so it's a bit nippy."

Edna grinned as Gloria put her arm around Edna's shoulder patting it with a caring touch. "Have a nice evening dear, I'll see you later."

Edna shivered against the crisp fall air as David helped her into the warm car. She snuggled into the seat. Heading down the tree-lined two lane road toward David's house, Edna looked out the window to the expanse of water almost hidden by houses. "It's a shame they've built so many homes. It's not at all the way things used to be." She sighed at the memories of her childhood years on the shores of the lake. Edna stared across the water to the vastness which lay beyond and diverged into a blur. "It's just not right. We used to have such lovely picnics here."

David reached across and took his grandmother's hand. "I bet it was a lot different back then."

"It was a more relaxed life." Edna settled back in her seat. "Are we taking the ferry today?" Edna's eyes squinted from the glare of the sun reflecting off the water as they came around the end of the lake, with a more open view.

"Grandma, we've been through this. There's no ferry on Lake Sammamish, we have to drive around the lake."

Edna pouted, squirming against the confines of the seat belt. "We always take the ferry across the lake to visit father." She opened the purse on her lap and fumbled around searching for change. "That's okay, I have money."

"You took the ferry on Puget Sound, and that was a long time ago."

Edna wrinkled her brow. "Oh, you." Frustrated by his response, Edna gripped her coins and watched out the window. The car moved away from the water and the scenery shifted. Edna studied the small businesses and houses along the way. Finally, the car turned down the gravel road lined with near naked maple trees with a few stubborn golden leaves holding on for yet another day. The serenity of the country returned. She couldn't wait to get home. She had missed her family while she was away.

Edna's body relaxed and she smiled broadly when the car pulled to a stop after the long ride. She ached for the warmth of the house where her mother always had a fire in the stove. With an arm helping her up the front walkway, the door flung open. The sharp burning smell of onions assaulted her, signaling meatloaf, which Mother always served on Sunday before Daddy had to leave for work again at the logging camp on Vashon Island. She looked around the surroundings, confused she didn't see her mother. "Where's Mother? Is she out in the garden?" Edna called to the emptiness of the house as she walked over to the wood stove in the living room, to take the chill from her hands. Edna rubbed them vigorously.

David walked in. "Your mother's not here, Grandma, remember? We can see if Jean is outside?"

Edna dutifully followed him outside. She didn't see her mother's old burlap harvest bag hanging by the door as she walked out. She must be gathering produce for dinner. Edna looked around the yard. Finally, mother came to the porch.

"Are you hungry? Dinner's about ready. I only have to make the biscuits."

Edna reached for the comfort of her mother's hand as they strolled inside. "May I help?" Edna loved the baking powder biscuits that graced the table every Sunday. She opened the cabinet door under Mama's cupboard and rummaged around. Out of the corner of her eye she saw her mother shake her head at the mess, but Mother said nothing, she simply smiled. Edna opened and closed the bank of drawers. Finally, in the third drawer she pulled out a yellow and orange apron. Someone had moved it. Her fingers fumbled struggling to tie the strings behind her back.

"Here, Grandma, let me help you."

Edna welcomed the help, tying the apron around her waist.

The flour slopped out as she dug deep into the canister with the white plastic measuring cup and with slow careful moves, scooped out two cups. She laughed as a dusting of flour settled on the countertop. Knowing the recipe by heart, Edna measured out two teaspoons from the red can of baking powder while watching her mother reach to the top shelf for the shortening.

"Let me help." Kind gentle hands guided Edna's hand helping dice the shortening into a coarse mixture.

With the warm milk poured in, Edna stirred gently with the wooden spoon until Mother stepped in and removed the spoon from her hand.

"That's stirred just about perfect. I'll take over now."

"I can do the kneading. I'm old enough." Edna pouted, feeling pushed away.

Her mother smiled, gathered the dough, and slapped it on the board. Edna reached for the baking pan to help place the cut biscuits on the pan for baking.

"How's it going in here?" David appeared in the doorway.

Jean pushed the pan of biscuits into the oven. "Dinner in ten minutes. Can you show Grandma where to wash up?"

Edna gripped David's arm and shuffled down the hall. She could hardly wait for her father to return from the town. He should have been home by now. She couldn't understand what had happened to him and why the family was gathering to eat without him.

David led her to her place at the table. The aroma of warm biscuits wafted into the dining room. Edna beamed with pride knowing she helped with the family dinner. "Where's Daddy? Shouldn't he be home by now? We can't eat without him." Edna's chest tightened. She stared at the blank faces looking back at her.

A strong hand reached out and grasped hers with a firm but kind voice. "Grandma, you're confused again. Your mother and father are gone. You're with your grandson, David and his family, remember?"

"Oh, you." Edna shot an indignant glance across the table. It wasn't her mother sitting there. She didn't understand. Jean looked nothing like her mother, whose eyes were green and her hair much darker. Edna blinked back the tears, silently cursing her confusion. Her cheeks burned. "I know that. I remember your family. I'm not senile you know."

With dinner eaten, the family retreated to the living room warmed by the heat from the wood stove. Edna smiled, wishing they could stay together always, but she knew soon David would take her back to that other place. "I wish I could see Alicia and Lacey again. But they're so far away. I hope they come to visit me soon."

David leaned forward in his recliner. "Have you talked to Alicia recently?"

"Oh, yes. She calls me nearly every week. Her last call was comforting. Lacey's getting stronger every day"

"That's good news. Alicia sent me an email keeping me up to date too. I guess Lacey's returning to school in a week or so."

"I should get a computer so I can learn how to do that email thing too. I was always very adept at typing you know. It's too bad Lacey's still not up to travelling. Did Alicia tell you that she's your half-sister? Larry was her father too."

"Yes, Grandma. She called and told me. It's nice for you to have more grandchildren, like Alicia and Lacey, isn't it?"

"Don't forget Lorraine, after all, she saved Lacey's life."

David nodded before kicking the foot rest of his recliner down. "It's getting late, Grandma. We'd better get you back."

She cast a downward look. It couldn't be time to leave already. A knot seized in her throat as David held out her blue quilted coat. Edna hated saying goodbye. Hugging Emily at the door, loneliness took hold and gripped her once more.

David opened the door and led Edna down the walkway, helping her into the front seat.

"When will we get to the ferry?" She fought to control the cracking in her voice and hummed to distract herself from the wave of sadness that swept over her. She had always been fascinated by the large white sleek vessel Daddy got to ride on. She loved to watch the boat as it bellowed smoke from the towering stack and listen to the horn blast its alert as the last minute riders dashed for the boarding plank.

The car pulled up a long drive and David announced. "We're home." He walked her to the porch and hugged her. "I'll see you next week."

The front door opened. Welcoming arms reached out to greet her, but she stood cold, alone, saddened as her father hung his head and walked away. When Daddy could no longer see her, Edna stiffened her resolve and wiped the small drop from her cheek. But she was brave, and next week he would be back to visit her again.

# Chapter 40

The ring of the phone interrupted the family Sunday evening cribbage game. Emily dashed to answer it. Handing the phone to her father, David noticed her usual smile had faded. Hearing Gloria's voice, his breath caught for a moment. She called only when there was something of concern regarding Edna. Gloria's calls had become increasingly frequent. His throat tightened and he swallowed to ease the dryness.

"David, I'm afraid your grandmother has wandered away again. Carl finally found her down by the lake."

David took a deep breath and exhaled as he counted slowly in his head. How could Grandma, who required a cane to get around, walk the four blocks to the lake without somebody stopping and realizing she was a confused old woman? "Where is she now?"

"Carl called from his cell phone. They're still at Vasa Park. Your grandmother's fine, but I thought it might be less traumatic for her if you came and calmed her a bit. She's pretty confused about things again."

"I'm on my way. Thanks for calling." David set the phone down with a huge exhale.

Noticing her husband's concern, Jean put her arm around his shoulder. "What's going on this time?"

"Grandma wandered off again. Do you want to go with me to pick her up?"

"Of course, you know I do." She headed for the coat closet.

David grabbed his keys and a coat and within moments they were on their way to the west side of Lake Sammamish for Vasa Park. "Don't you think people who are trained to take care of the elderly should be more aware of where their clients are?" David heard the irritation in his voice, knowing it was misplaced, but needing to vent, he continued. "Maybe we should consider moving her to an Alzheimer's facility where they can lock the patients in. I won't have to worry about her so much."

"Take it easy. You know they can't watch everyone every second. Don't get all upset over it. You're not doing your blood pressure any good."

"Well, what do you propose I do?" David glanced over at Jean almost daring her to come up with a better plan.

"Remember what we read about people with Alzheimer's? They are easily confused, and any change in routine can be upsetting, maybe, even set-them back. I think keeping her where she is, as long as she is safe, is her best option." Jean paused, reached for his arm and patted it. "You know it's only going to get worse. That's the way the disease works."

"You're right, but she can't keep wandering away like this." David's neck muscles tightened, he felt the tension creeping upwards sensing a headache coming on. "You can bet my blood pressure's going to be high when I take it tonight." David mulled over his current situation. His children were nearly grown, the oldest now in college. It should be a time for more freedom to enjoy leisure activities. But even with Grandma's move nearer to him, the time commitment of caring for her, which began as a slight imposition on his life, had grown like a sink hole, engulfing his whole life.

The sun was starting to descend as they pulled the car into the lot at the park. The sky wore a cloud tinged in gold and pink. David spotted Carl and Grandma sitting side by side on a bench, looking east, across the lake. The coolness of the late fall evening hadn't deterred the small crowd of parents who brought their children to the park to burn off some energy, before settling into bed for the night. David hurried down to the beach with Jean alongside. Across from a small white beach house, they joined Carl and his grandmother.

"Hi, Grandma." David squatted and patted her hand. She continued to look out into the distance. Her eyes lacked their normal feisty sparkle. David leaned in. Her face showed no sign of recognition as she turned and regarded him without acknowledging his presence.

Jean sat down next to Carl. "How is she doing?"

"She's been better. She's been staring out at the lake for the past ten minutes, talking about Pearl and her mother again."

"Thanks, Carl. Gloria said you walked here. Why don't I drive you home while David and his grandmother visit a bit?"

The cold night air made the blue veins bulge against Edna's translucent skin and her hands shivered. Jean took her coat off. "Here you go, Grandma. This will help keep you warm." Jean draped the coat across Edna's shoulders covering her red sweatshirt. "I'll be back in a few minutes to get you."

As Carl and Jean returned to the car, David took Carl's place on the bench. He put his arm around his Grandma's delicate frame, and followed her gaze. Her vacant eyes stared far off into the distance, across the vastness of the lake to the glow of lights dotting the other side. A twinge of sorrow overshadowed his anger, recognizing the complete helplessness of his grandmother in the grip of Alzheimer's. "What are you looking at?" He took her gnarled boney hand, cold from the chill of the evening, placing it between his hands, on his lap. David watched a young couple walking by the water enjoying a late evening stroll. Then he looked out across the dark calm lake, breathing in the crisp air.

"I can't see the school. I thought I would be able see it from here." His grandmother spoke with a wistful longing tone.

Turning to her, David's eyes and nose burned as he fought the feeling of despair. He sighed and continued to pat her hand wanting to help ease his grandmother's troubled mind. "What school is that, Grandma?"

"You know the one. I told you about my teaching job in Monohan. It should be right over there. It's not far from Pearl's house. Can you take me to Pearl's house now?" Grandma struggled to stand and shuffled closer to the water's edge toward the beach house. She pointed across the lake toward the flickering lights on the other side.

She was right. There once was a small lumber town called Monohan on the east side of the lake. The area still survived, though not recognized by many these days. Over the years it had given way to the rapidly growing sprawl of houses and commercial space surrounding Lake Sammamish. "There was a school there once, Grandma, but it's not there anymore." David's throat tightened with sadness at his grandmother's present situation, living more and more in the past.

"What are you saying? Of course it's there. I just got a job there last week when my teaching certificate came."

"You're right, Grandma, I forgot." David had learned not to fight the situation. It was much easier on everyone to go along with the flow and the time she was in. "I don't know if I can take you to Pearl's now." David hoped Grandma would forget about her sister soon so he wouldn't have to remind her Pearl had died over twenty years earlier.

Grandma's eyes widened and David saw a slight glint reflecting in her wet eyes. A slow smile turned up the corners of her mouth. "I can see the school and my students. Do you see it?" She grabbed David's arm for support, gripped her cane, and shuffled toward the small park facility building at the water's edge. Upon reaching it, she faced the building and ran her hand over the white painted surface.

# Chapter 41

Edna guessed the old country school was from the era of the children's grandparents, built around eighteen-seventy, or so. "I can't imagine this one small room holding all grades from one through eight." Growing up in Seattle, Edna never imagined her first teaching job would be at such a rural school. "You know I always imagined a larger school. Though I do like the opportunity to stay close to where Pearl and Stanley live."

"Yes, it is important to be near family."

Edna smiled at the man next to her. She guessed he had been assigned by the district to escort her to her new school. She looked over at the cistern at the corner of the building. It provided the water for the school. The stink around the area smelled like a ripe outhouse and drew flying insects. Edna bent over to inspect it. It was flavored with dead bugs and the like, obviously unfit to drink. "How can the school district allow children to drink this water? I know I certainly won't?" Edna looked down at the cistern and cleared her throat. "I suspect one of the reasons the small rural schools have a lot of sickness is from the water supply."

Her escort looked surprised at her direct manner. He shrugged and stuttered, "This faucet isn't drinking water." He looked at her confused, but Edna was not about to let him get away without inspecting the water. She demanded the district analyze the water and make it fit for drinking. She stood firm, until she heard the schoolmaster concede.

"I expect it analyzed immediately." Edna walked to the front door and ran her hand across the siding, where the white paint peeled away like birch bark on the weathered wood. "There are some other changes needed of course. Perhaps a fresh coat of paint for this tired building." The man's eyes widened. Edna suspected he wasn't used to such an outspoken, young, beginning teacher. He paused then muttered something. Edna knew about the limited resources of the district, but she didn't want to hear excuses. Nonetheless, he surprised her and quietly agreed.

"Of course, whatever you want."

The sounds and sight of children playing outside reminded Edna to prepare the classroom for the student's arrival. She pushed on the door. It groaned as it opened into the small room. The sun fought its way through dirt-encrusted windows, casting a dim light on the dirty, planked, wooden floor. A large, black, three-foot iron stove stood in the back of the room on a brick hearth. "I imagine in addition to my teaching responsibilities, I'll have to keep the stove going?" Edna looked over at her companion.

He smiled, but didn't answer.

She bent over the dirty black steel and struggled to stoke the stove with the coal that was delivered in loads of large pieces. She poked and prodded with an iron rod as the embers struggled to life like fireflies. She coughed. Her eyes burned as the gritty dust settled on the wooden plank floor and furniture, coating everything like a black snowfall. She inspected the benches and found they were etched with many years of students' names and initials, including the parents or other relatives who also had attended the school over its fifty years of existence.

The voices of the children got louder. She barely had time to compose herself before several children, from six to fourteen years old, dashed into the cold sparse room and stared up at her. "Settle down now children and be seated." She motioned for the children to sit on the old plank picnic benches. Edna brushed the soot from her nearly blue hands, her heart raced as she greeted the children. It was important to present an air of authority for her first impression, but her faltering voice threatened her position. "Hello children, I am your new teacher for this school year." Edna smiled at their polite smiling faces, eager to face a new year of education and immediately stood confident of her decision to teach.

Waiting for the warmth of the stove to heat the small room, she noticed the children were still in their coats. The commotion started early, Edna stood helpless as the children ran about without paying her any mind. She wasn't prepared for how the children might react to her. She had to devise a quick threat of consequence for any misbehavior. The stove came to life with small cinders burning with an orange glow. It would provide a sure chore for her students. "If there is any misbehavior children, you know what you'll spend your recess doing. There is always coal that needs breaking up." Edna smiled smugly at her wit, confused the children had failed to acknowledge her threat.

"Grandma. You're going to get burned if you stand too near the BBQ pit."

Edna looked up startled. She couldn't understand who was interrupting her instruction. She backed away from the hot surface. The children were gone. They must have all gone out to recess. She found a bench at a picnic table and sat down to rest.

# Chapter 42

David struggled with the role playing his grandmother had taken on. He was relieved for the reprieve when the sound of crunching gravel announced Jean's arrival. David urged his grandmother outside to the now darkened sky with the sun almost completely descended from view and the diminished crowd of park visitors. Her eyes twinkled with mischief and her smile flickered like the stars dotting the darkness.

"Are you ready to go home Grandma? Jean's here to take you home."

Grandma seemed puzzled at seeing him standing by her side. She snickered. "Dear, it's right across the street. Don't you think I can walk that far?' Her tone mocked David's apparent lack of knowledge.

"What's right across the street Grandma?" David raised his brows and studied his grandmother.

"The house the district has provided for me as the teacher."

David took her by the arm. "At least let us walk with you. Will that be okay?"

Edna didn't acknowledge him, but trudged along slowly with her cane, Jean supporting most of her weight. At the car, Jean opened the door. David helped Edna in. She didn't resist as they drove her home.

Gloria met them at the door with a blanket. "Let's get you warmed up." She draped the plaid wool wrap around Edna's chilly body.

Grandma swung around. "There is still a lot of work to be done at the school. The place is in need of a coat of paint."

# Chapter 43

"Ready, Edna? David will be here soon." Gloria walked into the room with Edna's coat draped over her arm.

Edna looked up bewildered. "Is it Sunday already?"

"No, dear, he's picking you up to take you to his home for Christmas Eve, remember?"

Flustered, Edna looked around her room, spying a big red bow hanging on her door. "Of course." A fresh wreath graced the wall behind her bed. She inhaled the delicate pine scent. "I just didn't realize it was that time already. I haven't done my shopping yet." Edna shuffled to the night stand and snatched her purse. Christmas had always been her favorite holiday, with all the gaily colored decorations and the sweet aromas of mulled cider and gingerbread houses. Looking at her now gnarled knuckles, she reminisced on all the years she spent the weeks after Thanksgiving making ornaments, to donate to Goodwill, for them to sell during the holiday season. When her children were small, their first clue she was starting preparations for Christmas was the whiff of cinnamon from the freshly baked snickerdoodles. Bernice had always loved pulling out the stool and rolling out the dough for the cut out cookies. Even Larry helped stir the walnut fudge and divinity. Edna ached for those days of long ago. She'd strung the cranberries for the tree and hand painted cards like she had in college, to sell for extra spending money.

Gloria grabbed Edna's stability cane and positioned it in front of her. "Come on, dear, let's get you ready. It's almost three-o-clock. David will be here any minute."

Edna frowned at the sight of the awkward aluminum cane, a constant reminder of her increasing limitations, and shuffled to the living room. "I need my hat. Somebody get my hat." She gazed out at the cloudy gray day which endeavored to dampen her bright mood. A winter chill radiated through the plate glass. The chiming of the doorbell brought a smile and she followed Gloria to the door. Edna shivered from the draft that swept in when the door swung open.

"Hi, Grandma. It looks like you're ready to go." David tugged at her hat, pulling it further down over her ears.

"I haven't had a chance to do any Christmas shopping. Nobody reminded me."

"Don't worry Grandma. You don't need gifts. We're just happy to spend Christmas with you." David helped Edna out the door and into the car. With her cane stowed in the backseat, David clicked on the radio, filling the car with holiday melodies and joyous voices.

Edna smiled. "Where's Nathan? Will he be there?"

"Yes, Grandma, he'll be there. Jean's whole family will be there too. There'll be a lot of people to share Christmas with this year."

The front door to David's house opened to a warmth which instantly took the chill off. Edna gazed in awe looking around the house taking in all the decorations. She didn't understand, Jean had never made such a fuss about their Sunday dinners like this before. "What kind of affair is this? Is it a summer affair or a winter affair?" Edna furrowed her brow as she studied Jean who appeared dressed for church or such. She looked down at her own navy-blue knit slacks.

"It's Christmas, Grandma."

"Oh, my." She blushed. "Christmas already. Someone should have told me. I don't have gifts for anyone."

"Having you here is our gift from you." Jean led her to the living room sofa facing the fresh pine tree which graced the corner of the high ceiling room.

A sharp cold breeze sent a chill across Edna's neck. She strained to turn around to see David opening the door. A crowd of noisy people rushed in with bags and armloads of gifts, along with plates and bowls of food. Never before had she seen such a commotion for a dinner. Confused by all the strangers, Edna's voice broke above the ruckus. "Who are all these people, David?"

"They're Jean's family, Grandma. We always spend Christmas Eve with them. This year you get to join us."

"Oh, I wondered about that." She relaxed into the comfort of the sofa watching the twinkling lights of red, blue, green and gold dance along the branches of the tree.

Jean sat down next to Edna. She looked over her shoulder at the door and called out to the crowd still arriving. "Just put the gifts under the tree. Rachel and Emily are upstairs playing pool, if the boys want to join them." Footsteps trampled up the steps.

Edna sighed at the sight of the tree dominating the living room. "It's quite a big tree isn't it?" Edna strained her neck to look up to the star adorning the top of the evergreen. She inhaled deeply taking in the scent of the pine needles.

"Come on, let's go look at it." Jean took Edna's arm and led her to the tree.

"Oh my, I've never seen anything like it at all. This is just lovely, dear." Edna fingered the assortment of ornaments. Jean removed several and told her where she got each of them. A gold angel they had bought in the German village of Oberammergau. The silver ball was hand painted by an artisan from the Bavarian village of Leavenworth. There was a small stuffed walrus bought in Alaska while visiting an old friend, and a silver heart from Florida, one of the last items Jean's mother had bought for her.

"You have quite a collection don't you? I need to give you some of the ornaments I made."

Jean searched the tree and retrieved a pearl beaded angel and a crocheted and beaded snowflake and handed them to Edna.

Edna's eyes widened and a broad smile appeared. "Gracious, I made these many years ago." She blushed. "I forgot I gave you these." Jean explained to Edna she had well over a hundred ornaments. She remembered where most of them had come from. Edna gazed at the room, soaking in the sights and sounds of the Christmas holiday. Evergreen boughs draped over the upstairs balcony rail overlooking the living room. Small white lights snaked through the greenery with red silk poinsettias poking through here and there. Jean led Edna back to the sofa so she could greet the guests. Edna didn't know this family. There were so many unfamiliar faces. She wondered when she was going to see Nathan.

As the crowd disbursed to other parts of the house, the room quieted except for the commotion from the kitchen. The robust smell of roast beef and garlic floated into the room.

The sharp knocking at the door made Edna flinch. Her heart fluttered at the touch of a hand on her shoulder. She startled, to see the smiling face standing beside her. Her heart leapt as she reached out to take Nathan's hand. "I'm so glad you made it. You're the spitting image of your granddad." This was the first Christmas she had spent with both of her grandsons in over thirty years and her emotions overflowed.

"Merry Christmas, Grandma."

Edna cheeks felt as warm as the glowing lights on the tree. She covered her eyes with her hand to control the waterworks that were coming. Nathan bent down and kissed her cheek.

"You're the last one to arrive again, I see." David laughed as he walked into the room and greeted his brother. "But not too late for dinner."

"I have a knack for timing that just right. It's good to be back home again to spend the holidays with family. It sure beats being with a bunch of soldiers." Nathan walked over to the tree and placed a small red foil wrapped box underneath.

Jean called from the kitchen. "Dinner's ready." A horde of kids stampeded down the stairs. "You kids can get your plates and go to the basement. The table is set and there are several bottles of sparkling cider down there in the fridge."

David reached out to assist his Grandmother. "I guess dinner's ready, Grandma. Let's get you seated." David helped Edna to a chair at a gloriously set table with a lace tablecloth and beautiful china and silver, enough places for ten. A platter of roast beef directed attention to the center of the table.

"Do you recognize your silver, Grandma?" David handed her one of the forks from a place setting.

"What is this?" She turned it over in her fingers.

"We thought it would be nice to have your beautiful silver out when you shared Christmas with us."

She thought about it for a moment. Her face lit up. "Is this my old silver or the new silver I bought?" She had given both sets to

David to keep for her. She guessed the silver would remain with him as she no longer had any use for it. Seated, Edna watched all the unfamiliar children and adults pile food on their plates, some scattering to find places to sit away from the table which couldn't hold the crowd of well over twenty.

"Can I get you some roast, Grandma?" David grabbed a plate and edged into the crowd of family members.

Edna sat at the end of the oval table and studied the plates and bowls brimming with all the makings of a real holiday feast. When her plate was set before her, she beamed at the piled-high plate, noticing all her favorites, including mashed potatoes almost swimming in gravy, just the way she liked them. Salad and vegetables sat on the other side. Her stomach gurgled and she laughed in embarrassment. She beamed at being the center of attention as everyone gathered around the table and talked with her, eager to hear her stories. Edna found an unexpected audience in one of David's sisters-in-law whom she learned was a second grade teacher. "I used to be an elementary teacher, too. I can still remember when I made the decision to teach. I taught for twenty-eight years."

"I've been teaching elementary school for nearly twenty years myself. I imagine children and teaching are a lot different these days."

Edna nodded. "When I first got my teaching certificate, married women weren't allowed to teach, only to substitute. But during the war there was a shortage of teachers, with all the men off fighting. I paid one dollar for an emergency permit that allowed me to teach until the war was over."

The sister-in-law laughed when Edna told her she had earned $1,500 for the nine-month contract. Jean's sister-in-law told Edna she had brought a pumpkin pie for dessert.

Edna straightened herself. "I don't much care for pumpkin pie. I never much liked nutmeg, though Mother used it all the time. I much prefer the old-fashioned fruitcakes filled with lots of fruits and liquors like Mother made when I was a child. She started preparing them in October to allow them to ripen."

A wrinkle formed on her forehead recalling earlier Christmases. "I always felt like Christmas was an obligation with Larry and his girls, but they were the only family I had. I was always taught Christmas is a time for family." Edna paused as the events of the past month jumbled in her mind. "I guess they really were my family all along." Her smile dazzled like the silver fork she held.

"Alicia and Lacey are your blood relations. But family can be anyone who cares about you and those you love. Now you can consider Jean's family part of your family too." David reached over and took Edna's hand. "How does that sound?"

Edna smiled. "Barbara always told me, families are created in the heart."

Everyone spilled into the living room. Adults sat in chairs carried in from the dining room. The children gathered around on the floor, each with a pile of gifts to open. Edna sat on the sofa facing the tree, a sparkling cider in hand, delighting in watching the children rip open their brightly wrapped presents. Several of the children smiled at her. She smiled coyly back as she turned and whispered to David, seated next to her. "They act like they don't know me, but I recognize some of them, especially those two boys. They were in my third-grade class when I taught in Monahan. I still have all the cards all the children made me that year for Christmas."

David smiled, then walked over to the tree and returned with his arms full of gifts.

"Oh, my." Edna brought her hands to her face, beaming at the sight of the gifts David piled in front of her. "How thoughtful you and Nathan are." Edna placed her cider on the end table and took the first of several gifts, ripping open the paper, revealing a lovely bottle of pink body lotion. Edna looked around the room. Everyone had stopped opening gifts and sat watching her. Feeling flattered, Edna tore open a flat box wrapped in green paper with red poinsettias. She giggled seeing the plastic plate of peanut butter cookies.

"I made those for you. Chewy, not crunchy, just like you prefer." Emily smiled from across the room.

Edna unwrapped a gold foil wrapped shoe box. She sighed deeply and held up a white knit scarf from Rachel. She fingered the delicate yarn, and ran it across her cheek. "This is like the scarves I used to knit. I also did a lot of crocheting, yokes for corset slips, doilies, and edges for handkerchiefs."

"I'm glad you like it, Grandma. I learned to knit after you told me how your mother taught you to knit."

Ripping open her last package, Edna gazed upon the framed photo of Lacey, clutching it to her chest. "To think, my great-granddaughter could have died without me knowing she was my family. It's a miracle she's still here, and in my life." She looked around the room at the large group of strangers all still watching her. "These are such wonderful gifts. Thank you so much."

"Just a minute, Grandma. There's still one gift left under the tree for you." Nathan walked over to the tree and picked up the red foil box. "This one is from all your grandchildren."

Still fingering the scarf around her neck, Edna smiled at the sight of the small red box which he placed in her hand. "All of them?"

"Open it." Everyone in the room quieted as their attention turned toward her.

Edna studied the box, carefully removing the adhesive bow from the top and setting it next to her on the sofa. Lifting off the top of the box, she saw a lovely ring with two rows of diamonds and a knot design wrapping around the band with six other gemstones sparkling and rimmed in gold.

Nathan squatted next to his grandmother and lifted the sterling silver ring from the box. He held it out for everyone to see while he explained what the stones represented. "This is a family tree ring."

"Look at all these diamonds. I am sure this cost way too much for you." Edna looked up at Nathan.

"No, Grandma. They aren't diamonds, only cubic zirconia and crystals. Each crystal represents the birthstone of each of your children, and grandchildren."

"Gracious." Edna brought her hands to her cheeks. "There's a ruby for Bernice's birthday in July, the aquamarine for Larry, and two diamonds for you and your brother for April. I don't know these other stones." She brought the ring close and bent over it, turning it over in her fingers. "Thank you so much Nathan."

Nathan smiled as he took her hand and carefully slid the ring onto the finger of her right hand, explaining the other crystals were Alicia's and Lorraine's birthstones. "I thought you would like them on your grandmother's ring. We can add your great-grandchildren too if you like."

Edna knit her brow in contemplation. "Alicia is my blood, my family, and Lorraine saved Lacey's life."

"That's right, Grandma. That makes her family too, don't you think?"

Edna sat erect. "I should think so." She held her hand out and beamed at the stones. "This is so beautiful. I don't recall getting jewelry with precious stones since Jacob presented me with my engagement ring." Edna's eyes moistened as she stared down at the beautiful symbol of love which had been placed on her finger.

Suddenly, Edna was taken by the scent of his cologne. Jacob had not worn cologne for her previously. It was a nice change of pace from the smell of a pub which usually accompanied Jacob, or worse, the faded scent of another woman's perfume. She noticed the champagne glass next to her on the table and frowned. She knew his game well. He was intending to get her to drink too much so he could have his way with her. This time, she wouldn't fall for it. He liked to put her on the spot in front of any group they were with. In order not to break up the fun or cause a scene, she smiled sweetly and went along with him, although she fumed inside. "It's warm in here." She wiped her hand across her forehead, wet from the hours of dancing. Her dance card had been quite full. She looked around the room. Dehoney's was a very busy place tonight. "I need to freshen up." She sensed all eyes in the dance hall were studying her. They could see she was angry and she didn't want to make a scene. So she calmed herself and excused herself to pin back her braids in the restroom.

Returning just minutes later, Edna couldn't believe her eyes. "What's going on here?" Another woman was sitting in her spot talking with Jacob. Her shoulders tensed as she strutted toward the table. Edna knew the game. She wasn't proud of it, but she'd enjoyed playing the game herself. She caught the eye of the offender with her gaze as she sauntered back to her seat. Standing over the woman, Edna stared at the floozy. "Excuse me, this is my seat." She couldn't understand how Jacob could be attracted to that other woman. She was much too old for him, nearly middle-aged.

"Is she another one of your many flirtations?" Edna stood hands on hips.

Jacob said nothing and offered no excuse.

Edna could tell his mind was involved with something. She feared what it might be. She looked down at her ring finger. Suddenly self-conscious, her face warmed, aware all eyes in the room were on her. She looked up and forced a smile to the large group of people who looked at her with puzzled eyes. She turned to her handsome beau. Shocked, she heard herself mutter. "Yes, my dear, I forgive you, and I will marry you."

He squatted next to her and held her hand. "Merry Christmas, Grandma."

# Chapter 44

Gloria led Nathan down the hall to his grandmother's room. The smell of age and its related problems assaulted him. Fighting the impulse to turn and walk out, Nathan choked back his stomach's urge to revolt. Walking toward her bedside he gazed at her pale expressionless face. If it weren't for the short shallow breaths that struggled and snorted with each exhale, Nathan would have thought he was too late.

Gloria stood next to him with a reassuring arm on his shoulder. "She's been sleeping a lot these past few days."

Nathan turned to Gloria. "Is that a good thing?"

"At her age, it's pretty typical, but she's not eating either. Based on the past few weeks, I'm glad you're here and able to visit with her before it's too late. Your grandmother will be happy to see you." Gloria patted his shoulder. "This is all pretty new to you, isn't it?"

He looked back at his grandmother and shuddered, still struggling with the rising uneasiness in his stomach. "I've never dealt with anything like this before." He wondered how David had managed to stay sane for the past few years, juggling work and Grandma's affairs. He finally fully understood the commitment which had been made and the patience and time his brother had dedicated to help make Grandma's last years of life as pleasant as possible. He stepped closer. Reaching out impulsively, he took her skeletal hand, startled by the chill of it. She stirred in bed, her eyelids fluttering.

Gloria reached across and stroked Edna's thin straggly hair. "Look who's here, dear."

Her eyes opened, only a sliver, relaying no hint of recognition.

Overwhelmed with a sense of helplessness, Nathan looked to Gloria for direction. "Are you sure she's awake?"

"Give her a few minutes, she'll recognize you." Gloria turned to leave. "Let me know if you need anything. I'll be here."

Unsure what he should do Nathan loosened his grip, exhaling loudly he released his jumbled thoughts.

Edna turned her head, her blank eyes staring his direction. "David?"

Her voice strained just above a whisper. Nathan bent over her and stroked her hair as Gloria had done. "No, Grandma, it's Nathan." Reluctantly, he again took her hand in his. "How are you doing today?" He forced a smile hoping she could read that, instead of the nervousness which his shaky hand expressed. It was an uncomfortable situation and he was unprepared to make idle chatter.

A tired smile crossed Grandma's face. "Nathan, is that you?" Her grip tightened. She clutched at the sleeve of his gray sweatshirt. "I didn't recognize you without your uniform." Her hoarse chuckle caught Nathan off guard. She was barely alive but her wit was still sharp.

Nathan relaxed. Perhaps the visit wouldn't be too bad after all. He was glad he came. Though well-intentioned, he hadn't visited as often as he should have since he moved back.

"I must be dying."

Her comment raised his eyebrows and he leaned in to study her face. "Why do you say that, Grandma?"

"You never come to see me. They must have told you I was dying."

Nathan watched for an indication his grandmother was being facetious, but her face was as solemn as her words.

"No, Grandma. You're not dying." He offered a self-conscious chuckle in a feeble attempt to make his words upbeat and convincing. "It's not easy for me to get away from the base that's all." He reached for a water pitcher and glass on the bedside table and poured a little of the thickened water. He grimaced at the appearance of the clear gelatin consistency before realizing it was the only type of fluid she could swallow without difficulty. "Here Grandma, would you like some water?" Adjusting the pillows behind her, and supporting the weight of her shoulders, he assisted her to a seated position. Then, holding the plastic glass, Grandma sipped slowly from the straw. He smiled at his small success until

Grandma began to gag. She coughed fitfully. Alarmed, Nathan called for Gloria.

Gloria came running. "It's okay, dear." She rubbed Edna's back between the shoulder blades until the coughing slowed to a minor irritant.

Nathan's heart beat slowed to normal. "Sorry. I guess I'm not too good at this."

"Don't worry, you'll feel more comfortable in time." Gloria reassured him.

With her breathing labored and the sound of gurgling still in her chest, Edna flopped back on the bed. Nathan reshuffled the position of the pillows behind his grandmother's head and shoulders. "How's that?"

She lay expressionless. Nathan shifted his weight uncomfortably, uncertain what to do next. Looking around the room, he noticed her cheery pictures and vases of silk flower arrangements sitting on her dresser and small table. Framed photos clustered atop the four drawer chest across the room. Nathan picked up the photo of the young woman he guessed was Bernice. A black and white picture of his father, Larry, stood next to it. Nathan studied them carefully. His Aunt Bernice had been a beautiful young woman, most likely favoring Edna when she was young. Nathan chose a more dated photo of another soldier long ago. He grinned. There was no doubt Larry took after his own father, Jacob. One more photo sat on the dresser, the color photo of him he had given her for her birthday. His resemblance to his father and granddad was obvious. He couldn't keep from smiling as he recalled his first meeting with his grandmother at the airport. He understood how the confused mind of an aging woman could deceive her. Though he and David were twins, there was no doubt he favored his grandfather's side. Heaving a sigh, he realized how much he had missed and how little time remained to learn about her.

"Nathan?" Edna's weak voice startled him back to his purpose. "Are you still here?"

He walked over to her bed side. "I'm here, Grandma. I was just looking at your room. David did a nice job fixing it up for you."

"Yes, David is such a dear. He's done so much for me. Did

you see my violets? I don't know where David put my violets."

Nathan glanced around and spied several large African violets in plastic trays on the window sill. "They're on the window sill, Grandma. Do you want me to water them?"

"Are they dry?" Grandma strained to look over her shoulder.

Nathan picked them up and fingered the dirt. "They seem like they need watering." He carried the plants into the bathroom.

"Don't get them wet."

Nathan stopped in his tracks. "They're dry, Grandma. I thought you wanted me to water them." Confused, he returned with the two plants in his hand. Edna's hand quivered and she reached for them. Nathan bent over and lowered the pots.

She fingered the dirt. "They need to be watered from the roots. Fill the trays with water and set the plant back inside. How do you think I've kept them alive for so many years?"

Nathan shook his head. Here she was on her death bed, and still concerned about her plants. David had said she loved plants and gardening. He found the whole experience ironic. He could see how David thought she was still such a sharp woman, even as her mind deteriorated. He did as he was told, and returned the plants to the window sill. Nathan looked down at his Grandmother's pale gaunt figure still struggling to find a rhythm with her breaths. "You look tired Grandma."

Her chest rose and fell in short rapid bursts, but for the first time since he had arrived he noticed a sparkle in her eyes. Bending over, he stroked her forehead once more. She beamed. He took another look around. Somehow in spite of what should have been a pleasant room, a gloom hung over it. It was just a matter of time, possibly a very short time, and the shadow of death would move in. With a knot in his stomach, Nathan bent over and kissed his grandmother's forehead as her eyelids drooped. "I'll be back again soon."

Her breathing slowed and quieted.

His jittery hands calmed and he breathed easier. Nathan walked out and departed for the base.

# Chapter 45

Grandma's health was deteriorating. She drank so little Carl diagnosed her with dehydration and had called an ambulance. David had sensed it coming over the past week, and Nathan had shared his concerns about her sunken eyes and confusion after his last visit. David struggled with his tasks at work, finding it difficult to concentrate on the graphs and data that lay before him. His brain refused to function as he reviewed the calculations. He glanced at his watch again. Nathan said he could meet David at the hospital around five. David either wished the time would fly by or his brain would kick in so he could concentrate on his work. He finally managed to push his worry aside and complete his report. With a sense of accomplishment, he phoned Jean to let her know he was heading for the hospital.

Pulling into the hospital parking garage, David grabbed his portfolio of legal documents. He found the lobby relatively quiet during the dinner hour and settled into a sofa that faced the main entrance. His stomach growled. He hadn't eaten anything except a small pre-made sandwich and box drink on the plane, during the flight test. He reread the brochure he had picked up earlier, regarding living wills and durable power of attorney, until Nathan walked over and joined him. "Let's grab a quick bite in the cafeteria before we go to see Grandma. I need to get some food in me while you look at something." David handed a folder to Nathan.

"What's this?"

"Grandma's directives to her physician. It certainly isn't the most clearly understood form I've ever seen." David grabbed a ham sandwich and coffee and they took a seat. He studied Nathan's face as Nathan reviewed the legal documents thrust on him. "Well?" David put his elbows on the table rubbing his temples with his palms. "I wish these damn things were more clearly stated than a standard box simply being checked. I don't know what Grandma intended. This whole thing is taking a toll on me." David regarded Nathan. "What do you think now that you've read it?"

"I can't make any sense out of all this legalese." Nathan scratched his chin. "The directives indicate if she is diagnosed with a terminal condition, she does not wish to be kept alive with life sustaining procedures which would offer no hope of recovery."

"If old age isn't terminal with no hope of recovery, I don't know what is. Is a feeding tube life sustaining? It would be the only means of keeping her alive at this point. Her life would be prolonged, and she would recover, but to what degree?" David struggled to interpret his grandmother's intentions. "Grandma's not eating enough to stay alive. I'm going to talk to her doctor about a feeding tube." David looked at Nathan to see his reaction.

"What's involved in putting in a tube? I don't think I would want one. Will it hurt her to put it in?"

David shook his head. "I don't know. The doctor mentioned it the last time he saw her." He rubbed the back of his neck and paused. "I do know she can't keep going like she's been. You've seen her recently. Don't you agree? We have only two choices. Either force feed her, or let her fade away naturally."

Nathan stood up, paced in front of the table a bit, then looked at his watch. "It's almost time for our appointment. Let's go talk to her doctor. I'll support whatever you think she would want."

David eyed him, resisting the urge to shout he didn't want to be the sole decision maker or play God. Instead, he took a deep breath. "It's time to make some tough decisions, and I don't want to make them alone." His ability to handle this responsibility was being tested. They took the elevator to the third floor. The disinfectant smell of the hospital by now familiar, still made him flinch when he exited the elevator. They walked down the hall to Dr. Bonner's office and knocked on the open door. Dr. Bonner waved them inside.

Dr. Bonner put his pen down and leaned back in his chair. "I'm glad you came." He extended his hand to Nathan and introduced himself before greeting David. "I'll get right to the point. If your grandmother doesn't receive a feeding tube, or start eating on her own, she'll most likely die within the week."

Feeling as if he'd been punched, David's words popped out without hesitation. "We have to do something." He paused. "Don't we?" David looked to Dr. Bonner. "What if she were your mother?"

"The feeding tube can be uncomfortable. There's always the possibility it will be pulled out. Knowing how stubborn your grandmother is, that is a distinct possibility. The alternative is just letting her pass on naturally."

David looked directly at the doctor. "You're saying let her starve to death. I don't think I could do that."

"It really is a very humane and natural way to allow someone to pass on. After the first two or three days, especially in her already deteriorated condition, her body will stop craving nourishment. We will continue to administer fluids. But as her system shuts down, the rest of the body begins to shut down, including the kidneys. The need for fluids decreases dramatically. There's no pain or suffering. She won't even be aware of her weakening state." The doctor walked around to the side of his desk and stood closer to Nathan and David. "Take a little while and think about it. Let me know what you decide. Soon."

They thanked the doctor and turned to leave. At the door, David turned back to the doctor. "What about discharging her? She's been staying at an adult care home, owned by a retired geriatric doctor, Carl Hoffmann. Do you think her need for fluids could be met in a home environment?"

"Of course. Hospice care providers are as capable as we are of administering fluids as desired. The last few days, fluids may actually increase nausea, vomiting, and diarrhea. Dr. Hoffmann may prefer swabbing her mouth with a damp sponge. This will help keep Edna comfortable at the very end of life. Dry mouth is what causes most people to feel uncomfortable and IV fluids don't relieve the experience of a dry mouth as well as gentle moist swabbing does."

David's mind raced as he mentally tossed dice in his head, attempting to achieve the right roll for his grandmother's fate, yet still uncertain of what that roll might be.

Grandma was in the bed farthest from the door. David pulled the tan curtain separating the beds open as he passed the bed table and blue chair. She lay propped up in bed staring wide eyed into space. This had become fairly common lately.

"Hi, Grandma, how are you doing today?" David and Nathan exchanged glances upon seeing how pathetic she looked. David walked over to the window allowing some sunlight to find its way into the depressing room.

Grandma turned her head toward the light. "I saw Mother again today."

"What did she want?" David turned to look at his grandmother.

"She took me to visit Larry and Bernice, only it was hard to understand."

"What's that, Grandma? What was hard to understand?"

"Well, it's just that I thought Larry and Bernice were dead."

David struggled to comprehend how his grandmother's mind was functioning. Her dreams or hallucinations, whatever they were, were becoming more frequent. Some of her statements made David think she was rational, though confused. But most of the time she seemed to be in her own place and time.

"We went to the 4-H fair. I watched Larry take care of the pig he got from the Future Farmers of America, he was showing it. Bernice won a blue ribbon for her bread."

"That's great, Grandma. I bet you're proud of your children."

David scooted a chair over and joined Nathan by Grandma's bedside. Nathan was stroking her forehead watching her labored breathing. Her wrinkled skin was almost translucent and her veins and bones showed through the ghostlike tissue. David picked up her frail hand and spoke softly. "Grandma, since you haven't been eating enough to stay alive we may need to put in a feeding tube."

"What's that? I don't want any tubes in me. I've had enough tubes in me." Her words were clear and abrupt. "What will happen if I don't get it?"

David's eyes widened. He hadn't heard her speak this coherently in many weeks. Feeling some relief, he swallowed hard and took in a deep calming breath before continuing. "If you don't get one, you'll die."

Her eyes focused directly on him. She didn't hesitate. "Well now, that would be okay with me."

Edna's words and calm delivery shocked David. He cocked his head and studied his grandmother's aged face. There was only one way he could interpret her words. He believed, at that moment, his grandmother was in as competent a state of mind as she had been in months. Her statement could not be taken lightly. Grandma was ready to join the rest of her family who had preceded her. He looked across the bed at Nathan for assurance.

"Grandma, do you understand what David said?" Nathan took her other hand and held it in his. Grandma shifted her gaze to Nathan.

"I'll be just fine." She closed her eyes. Within minutes she was snoring faintly, her mouth curled up in a wry smile.

A weight lifted, David wondered if she was off with her mother again somewhere. He recalled reading about death with dignity, having the patient's wishes honored. David thought about what Grandma had said and about Dr. Bonner's reassurance, there would be no pain or suffering. In the end, it was not his decision to make. It didn't matter if he agreed or not. Nathan and David walked quietly out of the room arranging to meet later in the evening to gather the family together, for possibly one last time. They stopped by the nurse station to relay a message for Dr. Bonner to make arrangements to have his grandmother discharged without a feeding tube.

# Chapter 46

Edna lay in bed; the room void of any color or sense of cheerfulness. Boredom blanketed her like a heavy veil. She missed David and Nathan. She didn't want to die. She thought about it a lot. She didn't wish to long for death, but sighed with an acceptance and willingness to move on to the next world. Mother understood, as she visited more frequently than she used to. Mother wanted Edna to go with her, but Edna puzzled over where exactly that was. Her mother kept insisting it was peaceful and there were meadows of flowers for her to stroll through.

"Come, dear, come with me. We'll visit Larry and Bernice and your father, too."

Edna looked up at her mother smiling. "Where are we going?" Edna wanted to know, but Mother wouldn't answer. Instead Edna followed her out to the old farm Jacob and she owned when the children were young. Edna watched the wheat fields parting. Something was moving through them. She recognized the car. It was their jade green Ford. The kids didn't think she could see them. She wanted to scold them but it was hard to stay mad.

"Don't be upset, Mother" Larry faced her boldly. "Bea wanted me to teach her how to drive."

She found herself laughing instead. She stood and watched as Larry and Bernice wove the car back through the wheat fields.

"You can stay here and be happy with your children again," Mother kept insisting. "Stay and watch Bernice in the garden. We can make zucchini bread for the bazaar next week."

A voice called from across the dusty air of the wheat fields. She closed her eyes struggling to hear the voice.

"Mrs. Pearson, are you okay?"

Edna opened her eyes. The golden stalks blowing in the wind were fading. She searched for her mother. "Where's Mother?" She was gone. In her place was a younger woman wearing blue hospital garb.

"I'm sorry, Mrs. Pearson, I don't understand. There's no one here visiting you right now. Your grandsons were by earlier."

The voice from the wheat field was no longer her mother's. "Never mind." The pain deepened. Edna knew her mother had left again. Mother had said she could stay with her and her children. Edna strained to lift her head and look around, but Mother was gone, and she was back in the dreary hospital room.

"Someone will be in shortly to take care of you." The woman in blue rushed out. Edna became aware of a wet, uncomfortable situation. Disgusted with herself and her lack of control, she burned with anger and shame. The door opened. Edna was incensed with the realization a male nurse was coming to clean her. How humiliating, to be like a newborn with no control, and no dignity.

"Where's David? Where's my grandson?" Edna brushed away the tears with her hand.

"Mrs. Pearson, stop moving. You're making it worse. You'll be cleaned up in no time."

Ninety-six years of independence, reduced to this stage. This was not the way a person was supposed to live. There was a knock at the door. The nurse responded to the caller to wait for a few minutes.

When the door opened and the nurse departed, David poked his head in the door and greeted her.

Aware of the mist of Lysol melding with the odor of her mishap, Edna reddened as she turned and reached out for David. "Thank God you're here."

"It's okay, Grandma. Don't cry. You're not having a good day are you?"

David's wrinkled nose and frown told Edna he was aware of the situation.

"I want to go home. I don't like it here. I've had enough." Edna struggled to free herself of the confines of the fresh bedding, now tightly tucked in, restricting her movement.

"I've spoken to your doctor. Do you think you can eat something?"

"Oh, you." Edna pouted. "You're just like Jacob, always telling me what I can or can't do." David didn't understand. She had no desire nor hunger for food or water. Besides, she was never one to like being told what to do. Jacob had always tried to dominate her. "I just want a glass of water."

David handed her the glass by her bed. She tasted the syrupy fluid.

"This isn't water." She pursed her lips, handing the glass back.

"It *is* water, Grandma. You know you can't swallow liquids without almost choking. That's why the doctor says we have to add thickener to anything you drink."

"I don't like it. It tastes awful."

"Grandma, there is no taste to it at all. It's just your imagination."

What did David know? Edna fumed. She didn't see him drinking it.

The door creaked open a little further and a small crowd piled into Edna's room which was already cramped with machines and tables. Nathan and the rest of her family were all there to see her.

"Hi, Grandma." The voices melded.

Edna looked around. "Where are Alicia and Lacey? How come they're not here?"

"Alicia lives too far away to make it right now. She wants you to know she's thinking of you."

Edna wished she could see her great granddaughter again. She longed for just one more chance to make peace in person for all the tension between her and Alicia. She looked down at the ring finger on her left hand. "David. You see my wedding ring?

"It's very nice Grandma."

"It's old. From 1922. I want Lacey to have it when I'm gone. It should go to her."

David nodded. "I'll make sure she gets it. It's a wonderful gesture of peace. It's strange how Lacey's illness has brought healing to the family."

With everyone at the hospital at the same time Edna knew what it meant. They thought she was going to die. David must have told them she wasn't eating and didn't want to prolong her life. She studied the forced smiles staring down at her, uneasy in what to say. Tears welled up in the corner of her eyes. "I love all of you. You are my family."

The nurse poked her head in and smiled at the group, reminding them the evening was getting late, and to be aware of the time. The lateness didn't matter to Edna. The people who were gathered in her room were all that mattered. She wanted their visit to last as long as possible so she wouldn't have to face the quiet starkness of the room in isolation again. But their visit couldn't last forever and her eyelids were getting heavy.

Edna woke early, just as the sun was starting to poke through the window blinds. It had been a fitful night, but she smirked realizing she had fooled everyone. She was still around to face another day. The doctor came in with the good news. She was strong enough to leave the hospital. David came soon after and took her back to Carl and Gloria's. Edna ached for her own house, but had accepted her small room at their place was as close to home as she was going to see. She immediately sank into the boredom of her standard routine. She wasn't getting around much anymore, and her Sunday visits to David's had ceased. Her bed and wheelchair were where she would be spending her remaining days. The television, on all the time, was only a distraction. Edna saw only blurry images and heard only muddled sounds. She was unable to concentrate and held no interest in the news which once enticed her. A general weakness overcame her and she spent most of her days sleeping. Eating would probably help her strength, but her stomach and her mind had stopped craving food.

# Chapter 47

David didn't expect Grandma to leave the hospital, but Grandma didn't live to be ninety-six by being weak. She'd spent her entire life fighting for what she believed, and spent the last few years, in particular, contradicting everything and everyone, especially David. Determined to fight the doctor's prognosis, she wasn't about to stop now.

After her release back to Carl and Gloria's, David received urgent calls twice from Gloria that Edna was dying. Twice, David rushed to Grandma's side. Still, she lingered, continuing to eat just enough to hang on as the days turned into a week and beyond. Every day after work, David stopped in to see her, each day uncertain what he would face. Sometimes he found her alert and sensible, other times she was entirely lost, only babbling a string of guttural sounds with random words not tied to any coherent thought. His nerves were like exposed wires, ready to spark at any time from his emotional roller coaster of having to face Edna's imminent death.

As the days went by, it was obvious they were only playing a game of Russian roulette against time. The only unknown was how long she could hang on. After almost a year of enjoying Edna's company and enchanting stories every Sunday afternoon, it was heartbreaking to watch her lose her will to go on. Grandma had very little cognitive quality left and David sensed she knew her mind had surrendered to advancing age. The ultimate end which everyone faces, was near for his grandmother. David called Nathan to share his concern. The sudden emptiness he felt surprised him, as he faced the prospect of his grandmother no longer being an integral part of his life.

It was her second Sunday back home when Gloria called. "Edna is unusually disoriented and agitated. She hasn't taken any liquids for the past two days. We've only been able to keep her comfortable with the moistened swabs. I think you should come soon. I'll call Nathan for you."

David and Jean rushed out the door. David focused on his breathing, fighting back the burning sensation behind his eyes. His brain clouded with a sense of foreboding as they drove. "Maybe I should have agreed to the feeding tube." David poured his guilt out to Jean.

Jean glanced across and rubbed his shoulder as he drove. "You made the right choice for her. But that doesn't make it any easier."

His heart pounded fast and frantic by the time he pulled his car into the driveway at Gloria and Carl's house. He took one last deep breath, and with resignation, climbed out and walked to the front door. He knocked twice before opening the door and walking in. An unfamiliar faint odor greeted David. He gulped in fresh air and courage before heading to his grandmother's room. Gazing down at her body, ravaged by time, something inside David's throat lurched. Unsure of the basis for the overpowering urge, David rushed to the window, pulled back the curtains, and flung the window open. The cool late afternoon air brought welcome relief. The light added a sense of life to the aura of death in the room.

"Hi, Grandma, it's David." He inched closer, with Jean on his arm. He gazed upon his grandmother's pallid face, not sure if she were aware of him. Leaning in, he studied the dark sunken eyes that looked as if she were staring straight through him. He reached out for her bony arm and patted it. The chill of her flesh forced him to look one more time. He pressed his finger tips to her wrist. Cool relief washed over him at the realization her heart was still beating and she was still breathing. "It's okay Grandma, I'm here. How are you doing?"

"Are you there? Is that you ... ?" She quivered all over, her gaze fixed and emotionless.

David and Jean sat by her side stroking her arm and her hair, soothing her like a frightened child. Suddenly, she shifted and yanked at her clothes, struggling to throw the blankets off and tearing away at her bed clothes.

"Help me Jean. Why is she acting this way?" Panicked, David tried his best to calm her, patting her shoulder. "It's okay, Grandma. Are you too hot? Do you want some water or anything?" David went cold. He shot a glance to Jean. He'd never experienced anything like this. His neck tingled from fear as if he had seen a ghost, not just the pale skeleton of the woman he had grown to love, so much.

"She doesn't know where she is, dear. She's frightened. Keep talking to her to calm her down. Right now you are the only familiar thing she has." Jean helped restrain Grandma with a gentle pressure on her shoulder and a gentle stroking of her hair.

David's heart regained its normal pattern, his neck muscles relaxed, thankful Jean had an understanding of his grandmother's bizarre behavior. Her reading about Alzheimer's patients and the elderly had prepared her for this. Gripped in helplessness, he wanted to flee, to be released of the inevitability of what he predicted would follow shortly. But he knew his place was by her side. David and Jean sat by her bedside for the next few hours, reluctant to leave as long as she was awake and responding on some level. Their vigil was interrupted by a soft knock on the open door. Nathan started to step inside. David motioned with his head toward the hallway. He met Nathan outside the door with an update on their grandmother's state.

The increased activity in the room made Grandma stir and she became aware of their presence. She lay quiet, listening to her grandsons' recount stories of the times they shared with her.

As Edna began to fade off again, Nathan offered a reprieve. "You've probably been here quite a while. Why don't you take a break?"

Nathan's words were a welcome invitation. David needed to get out of the house, away from the smell of salty perspiration, away from the musty bedding, and stagnant air, away from the ghostlike figure who was once his spunky grandmother. A quick break would be nice in spite of his churning stomach and lack of appetite. David and Jean nodded their goodbye to Nathan, and escaped outside to soak in the fresh air.

After a quick stop for a deli sandwich and a cold drink, they returned to Edna's bedside again. "How is she?"

Nathan stood as they entered. "In and out."

David stared at her for a few moments unsure what he should do next. She turned, smiled, reached out for David's hand, and mumbled some faint words, then, dozed off. Nathan and David realized from past experience that as bleak as things looked, she could still linger for days. Satisfied, and relieved she was peacefully asleep, they said their goodbyes and departed for home.

# Chapter 48

Lying in bed, a shroud of loneliness veiled Edna. Darkness cloaked her room except for the dim stream of light which spilled in from the hallway. She dreaded the darkness. The specter of solitude haunted her nights as dementia induced ghosts and shadows of reality drifted in and out of her weakened mind. David had told her she wasn't crazy, just confused. The doctor had warned her the Alzheimer's would only get worse. She sighed as she looked up at the ceiling, half expecting to see her mother. She had seen her with increasing frequency lately. Edna tried to reminisce on her life, but only fleeting thoughts danced across her mind. She hummed a melody from her long ago past attempting to stay in touch with reality. Salty tears tracked down her cheek. She blocked out the vague surroundings and allowed her mind to dwell on the happy memories of her loved ones. Familiar faces flashed like strobe lights through her mind which had long outlived its useful life. Now, at ninety-six, her body was catching up as her passing days continued to eat away like moths on the fabric of her life.

Her once acute vision that delighted in the beauty of nature and the intricacy of her needlepoint and crafts, now narrowed like a dark tunnel with only blurry images cavorting in and out of its constricted scope. She sensed the presence of people surrounding her. Her heart skipped knowing loved ones gathered for her. She shifted in bed, attempting to sit. Garbled tones spilled from moving lips, Edna struggled to decipher them. The caring tones were familiar, but their names had slipped from her mind like so many of her memories. A soft touch of lips brushed against her cheek. She reached out into the shadows and held a warm hand, her sole connection to reality. She knew the hand and she stroked it. She fixed her attention on the figure. "I'm so glad you came to see me." Her garbled words struggled to emerge past her droopy lips and thickened tongue. Her breathing became shallow. She allowed herself to relax as her visitors held her hands warming them and stroking her uncombed hair. She was at peace.

All the prayers of her last years had been answered by the love she had shared with David and Nathan. She had made peace with Alicia and Lorraine and had come to know Rachel and Emily as well as Lacey. She fumbled with the fingers on her right hand feeling the ring which all of her grandchildren had given her for Christmas. She had lived to experience the love of family, a love that she thought she would never truly know. She had been given a second chance to make peace with each of them. She willed her lips to move and words to come. She needed to tell her visitors she knew they were there and she loved and appreciated them, but she sensed the coordination of her thoughts and words were not in sync. She reached out and grasped the warm hand, attempting to focus and manage one last smile toward those she loved. Surrendering, she closed her eyes in defeat. She wiped her damp cheek with her nightgown sleeve. She was tired. It was time. Contentment cocooned her as she lay still and listened to the slow faint pounding in her chest. Tiredness overtook her and she drifted off.

# Chapter 49

Minutes after Jean and David arrived home the phone rang. An uneasy feeling swept over him. A lump formed in his throat. He swallowed. His chest tightened as he stared at the phone for a beat before picking it up.

"Edna passed away a few minutes ago." Gloria's compassion carried across the line.

The words stung. "Is there anything you need me to do?" David sat down at the dining room table, already with a pen and a note pad in hand. His look and actions drew Jean to his side.

"No. I've already called the funeral home, they'll pick up her body tonight. You can call them tomorrow to coordinate the rest of the arrangements. They'll be expecting your call. I told them she probably was going to be buried in eastern Washington, not locally."

David scribbled the name and phone number of the funeral home on the pad. He thanked Gloria, relieved that the immediate need had been met. A pang of guilt struck him as he returned the phone to the receiver and faced Jean. Grandma had skirted death for weeks, possibly months. Everyone knew her time was looming. Nonetheless, the finality was not easy to face. It had been just a half hour or so since David and Nathan left Grandma's bedside. Her last words to them were incoherent. Her rambling had been increasing over the past few days. Yet, David remembered her final action. When he bent down to kiss her goodbye on the cheek, she gripped his hand and looked intently into his eyes. He searched for a sign of recognition. She had smiled. He sensed for that brief moment she knew him again, as her eyes sparkled from her pained thin face. The thought comforted him. "We should have stayed 'til the end." David looked over at Jean, fighting an emotion that was new to him.

"It wouldn't have mattered." Jean's voice cracked. "We've visited every night since she left the hospital. You know how long she lingered. There's no way we could have known it would be tonight."

"You're right. Besides, knowing Grandma, she hung on until she'd seen Nathan and me one last time, and she hung on until we left, before she allowed herself to drift away." David recognized she had planned the timing of her last moments as much as she could manage. It was all according to her design and her being in control, as so much of her life had been. She had lived independently for so many years and liked things her way. It was fitting and proper her final moments were according to her wishes.

The small white tent did little to break the icy chill of the winter wind as the brushed stainless steel casket was lowered into the hard snow covered ground, alongside Jacob and Bernice. All of Edna's remaining family were there to pay their respects and say their goodbyes. Nathan joined David, Jean, and their daughters. Lorraine had gathered along with Alicia and Lacey. Only Kora-Lee was absent. The crisp air chilled David on the outside but he was warmed inside as he looked out at the bare trees and early budding flowers surrounding Edna's plot. He sighed remembering how badly Grandma had wanted Larry's remains to be buried with the Pearson family and how his cremation almost severed all ties with Larry's daughters. As the last of Edna's remaining friends and few neighbors departed from the site, David turned to his brother and sisters.

"I'm sure Grandma is happy. She's finally with Larry, Bernice, and Jacob. She is at peace with her parents, and her sister, Pearl."

David removed the funeral wreath from the large metal easel and placed the circle of vibrant flowers on the grave. He whispered one final goodbye to Edna Pearson, his grandmother, who left behind, as the obituary read, "four grandchildren and three great-grandchildren." He looked up to the faint rays of sunlight breaking through the mantle of gray clouds. He knew his grandmother was no doubt picking wildflowers in a meadow somewhere, smiling.

She had finally made it to her own family reunion, for which she had waited so long.

47244872R00144

Made in the USA
San Bernardino, CA
25 March 2017